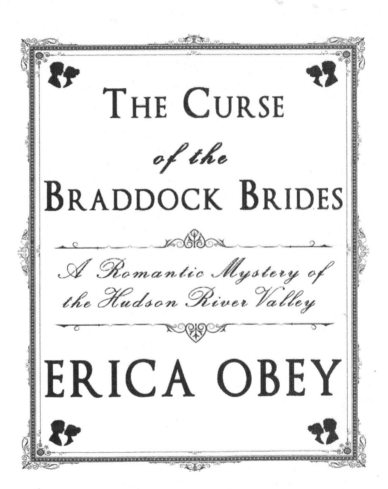

THE CURSE

of the

BRADDOCK BRIDES

*A Romantic Mystery of
the Hudson River Valley*

ERICA OBEY

Walrus Publishing| St. Louis, MO

Walrus Publishing
Saint Louis, MO 63116

For information, contact:
Walrus Publishing
4168 Hartford Street, Saint Louis, MO 63116
www.amphoraepublishing.com
www.ericaobey.com

Walrus Publishing is an imprint of Amphorae Publishing Group, LLC
www.amphoraepublishing.com

Manufactured in the United States of America
Cover Design by Kristina Blank Makansi
Cover art: Asher Brown Durand, *The Catskills*, [Public domain or Public domain], via Wikimedia Commons
Set in Adobe Caslon Pro, OptimusPrinceps, and Exmouth

Library of Congress Control Number: 2017900797
ISBN: 9781940442181

For George, who helps with the research.

THE CURSE

of the

BRADDOCK BRIDES

Chapter 1

At first glance, The Old Grange scarcely looked like the picturesque ruins steeped in mist and legend that Miss Eustachia Ripley had assured Mama would awaken even Miss Libba Wadsworth's long dormant talent for sketching. Nor did it look like the desirable leasehold Miss Ripley promised would offer *entrée* to the First Circles of English Society. It was, rather, one of those overgrown farmhouses that had been added to over the years in order to accommodate additional generations of sons and daughters until better opportunities beckoned. Back home in the Hudson Valley, it would have been converted into a hotel or rooming house, in order to accommodate tourists who could not afford the grandeur the great Mountain Houses offered.

Here, on the border between Devon and Cornwall—or as Miss Ripley insisted on putting it, on the border between this world and the Other—the situation was more delicate. It was not as if the ladies currently occupying the crumbling ruin that was the New Grange were in enough financial embarrassment to set themselves up as landladies—nor was there even the slightest hint they were offering anything so vulgar as a *quid pro quo* round of introductions in connection with the lease, but it was well known that the old Earl had left things in such a state that the year's mourning had already passed without the heir to the title having been sorted out. And now that the ladies were in half-mourning, so to speak, what better excuse for their return to Society than to obligingly introduce an American protégée with Vanderbilt connections?

Or so Miss Ripley had presented her case back at Braddock House as she also presented the letter of introduction from Cousin Cornelia. A six week stay. Six weeks of title and husband hunting. It was no secret that Libba would rather have been guillotined in a public square with naught but her bloomers on, but strangely, it was Mama who looked askance at the idea. Mama, who had spent the past five years wangling invitations to any party that might include gentlemen susceptible to a debutante whose main charm was that she was the daughter of the richest quarryman in the Hudson Valley. "These Hardcastles," Mama demurred, "how exactly are they connected to Cousin Cornelia? Are they the same family as that English gentleman who visited years ago...?"

Mama flushed as her voice trailed off, but Miss Ripley dismissed her objection with a wave. "Oh, he was the cadet branch. This is the Earl's family itself. Quite different. There will be no possible cause for embarrassment. In fact, the *on dit* is that they have broken with him entirely."

But Mama looked unconvinced. Even more strangely, it had been Papa whose face grew wistful. "Tavistock," he said. "Right on the border of Cornwall. Been wanting to see the place for some time now."

Miss Ripley turned on him, her hands clasped with a rapture that befitted her status as the local poetess. "Why, Mr. Wadsworth, I never thought you had a penchant for romantic landscapes."

"I don't," Papa said. "I care about tin. Tin mines all over the place in Tavistock. That's the sort of landscape I care about."

Well, at least the house was clean, and had been prepared for them—a cold collation laid out in the kitchen, and the rooms freshly turned. And it didn't *sway*—as everything else that had brought them from New York to Tavistock, from the steamship to the railroad to the hired carriage. Libba slunk upstairs after dinner intent only on throwing herself onto a bed that didn't move.

If she had been less intent, she might have noticed the faint flush of cool air that came from beneath the door. Or heard the muffled curse and quick footfall as she touched the handle. Instead, she threw open the door to see a man etched in the moonlight of her open casement window, a dark muffler obscuring his face. One of the famed Cornish smugglers, stepped straight out of one of Miss Ripley's legends? It didn't seem likely. None of Miss Ripley's stories featured brigands undignified enough to get hopelessly entangled in heavy draperies.

"Stop," Libba said with an aplomb she did not feel. "Or I'll shoot."

He stopped. And surveyed her. "Have you really a gun?" he asked curiously.

"I'm American," she said. "I'm sure you've heard the rumors."

"A derringer tucked in the lace of your bosom, as they're said to do in the saloons out west?" he mused as he disentangled himself and raised his hands with exaggerated ceremony. "Then I must confess myself the prisoner of the possibility alone. I am yours to command, Miss . . ."

"Then I command you to remove the scarf and walk downstairs to explain yourself to my father."

"Are you quite certain?" he asked. "I've experienced such scenes, you know, and they're deucedly uncomfortable all around."

"My father is not a man given to making scenes."

It was, in fact, an understatement. Papa evinced no more reaction to his daughter forcing a sheepish looking man clutching a muffler into his presence than to cast a long look at his dusty riding breeches.

"Housebreaking in boots?" Papa said. "You must not have been long at this game."

"I can explain."

"I gather that's why she brought you here."

"She said she had a gun tucked in her bosom," the man said. "I'm beginning to believe she lied."

"Ought to be grateful for that," Papa said. "The girl's never fired a gun in her life. She's likely to have killed you."

The man forced a smile. "Then I am profoundly grateful for her duplicity."

His hair was overgrown, and he was in need of a good razor. But his boots were first quality and cared for, if worn and dusty. And from what Libba knew of English accents, he spoke like a gentleman.

"And what were you doing upstairs?" Papa continued his grim critique. "Silver, such as it is, is down on this floor. Unless you were planning to abduct my daughter."

"No!" The man seemed to notice that perhaps his vehemence was more than unflattering. "I mean, not that the young lady isn't charming, and that I wouldn't be delighted to make her acquaintance under circumstances other than gunpoint."

"Better off abducting the silver," Papa said, a glint of affection warming his eyes. "Give you less trouble. Libba's got a steady head on her shoulders. She can take care of herself."

"So she has so aptly proved."

"Enough with the parlor talk," Papa said. "Explain yourself. Why are you here?"

The man drew a deep breath. "Orchids," he said.

And unflappable as Papa might have been at being confronted with an intruder having been captured not entirely at gunpoint, that single word made him pause.

"Orchids? You were trying to steal a flower?"

"Roots, actually," the man said. "Rare crate of dendrobiums smuggled over here from Borneo. Didn't dare bring them straight into London; Sander would have snapped them up for one of his auctions, and where would we have been then? So we arranged a drop-off here. Unfortunately, my . . . contact was unaware the house was to be let. I assume that's why he never showed."

"You're a smuggler?" Papa asked, sizing him up in patent disbelief. "This is what Cornwall's famous free traders look like now?"

"An orchid hunter," the man corrected him. "Although sometimes we are forced to use similar means. For all their delicate beauty, it's a down and dirty business."

There was a long, incredulous silence. Then Papa laughed. "Well, that's certainly a better excuse than your being driven to evade Her Majesty's excise in order to put food on the table for your aging mother and widowed sister with her brood of orphans."

"I assure you, sir—"

"And I can tell you what your assurances are worth," Papa snorted. "But it doesn't matter. Go. And don't let me see you around here again."

"Thank you, sir. But although I know it sounds odd, sir—"

A glint of humor lit Papa's eyes. "It sounds more than odd; it sounds like a damned pack of lies. Just your good fortune that I come from that peculiar class of the American gentry they like to call robber barons, and there ought to be honor among thieves, wouldn't you say?" As quick as it was there, the humor was gone. "But if I catch you around my daughter or this house again, I'll horsewhip you straight to the magistrate, ye hear?"

The man opened his mouth to argue, then thought better. "Yessir," he said, turning toward the window that was open to the night air. "Much obliged, sir. I'll be on my way, then, shall I?"

"Save us all a bit of gossip if you'd be so obliging as to leave by the door," Papa said.

Chapter 2

Papa left before breakfast the next morning, unable to conceal his eagerness to inspect his precious tin mines, leaving Mama and Libba to spend the morning poring over guidebooks that enumerated the various attractions of Tavistock. At least one of these had been penned by one Mrs. Bray, a well-known novelist and wife of a previous vicar, who had been an authority on the presence of druids in the environs. It was unlikely, Libba thought ruefully, that she would be able to persuade Mama to venture an excursion onto Dartmoor in order to view the various processional ways, menhirs, and altar stones that the adventurous Mrs. Bray had visited on her sturdy moor pony, charming adders and rendering them harmless with a flick of an ash bough. Instead, Mrs. Bray's successor was engaged to collect them in her carriage to take tea together with their promised sponsors at the New Grange.

Alas, no sooner had they settled amidst the comfortable cushions, than the new vicar's wife confessed there had been an unexpected change in plans. The Hardcastle ladies had been unavoidably detained in Exeter, where they had been forced to journey in order to clear up an awkward matter of family business. As a consequence, tea would have to be postponed until the following day. In the meantime, Mrs. Humphries hoped to make it up to the Wadsworth ladies by giving them a tour of the rest of the Hardcastle estate.

If Mama was disappointed, she gave no sign of it. Then again, nothing seemed capable of disturbing Mama's serene beauty. And Libba certainly had no cause to object to the change in plans. She might have preferred a brisk tramp after the daring Mrs. Bray's druids, but a carriage ride through the estate's most scenic vistas was still preferable to an afternoon perched on a settee, struggling to balance a teacup on its saucer with the same effortless aplomb as Mama.

The driver had barely urged his horses back into a trot before it became clear that the current vicar's wife shared her predecessor's taste for romantic legend, albeit with more of an affinity for smugglers, midnight elopements, and mad, bad baronets than was quite consistent with Christian charity—or with Mama's perception of polite conversation.

"Tam's Bane," Mrs. Humphries said, signaling the coachman to stop and waving her hand at a bluff that arose above them. "Where the Free-Trader Tam Jenkins at last met his end. All for love of a woman, of course. As is so often the case."

"Free-trader?" Mama inquired.

"A smuggler—although the word scarcely does him justice. In the day, Tam Jenkins ruled this area, from the tip of Cornwall to the border of Devon. Beloved by all, he was another Robin Hood, robbing the rich to give to the poor. The Old Earl had no choice but to tolerate him; Her Majesty's Revenue Service never could catch him. The stories of his exploits were endless. The caseloads of brandy he secreted in the very wagons sent to assist in his capture. The condemned Fenians he helped escape to the New World. The wronged women who were suddenly supplied with a marriage portion upon which to raise their babes. Oh, yes, Tam Jenkins might not have been the law, but he was the heart of justice 'round these parts. And it was that love of the right that at last proved to be his undoing, when he dared all to save a lady from being ravished by the wicked Viscount Naughton."

Mama's face paled. "Has the Hardcastle family a Wicked Viscount then?"

"Oh, only on the cadet branch. That much is unfortunately attested to by the more than a few children in the neighborhood with his coloring . . ."

With a gentle cough, Mama turned the conversation back to smugglers. So like the Hudson Valley, really. Renegades and outlaws hiding behind every cliff. Not literally, of course," she hastened to add, "but the area does have a penchant for legend. Perhaps 'tis something in the geology."

The geology? Libba glanced sharply at her mother, who really hadn't been the same since they had decided on this trip. Indeed, she had been so much altered that Libba and Papa had agreed not to mention a word of the mysterious visitor of the previous evening, so as not to upset her further.

"We have a ghost brought low by love right in our own home," Libba said helpfully, turning back to the vicar's wife. "But he was betrayed by a Hessian rather than a Wicked Viscount. And he cursed the lady rather than saved her. Cursed all the brides of the Braddock family actually. We're most unlucky in love."

An awkward silence ensued before Mrs. Humphries valiantly took up the conversational baton again. "Some say the spirit of Tam Jenkins still haunts the caves that lie buried beneath the cliff. And some say the Wicked Viscount is trapped there with him, the two of them doomed to an endless chase, down into the bowels of hell itself. But others say Tam Jenkins will rise again when the need is greatest and a pure lady's honor is imperiled."

This time the ensuing silence was that which greeted any ghost story well told. And then Libba's mind went back to that stranger trapped in her bedroom window. "Is there much imperiling of ladies' honor around Tavistock, then?"

"Libba, dearest—"

At least that was the most Libba could make out of Mama's choked syllables. Immediately, Libba found herself overwhelmed with guilt. But why were vicar's wives and poetesses allowed to prate on most improperly while she could only blunder into one gaffe after another?

"I apologize—" Libba began.

But Mama cut her off with a laugh. "Perhaps we should eschew any more legends, lest you lead us to believe that our new benefactresses are something straight out of a novel from a circulating library."

She spoke gracefully enough, but Libba knew from long experience that there was no worse epithet in Mama's vocabulary. Libba and her mother held quite divergent opinions on the merits of visiting circulating libraries. With a glance between her two guests, Mrs. Humphries, too, seemed to at last sense that she might be treading on dangerous ground.

"You must forgive my passion for the old tales. I meant to cast no shadow on this branch of the family, of course," she said hastily. "Strictest of propriety, I assure you. All these problems were long buried in the past."

"As well they should stay," Mama suggested.

"Well, of course, of course. But that's the thing about such problems, isn't it? They don't like to stay buried."

Mama's smile grew fixed. "I'm sure I wouldn't know."

"Well, of course not. Of course not." Mrs. Humphries glanced around, as if one of those problems might be about to rear in front of their carriage and demand they stand and deliver, before lowering her voice to add, "Of course, one does not like to gossip. But given your proposed intimate relationship with the ladies it might be best if you understood the position more completely. It is one of those problems that has driven the ladies to Exeter. And I fear the delay in their return suggests it has not been buried quite to everyone's satisfaction."

This time even Mama could not keep her face from setting in horror. "I trust you do not suggest that your Wicked Viscount is predicted to emerge from his underground caverns along with your heroic smuggler."

"Oh, you shouldn't worry about that. 'Tis nothing but an old wives' tale. The Wicked Viscount was dispatched to America, where it was said he found plenty of opportunity to satisfy his taste for American heiresses. That is to say, he has never been heard from since," Mrs. Humphries amended herself hastily. "And surely, if he were still alive, he would have been among the first to advance his claim on the earldom."

"But who else might claim the succession?" Mama asked.

"Oh, it seems every time you turn around there's another one crawling from the woodwork," Mrs. Humphries said. "By-blows and lost cousins. Adventurers the lot of them.

Borrowing against their expectations and generally making a nuisance of themselves."

Crawling from the woodwork or through a lady's bedroom window? Libba thought suddenly. But to what purpose? Orchids? The idea was preposterous. But was she seriously to think she had been confronted by an adventurer bold enough to make off with an American heiress as the Hardcastle's Wicked Viscount had sought to do?

"Not that they seriously want the title; more likely they simply want to be paid to go away. All that was necessary was a firm hand, but alas, such is not a gift that Claudia, the bereaved present countess possesses. Fortunately, the Dowager Countess has recently come down from London to set things right. And she, it is said, is possessed of a very firm hand indeed."

"Then we must hope that matters will be settled to the satisfaction of all soon," Mama said with a firm smile that signaled the end of the discussion.

"Of course, of course. It's just that ..." Mrs. Humphries broke off with a quick shake of her head. "One does not like to gossip."

"No," Mama said, with an unaccustomed hint of asperity. "One does not like to gossip at all."

Chapter 3

By week's end, the continued delay of the Hardcastle ladies' return from Exeter had grown into something of an embarrassment. Mrs. Humphries made an effort, inviting the Wadsworths to tea at the Vicarage, where her husband had taken time out of his pastoral duties to personally decipher the runic inscriptions on the standing stone that had been discovered when they had dug out a new garden. But Mama, in an effort to avoid her persistent gossip, allowed Libba to persuade her to engage their own carriage to tour several of the more interesting locales mentioned in Mrs. Bray's historical romances. At the top of Libba's list was the Abbot's Oak in Hartland Forest, where the Spectre Horseman was said to ride past on his way to Hell, and the remains of the monastery of Tavistock, whose independence from Exeter had been defended by the Ordeal of Bread and Cheese.

Papa had always been a shadowy presence in family life, but now he was distant and preoccupied in a way that suggested that whatever the business in the tin mines was, it could not have been good. Still, nothing could have prepared Libba for his reaction to the man who sheepishly introduced himself, "Begging your apologies for intruding, but I am Sam Burr, under-bailiff around here, and I'm afraid I must trouble you with some distressing business."

Papa blanched. And then he rose slowly to his feet, his face suddenly drawn and old. "If it's not too much trouble, I would beg you the courtesy of stepping outside," he said. "So as not to distress the ladies."

"Distressful as it might be, I need to speak to the ladies, too. Might be possible one of them saw the tramp instead of you." The bailiff was a heavyset, genial farmer, clearly more used to dealing with runaway cattle than villains, and he spoke with a cow's slow steadiness.

Papa frowned. "Tramp?"

"Well, sir, you know how it is in a small town. My wife did for the Hardcastles for years, and rumors have a way of getting around. Word is that a tramp has been seen around the Old Grange, and I need to ask whether anyone saw him here last night."

And all of Papa's coiled tension abruptly vanished. "Did something untoward transpire last night?"

"More than untoward. Unholy. Someone broke into the registry office at the church."

"Only a fool or a madman would do a thing like that," Papa snapped. "Ought to know that if there's anything worth stealing it would be in the treasury or the poor box. And I wish luck on any man desperate enough to try the second. Stealing from the poor is not just unholy, it's bad business."

"Oh, our lot of rogues are too canny for that, to be sure." the bailiff assured him. "But this new lot that's come to town, ever since the earl died so sudden-like, they're an entirely different class of blackguards. Mind you, the ladies themselves are nice enough, there's no denying that. But they seem to have brought a whole lot of trouble in their wake."

Papa's eyes glinted with humor, as the color seemed to remount to his cheeks. "There'd be some who'd argue that's why ladies were put here on earth."

Mama cast him a repressive glance. "I believe Mrs. Humphries mentioned there were several unfortunate claimants."

"Seems like there's a new one each week," the bailiff sighed. "And each week they get worse. I don't know what a cadet branch is, but I can tell you this newest one's the worst I've had to deal with yet."

And suddenly Mama's face went as white and stiff as Papa's. "You are referring to the earl's Naughton connections?"

"Begging your pardon, I'm sure. I was unaware you were acquainted with them."

Mama forced a smile. "Only in passing. And that was many years ago, when he visited New York."

"Oh, well, now that would be old Sir Roderick. No saint, to be sure, but at least he was who said he was. This new one is one of his by-blows—begging the ladies' pardon for any indelicacy. All out of the blue, he claims that his mother was secretly married to his father, and so he has a legitimate claim to the Hardcastle title—and making a nuisance of himself doing it."

"By breaking into the church registry?" Papa asked.

"I told you they're a worse kind than our locals. Poaching and smuggling's one thing. I'd like to say we all know when to turn a blind eye. But this business of secret marriages—"

Mama had grown increasingly pale as he spoke. "I should say so. But now you tell us, he might come here. Why?"

"Old Sir Roderick had the living of this house for some time, before his misdeeds grew so bad the family packed him off to America," the bailiff said. "His son's claim is arrant nonsense, of course, but he's a stubborn one, I'll give him that. It's possible he might come here looking for those marriage lines if he found nothing at the church."

Possible? It seemed he already had. That must be what the masked intruder had been looking for in her bedroom. Libba was surprised how disappointed that made her feel. But before she could open her mouth to speak, Papa cut her off with a warning glance.

"You have my word he'll never gain entrance to this house, as long as I'm here,'" he said firmly. "Still, I must say I don't envy you the situation. Seems like a bad business all around."

"Quite so, sir." The bailiff sighed as he turned to go. "I'll be glad when this business is over and a proper earl is in place. Whole county seems to have gone mad. First, it's breaking into a church. Next thing you hear, it's Tam Jenkins returned to do it."

"Has someone proposed such a thing?" Papa spoke casually enough, but there was no mistaking that he stiffened, just as he had when the bailiff had first announced himself.

"Old Mary Lewis swore she saw him riding across the Tamar back to Cornwall. Which, if you believe the old stories, means nothing less than the end times are coming to Tavistock—although between you and me, sir, I'd say it means that she's given to taking a dram too many. Still, as bailiff, 'tis my duty to follow the fewmets wherever they lead me. And so I'm off, and I bid you a good day."

"I confess I don't know what to make of it." Mama said, finally breaking the silence that followed the bailiff's departure. She shivered as she glanced around her. "I do wish Miss Ripley had at least bothered to mention this house's . . . unsavory connections. Secret marriages. Missing wedding lines . . ."

Papa had said nothing since the door had closed behind the bailiff, simply folding his arms and bowing his head, lost in thought. Now, he finally looked up. "My apologies, Mrs. Wadsworth," he said. "This is entirely my fault. Had I not given in to a sentimental impulse—"

Papa? Sentimental? Over what? Tin?

"Your fault? How can you say such a thing?" Libba said hotly. "What have you to do with smugglers? Midnight elopements. Wicked viscounts. Concealed wedding lines. Claimants. *By-blows.* Why, it all seems to have stepped straight out of a novel from a circulating library! We should leave immediately, and count it a blessing that we were never forced to meet these Hardcastle ladies—whoever they might be."

Her words died off into silence, and for a moment she feared her family would be trapped forever in this strange communion. Then Papa nodded, and the preoccupied look in his eyes was replaced by a warm glint. "Always said the girl had a head on her shoulders. Absolutely right of course. We should head directly back to London, book a respectable hotel, until I can arrange an earlier passage back home."

"Without *introductions*? Mr. Wadsworth, I pray you think of the scandal. Cousin Cornelia would be mortified."

Papa flushed. "That seems to be her regular condition when it comes to me."

"It seems to me we court far more risk of a scandal here," Libba said. "I admit I know nothing about how the first circles of English society behave, but if this is an example, I think I would prefer not to be introduced. And I would tell them to their faces."

"Tone, Libba, dear," Mama corrected her reflexively. "Always better to contrive an excuse."

But Libba was pleased to see that Mama's color was returning, and that she was already calculating the right words for their letter of apology.

"Demands of my business," Papa said. "Constant danger of an accident at the quarry. I'll receive an urgent cable tomorrow."

Mama nodded slowly. "Surely Cousin Cornelia couldn't take offense at a natural concern for your workers."

"Cousin Cornelia would call it sheer Fabianism. Or at least her man Gaddis would," Papa said. "Cousin Cornelia doesn't care how her dresses are paid for, as long as they are. Gaddis takes care of all that, and that's how he can rob her blind."

"Mr. Wadsworth!"

"Apologies, Mrs. Wadsworth. I spoke without thinking. Never meant to trouble you with sordid business affairs."

"I think most would say we are the ones who are owed an apology," Libba defended Papa angrily. "Why . . . we've been thrust into a nest of adventurers!"

"Tone, dear," Mama corrected her again. "Still, you're quite right. 'Tis an entirely unsuitable situation. I can't imagine what Miss Ripley was thinking, introducing us to such people."

"That woman always has been a meddling trouble-maker," Papa snapped. "See if I won't have quiet word in her ear when we get back."

"Please, Mr. Wadsworth. I must have your word that you won't do anything to embarrass us."

And suddenly, all the life seemed to leach back out of Papa. "I trust I have never given you cause to accuse me of doing that," he said stiffly. "And if I have, I can only offer my most sincere apologies. Now if you ladies will excuse me, I should inquire as to when the telegraph office opens tomorrow."

Chapter 4

Ransome was not happy to return to the solicitor's office in Exeter. No man liked to revisit the scene of his worst defeat. And now it was impossible not to admit that the issue of the putative Lord Hardcastle was rapidly proving to be an even worse defeat than Micholitz beating him to that last cache of *Dendrobiums* simply because Ransome had taken the time to negotiate the rather more delicate matter of the King's tastes in boon hunting companions. The King's business had been settled satisfactorily, but he could not tell the tribunal he now faced that. The King's affairs? they would ask, incredulous. What have you to do with that? And because he could not reveal that matter, he must endure their derision. Besides, he had not the slightest hope the tribunal would be any less scathing in their critique of his attempt to unmask a spurious claimant to the Hardcastle estate even if they knew he was possessed of talents beyond a willingness to prowl the bogs of Cornwall and the heights of Dartmoor in search of the Western Marsh Orchid. He knew well they were a querulous group.

"Breaking into a church," the Lead Inquisitor, more conventionally referred to as the Dowager Countess of Hardcastle, queried, "to steal baptismal records?"

"Marriage records," Ransome corrected her. "And I didn't steal any. There were none to steal—a fact I merely *ascertained*."

"The bailiff's term for it was desecration."

"Which only points to the bailiff's lack of education. You cannot desecrate a space that is not already sacred, and I did not set foot in the sanctuary. Lord knows, I know enough not to do that, especially after that episode in the Shaolin monastery."

A gentle cough from his mother reminded him that perhaps talk of such episodes were not best calculated to soothe the injured feelings of the vicar, who had insisted on purifying and reconsecrating the church with a ceremony that had his parishioners murmuring about the unfortunate similarities between druids and Papists.

"And this was your plan to put paid to this poser?" the Dowager Countess asked.

"Only a part of it," Ransome said. "I spent not inconsiderable time and effort investigating other aspects of the man's story. I had been told that he claimed to have been born in the Old Grange, and I broke in there hoping to find something that would put paid to the matter for once and for all—."

"Through a young lady's bedroom window."

There was a long pause before Ransome was forced to concur. "Yes, through a young lady's bedroom window."

"May I be permitted to ask," the Dowager Countess went on with annihilating courtesy, "what led you to believe these efforts would prove a simpler solution than meeting us at the solicitor's office, simply presenting your *bona fides*, then returning with us to share a country house weekend with our American guests—as I believe both I and your mother have previously suggested."

And that, Will Ransome—or William, Lord Hardcastle, as he was more correctly known since his cousin, the Ninth Earl, had done him the signal unkindness of breaking his neck while riding to the hounds—had to agree was an unanswerable question. Unanswerable, that was, if he did not want to risk explaining why his most recent journey to Borneo would have been considerably complicated by being a Peer of the Realm. And while he was emphatically not interested in offering any further explanations on that particular issue, he had little idea what other explanations might prove acceptable to the tribunal he now faced.

The Dowager Countess studied him through her quizzing glass as if she were tasting a questionable wine. The recently widowed Countess of Hardcastle, against whom the newly minted Tenth Earl already held an unreasonable grudge for having produced an endlessly increasing succession of daughters instead of one simple male heir, had developed the rather insulting habit of bursting into tears every time she looked at him. His own mother did her best to excuse him, anxiously murmuring that, of course it was hardly his fault that the responsibility had been thrust upon him so unexpectedly. So it struck him as the height of unfairness, when she was the one to complain, "But smugglers? Climbing in windows? Pretending you were the reincarnation of Tam Jenkins? Do you not think that could be described as the slightest bit . . . theatrical?"

"I was never pretending to be Tam Jenkins!" he was stung into protesting. "I was simply trying to discreetly investigate this poser, and unmask him. All that bit about smugglers and abductions took off of its own accord."

"As things so often seem to do with you," his mother said reproachfully.

Justifiable as the point might be, Ransome felt it was more than a little lacking in the matter of maternal sympathy.

"I was somewhat pressed for time," he said, more or less truthfully. "I was forced to set sail quite urgently for Borneo within the week."

"Borneo?" The Dowager quelled discussion. "Is it not rife with Ourang-Outangs?"

"And remittance men. Had some delicate business with the latter, although frankly, I find it easier to deal with the former."

Another pause, another anguished glance from his mother.

The Dowager finally broke the silence by raising her quizzing glass, and Ransome had the uncomfortable feeling they were at last reaching the heart of the matter. "Where you *were* is not what matters. What matters is where you *are*." "And where you most decidedly are is not on the steamship *Atlas*, setting sail to cross the Atlantic in order to pay a reciprocal visit to the Wadsworth family whose visit to Tavistock had been so abruptly interrupted."

Ransome studied her, but he could see no hazard in agreeing to the truth. "No," he allowed, "I am not."

The Dowager Countess was at least good enough to deliver the blow quickly. "Then why is William, Lord Hardcastle listed on the passenger manifest of the *Atlas* as it departed Southampton yesterday?"

Silence fell as Ransome found himself forced to agree that it was indeed an excellent question. As well as one that threatened to offer singular complications to his future well-being. "You think it is this poser," he supplied the answer.

"It does seem to be the simplest answer," the Dowager opined.

"Occam's Razor, you know," the Countess offered, in an unexpected paroxysm of learning.

"Unless perhaps you missed your embarkation," his mother suggested hopefully. "And you're here to try to find another passage."

Her eyes pleaded with him for that to be the case, but as much as he longed to present her with the son she kept trying to excuse him into being, he couldn't bring himself to lie. "I'll sail for New York tonight," he told the ladies. "And I have a boat that will move a lot faster than a steamer. I will catch this man and put an end to his machinations for once and for all."

He spoke decisively, trying to demonstrate he had the matter well in hand. But once again, his mother betrayed him by asking, "How?"

"As discreetly as possible," he prevaricated.

"No churches," she pressed. "No windows."

"No complications whatsoever," he agreed. "I shall voyage straight up the Hudson and place myself directly in the Wadsworths' confidence. Surely they should be as eager to avoid a scandal as we are."

Another silence fell.

"And as for Miss Wadsworth?" his mother asked.

Senses honed over a lifetime of adventuring went on high alert. "What about Miss Wadsworth?"

"Presumably, she would feel entitled to some kind of explanation."

"Explanation as to what exactly?"

His mother waved a hand. "The unfortunate incident of the bedroom window."

"There was no unfortunate incident. At worst, a misunderstanding—"

"As happens so often with Americans, of course," the Dowager Countess harrumphed. "Sometimes one wonders whether one even speaks the same language. Still, one feels that perhaps matters might have gone more smoothly, if you had been a little less *improvistory*."

Ransome's eyes widened. "Are you accusing me of having designs upon the lady?"

"Sailing across the Atlantic to pay your respects can scarcely be called a design," his mother said.

"Especially when the family originally sailed to England for precisely the same purpose," the Dowager pointed out. "No reason to think they wouldn't be eager to return to the topic."

"And they do say Mr. Wadsworth is quite the richest quarryman in the Hudson Valley," the Countess ventured to suggest. "One would not like to convey the impression that we somehow held ourselves above those in trade. No reason to suggest that bluestone is somehow lesser than the tin from which our family's fortunes once arose."

Once arose. That was the salient point. For it was not that the Hardcastles held themselves above trade. It was that they were peculiarly inept at it—leading to their present situation. Along with the unfortunate implications of what the Countess was saying.

"You're saying that after I send this imposter packing, you want me to take up where he left off?" Ransome said. "You want me to *court* Miss Wadsworth?"

"It is not the *what* of this poser's going to visit them that's the problem," the Dowager Countess said succinctly. "It's the *who*."

"No real shame in heiress hunting," the Countess agreed Jesuitically. "It's the false claim that's the problem here. Not done. Simply not done at all."

Arguably so, but there were other, more risible, matters at stake here.

"You are aware that when I first met Miss Wadsworth, she was pointing a derringer at me in her bedroom?" Well, an imaginary derringer, but that fact still stung, so he was inclined not to rehearse it.

"We had suggested you just meet for tea," his mother pointed out apologetically. "It was you who decided to . . . swing through windows."

In other words, this entire debacle was all his fault. And he supposed it was. Just as he supposed his mother was right in nobly refusing to once again point out that his protests that he had never been born to become an earl were rapidly descending to the point of selfish childishness.

"I suppose," he said, grasping at whatever vestiges of dignity might be left to him, "if nothing else it would be right to at least explain the situation."

There followed a long period of wordless appraisal that left no doubt as to the assembled ladies' opinion of his chances of success on that front. And then the newly-widowed Countess burst into tears again.

"Come, come my dear. Show some faith," the Dowager Countess said bracingly. "The man has wrestled Ourang-Outangs in Borneo. Surely, he can handle a few Americans."

Chapter 5

Libba winced as Annie Morgan stuck yet another pin perilously close to her skin. Annie was not a *modiste*, and would not hear herself called one, but she would defy you to find anyone in Braddock's Landing who wouldn't say she was as clever with her needle as any Frenchwoman. More clever, in Annie's own opinion, to judge from the way she shook her head at the workmanship of the gown that had been copied by a Ladies' Mile atelier directly from the design of a French *modiste* last year. Annie was equally impressed by Mama's suggestion that a seamstress of her caliber could easily update the gown with the newly fashionable leg of mutton sleeves before Mrs. Philipse Braddock's Midsummer Ball tomorrow night, and in her countrywoman's way was making no bones about it.

"Miss Libba doesn't want sleeves and ruffles," Annie snorted, taking as little notice of the young woman wearing the gown as if she were a leg of mutton herself. "Simple lines are best for her. A Grecian effect, your *modistes* would call it," she concluded with heavy-handed irony. Which was Annie's way of saying that while Mrs. Braddock seemed to have been created by Heaven itself in order to wear fripperies and flowers, Libba could be most politely described as having had inherited her father's handsome looks. As well as her father's patience with clothing.

Libba sighed, and several of Annie's pins stabbed her in reproach. She had also hoped—arguably unworthily— that their adventures in England might have finally put the notion of finding her a husband to rest. But upon their return home, the coveted invitation from Mrs. Philipse Braddock—Cousin Cornelia—lay on the silver salver in the hall. The invitation to a ball to which several English gentlemen in possession of a title rather than a fortune were rumored to have been invited, had instantly restored the scheming twinkle to Mama's eyes.

"I suppose you're right," Mama said, casting Libba an apologetic glance. "We must remember how vulgar it is to gild the lily."

"And I only wore it in London," Libba added. "No one has seen it here in America, so there's no reason to waste money altering it."

She bit her tongue. Ever since their return to Braddock's Landing, there had been an unspoken agreement among them not to mention the events in Tavistock. But Mama merely murmured, "So like your dear Papa. Pity. You would have made him such an excellent son."

And that, of course, was the heart of the problem Libba reflected, as she was at last released back into her comfortable walking skirt, and allowed to escape into the breeze that rose from the cliffs overlooking the Hudson River. Excellent or otherwise, she was not her father's son. Unhappily, however, neither was she her mother's daughter.

So immersed was she in her own unhappy thoughts, that she did not notice her feet carrying her toward Cora's Leap, the locally famous outcropping which marked the boundary between Braddock House and Cousin Cornelia's far grander adjoining estate. But consciously or unconsciously, it was an appropriate enough choice of destination. Libba's eyes went to the place on the cliff's edge over which the first unhappy Braddock bride had thrown herself after, in Miss Ripley's immortal words,

The Renegade died,

And with his last breath he sighed,

A CURSE ON ALL BRADDOCK BRIDES.

Libba heaved another sigh, and what felt like half a dozen pins Annie had overlooked pricked her. Or perhaps it was Mama's disappointment that pricked at Libba every time she drew a breath of fresh air. She knew Mama only wanted what was best for her. She knew that if she could not find it in herself to be happy, she should at least be grateful. Thousands of other unmarried women were already looking reluctantly at the possibility of taking positions as telephone operators or typists down in Manhattan. And while much ink had been spilt— especially among the forward-thinking ladies of Seneca Falls—on how these New Women were much happier and more independent than many wives, Libba couldn't honestly convince herself that she envied those girls in their tailored suits and shirtwaists striding off every morning to the same job in the noisy city.

But what *did* she want? A renegade to sweep in through her window and carry her off? Had she not had her fill of that in Tavistock? Some renegade he had been, feet tangled in the draperies and offering a ridiculous story of searching for rare orchids hidden in the bureau or some such nonsense. She was almost embarrassed for the poor man.

She bit back a surge of superstitious dread when, as if summoned by her questions, a figure arose on the far side of the cliff, just beyond the Grecian Folly that Cousin Cornelia had erected as a clear line of demarcation between their houses. This was no renegade in a swirling cloak—no masked intruder either. He was simply a gentleman impeccably attired in afternoon dress standing at the cliff's edge, smoking. Was this to be one of Mrs. Philipse Braddock's eligible English gentlemen?

Libba could not have explained what impulse drove her to go over and find out. But as she passed the Folly, motion surged behind one of its ivy-covered pillars. A hand closed over her mouth, and a hard arm snaked around her shoulders, pulling her inside.

Shock paralyzed her. Was she about to be kidnapped? Ravished by a mad, bad baronet? Well that was one thing in the smuggler-infested wilds of Tavistock. But this was Braddock's Landing; this was her home. How dare some bad English earl invade it?

Furiously, she kicked out at her captor as hard as her skirt would allow.

Something hard and round jammed into her ribs.

"Hush and spare your frock," a disturbingly familiar voice murmured against her ear. "I have no desire to harm you. But I do need you to be silent while I listen to a conversation of particular interest to me. And this is a flintlock, which I will not hesitate to fire if you kick me again. Is that understood?"

Without waiting for her answer, he concentrated on listening as another pair of footsteps crunched closer, and a new voice said, "Lord Hardcastle, is it? Allow me to introduce myself. My name is Gaddis, and I handle Mrs. Philipse Braddock's business interests."

Gaddis. What had Papa said about him? Robbing her blind.

"And how may I help you, Mr. Gaddis?"

"Please allow me to speak frankly, Lord Hardcastle, in the interests of time. Rumor has it that you were so smitten with Miss Libba Wadsworth in England that you have prevailed on Mrs. Philipse Braddock to invite you here so that you can pay court to her at your leisure."

"Dear, dear," Lord Hardcastle said. "From that am I to infer I have a rival?"

"You'll not be likely to find many of those," Gaddis laughed. "That girl has been on the shelf so long she is in need of a miracle."

"How *dare* he—"

Her captor's hand tightened over her mouth and nose, cutting off Libba's muffled protest.

"So, you must allow me a certain incredulity that you are so smitten with the girl that you have voyaged across the Atlantic to woo her."

Lord Hardcastle laughed softly. "And what if I'm smitten with her father's business interests rather than her? It seems to be rather an American industry these days."

"Because I have interests in her father's business as well. And I must needs make it perfectly clear that while I care nothing about Libba Wadsworth, I will not tolerate you interfering with my plans. I suggest you make your excuses after the ball, and remove yourself to New York City where there are more fertile furrows to plow."

"But I am Mrs. Philipse Braddock's guest, not yours. Which means, that it is up to Mrs. Philipse Braddock to decide. And she seems to be amenable to my spending the entire summer here. Now, if you will excuse me, I have a bride to woo."

Of all the—

Libba was so furious that it took all of her captor's strength to pull her back into the shadows of the Folly, as Lord Hardcastle's footsteps crunched past.

"Tread carefully, Lord Hardcastle," Gaddis' voice rang after him. "You have no idea what you're bringing upon yourself. The mother is a fool, the father a stubborn nobody, and the girl cannot decide whether she's a bluestocking or a hoyden. And you, Lord Hardcastle, are attempting to navigate waters that are far too deep for you."

His footsteps hurried off in the opposite direction, and briefly, the only sound to break the silence was the lapping of the waves of the Hudson against the shore at the foot of the cliffs beneath them. And Libba's outraged splutters.

Cautiously, the man released his grip, and she whirled to strike him, angry enough to want to hit something, anyone, even if he were wielding a flintlock.

"You!" she snapped. "What, has all of Tavistock decided to convene on Braddock's Landing at once?"

For it was indeed the masked man she had surprised in her bedroom. But instead of a gun, her captor carried nothing more harmful than a botanizing tube for collecting flower samples.

"So it would seem," he allowed, tossing it aside.

"That's a vasculum, not a flintlock," she said. "You lied."

"Well, I owe you that much, wouldn't you say?" he asked

with a grin. "Besides, in fact, I spoke the absolute truth. I told you I had no intention of hurting you. And I haven't. Haven't even wrinkled your skirt."

The same could not be said for him. He was no better attired than he had been when she had surprised him in her bedroom, for all that he was not wearing a mask.

"But . . . who are you?"

He hesitated in a way that suggested he was about to lie. Again. "I'm Will Ransome."

"That's a name," she said. "It's hardly a proper introduction. Or so Mama would say."

"I'm not a very proper man," he conceded, then grinned again. "On the other hand, at least in one man's opinion, neither are you. Perhaps I'm prejudiced by that little matter of the derringer that never was concealed in your bosom, but I am assuming that there is no doubting that you are a hoyden? I mean, of course, the hoyden so central to his Lordship's matrimonial plans."

She glanced down unhappily at her sturdy boots and the grass stains on the hem of her walking skirt. Felt surreptitiously for the hair that had fallen free of its pins, as she said stiffly, "I am Libba Wadsworth. I live here at Braddock House. And no, sir, I am no hoyden. I can assure you Mama would not tolerate such a thing."

His grin deepened. "Bluestocking then?"

And suddenly she was smiling as well. No, she was ready to burst out laughing, despite the fact that she had just listened to herself and her family being mortally insulted by some bounder who apparently had designs on her. "I don't think I should divulge such intimate details until we are more formally introduced."

"Of course. Forgive me. How could I have forgotten

my manners at a time like this?" He took her hand. "Miss Libba Wadsworth, may I present myself. I am—"

"Sir, do you propose to kiss my fingers?" she asked, as she snatched it away.

His eyes sparked with humor. "I agree there are much more interesting places to kiss . . ."

"Mr. Ransome! Perhaps you fail to recollect that my father has already threatened to have you horsewhipped."

"And what sort of suitor would I be if I would not risk far more for a fair lady?"

Flushing furiously, she fought for the icy tone a lady used to discourage unwanted attentions. "Perhaps instead of this . . . japery, you could explain what you are doing here? And don't waste your time trying to convince me you're smuggling orchids. Were you following those two men?"

Her sternness did nothing to chasten Ransome. "Obviously," he said.

"Why?"

He shrugged. "It's complicated. And delicate."

Her mouth twisted. "Involving a lady's honor? Save your worries on that matter. The travails of the Braddock brides are well known here in Braddock's Landing, ever since Cora Braddock threw herself off right over that cliff." She waved her hand toward the abyss in the distance. "It's nothing new."

"Is that what brought you here? Did you intend to leap?"

"Over unrequited love?" She laughed. "You can trust that I will fall into no such trap." Her eyes drifted longingly toward the cliff's edge. "Although I will confess to a strong temptation to see those two gentlemen fall to their deaths."

"Now, that's a bit bloodthirsty, wouldn't you say?"

"I could shoot him instead." Libba brightened. "The renegade's pistol—that's Cora's fatal lover, of course—still lies in the Braddock House Library, awaiting the moment the renegade will return to fire it in order to save a Braddock Bride's honor. It would be nothing less than poetic justice to kill the ambitious Lord Hardcastle with it, would you not say?"

"Poetic or not, I think they'll hang you if you try."

"Well, that won't accomplish anything then, will it?"

"It wouldn't seem so," he agreed. And suddenly all the laughter vanished from his face, "Miss Libba Wadsworth, I would beg you to allow me to handle this matter. Consider me your sworn servant if you will."

And before she knew what he was doing, he had taken her hand and was kissing it. But instead of brushing his lips decorously across her knuckles, he pressed his lips to the inside of her wrist. It was only a fleeting touch, but it was enough to make her heart race, and her voice a bit ragged. She disengaged her hand and said, "Forgive me if I speak from a cynicism born of being too long on the shelf—in my new suitor's kind words. But I would prefer it if you would just speak directly. Why? What is your interest in all this?"

"As I told you, it's complicated. And delicate." He considered his words for so long that she was certain he was prevaricating again. "For now, will you simply take my word that this Lord Hardcastle is not to be trusted, and I would urge you to avoid him until I can set matters right."

"How? Do you intend to kill him?"

"With a botanizing vasculum?" He laughed. "I have no more desire to hang than you do. Or throw myself off a cliff in an agony of betrayal, when it comes to that. I'm fond of my skin, Miss Libba Wadsworth. But I am not fond of this Lord Hardcastle. Nor am I fond of scandal. And handled wrongly, this could result in a very bad scandal indeed. So I must beg you trust me until I can find a way to handle things quietly—for all our sakes."

Chapter 6

Hoyden. Bluestocking. Stubborn nobody. Fool. The memory of the ugly words echoed more loudly than the chatter and the music that wafted across the lawns as the Wadsworths' hired carriage moved slowly up the cobbled drive toward the white Georgian columns of Mrs. Philipse Braddock's *porte cochere*.

Not that Libba hadn't already known that such was polite society's opinion of her family—ever since the snippets of gossip she had unhappily overheard during her first Season.

"In most weddings, it's the bride that changes her name, not the groom."

"Lucius Wadsworth indeed. I remember when it was plain Luke Watkins when he was just her father's quarry manager."

"Snatched her up quickly enough."

"Like one of his undervalued quarries."

"The daughter didn't arrive until two years after that, so her worries were unfounded, at least in that regard. But there's no question she was desperate."

"She honestly fancied herself Lady Lydia?"

"Lydia always was a fool."

"Pride goeth before a fall. They say he falls asleep at the opera. When she can curry an invitation."

Well, Libba fell asleep at the opera, too. But there was no danger of falling asleep at the ball tonight. She should have warned Mama that Lord Hardcastle would make an appearance at the ball tonight. But how could she without introducing midnight visits and orchid smugglers and horsewhips? Better by far to simply trust Mr. Ransome and do her best to avoid Lord Hardcastle until Ransome could handle matters discreetly, as he had promised. What matters they were, she had no idea, of course, but she hoped all would be settled quickly and Lord Hardcastle sent packing back to England post haste.

Besides, Libba was loath to shatter the magic of the evening. The invitations had been decorated with images of Titania and Oberon to suggest the night's theme, and even Libba had to admit that stepping down from the carriage felt exactly like stepping into Shakespeare's Fairyland. Every detail was just as it was described in the society pages that Mama read so religiously each morning. Garlands of hothouse flowers swathed the portico, while fairy lights picked out the edges of Mrs. Braddock's intricate parterre gardens. The stairway in the grand foyer was lined with palms, and the ballroom was even more spectacular. Its faux marble walls had been hung with tapestries, interspersed, at regular intervals with white pilasters with gilded capitals whose bases were jardinières filled with roses and lilies. The musicians were hidden behind a screen of azaleas. Overhead laurel and rose wreaths swung from the chandeliers. Mirrors sparkled from every side, reflecting the dancers who were enjoying, according to the list on Libba's dance card, a Grand March, followed by a quadrille. A Newport and a Berlin, three plain Lancers and a Saratoga Lancers, a waltz-quadrille and a double quadrille, as well as such partner dances as waltzes, schottisches, and a rather alarming sounding Danish polka.

She glanced down unhappily at the frippery booklet with its cover decorated with an image of Puck, a gilded pencil appended to it by a silken cord. Another silken cord manacled it to Libba's wrist, where it seized every chance it could to tangle with Libba's reticule. Mama, of course, had no such problem, managing reticule, fan, and dance card as if she had been born to do nothing else. Libba watched her with an obscure sense of pride. From the moment she had been handed down from the family carriage, Mama had been transformed. Happiness and hope replaced her usual expression of tight worry, and her smile was as incandescent as the hundreds of lights that studded the cornice that connected the pilasters in the ballroom. Tonight, Mama was ravishing. Even Papa seemed to have fallen under her spell, Libba noted in disbelief, as she surprised him watching his wife with a look in which pride of possession warred with inexplicable longing. Papa, who had at least once indelicately pointed out the similarities between the marriage mart and horse breeding? What more could Mrs. Braddock transform with a wave of her wand?

Unfortunately, the person who knew the answer to that question was bearing down on them, determined to usher her unfortunate Wadsworth relations personally into the refreshment room whose walls were lined with fir trees in order to create a grotto-like effect for those who sipped lemonade and ices at small filigreed tables. Mrs. Philipse

Braddock—Cousin Cornelia, as she was suddenly insisting on being called—was laced into a dowager's purple silk that flattered a ramrod straight posture as unbending as her social pronouncements. Even worse, the Wadsworths' only other acquaintance at the ball slithered in her wake: Miss Eustachia Ripley, the Sappho of Braddock's Landing, her mandarin-cut yellow satin meant to call to mind her interesting adventures in the Orient, as well as her reputation for singularity.

Her eyes focused on Mama's coiffeur, which Annie Morgan had spent all afternoon creating, and a particularly unpleasant smile twisted her lips. "Lady Cora's tiara," she said. "Is that quite *wise*?"

As jewels went, Lady Cora's tiara scarcely compared to the rampart of diamonds that graced Cousin Cornelia's hair. But it was the same slender circlet depicted in the portrait of Lady Cora that hung on the first floor landing at Braddock House—the same circlet that, as legend had it, she flung angrily at her husband before throwing herself from the cliff in despair that her lover died believing she had betrayed him.

"Why would it not be?" Mama enquired.

Miss Ripley's voice grew insinuating. "Well, taken wrongly, it could be seen as . . . rushing your fences a bit?"

Mama's face stiffened. "I'm not sure I entirely understand your meaning."

But Libba did. In England, only a countess would wear such a tiara. An earl's wife. But she barely had time to bitterly regret not having warned her parents before Cousin Cornelia had snatched them up and was propelling them straight toward Lord Hardcastle—impeccably turned out in evening wear.

"I am so sorry circumstances prevented you being introduced in Tavistock," Cousin Cornelia said. "But I am delighted to be the one given the chance to right that wrong. Lord Hardcastle. May I present Mr. and Mrs. Wadsworth? And their lovely daughter, Miss Wadsworth."

All the joy leached from Papa's face. But if Mama was shocked, she evinced no sign of it. If anything, her smile grew even more enchanting as Lord Hardcastle bent over her hand, lingering just long enough to convey the grave pleasure he took in making their acquaintance. And then it was Libba's turn.

No! She couldn't bear the thought of the lips that had spewed those reptilian words touching even her glove. And yet it would have been unthinkable to snatch her hand away. All she could do was endure, her smile frozen into place, as he deftly turned her wrist in order to consult her dance card. "Enchanted," he said. "You will allow me the pleasure of at least one dance? Perhaps the Comus Waltz?"

Since her card was manifestly empty, she had no choice to but to allow him to pencil his name next to the dance, before he turned back to Mama. "And perhaps, Mrs. Wadsworth, you would gracious enough to guide me through the difficulties of the Lancers?"

"It's been quite some time, but I shall strive to remember it," Mama said, as Miss Ripley cast her a sour look.

"The Comus Waltz is a bit of a daring choice, isn't it?" Miss Ripley murmured, as she took Libba's arm once again, as Cousin Cornelia swept them off to their next introduction. "Or perhaps you were unaware that Comus was the god of festivity, revels, and nocturnal dalliances . . . every kind of excess. Or perhaps your Mama does not think such . . . episodes befit her own daughter's innocent ears."

Libba did not need to see Mama's face to know her smile had rapidly become as fixed as Libba's own. "On the contrary, Mama and Papa have gone out of their way to provide me with a thorough grounding in moral literature," she retorted. "Which is why I wonder how you could have lost sight of the fact that in Mr. Milton's famous Masque of that title, the Lady manages to vanquish the Lord of Excess simply by exercising the freedom of her mind. Which many would argue is a salutary moral lesson indeed."

Despite her brave words, waltzing with Lord Hardcastle scarcely felt like a salutary moral lesson—unless the lesson in question was that offered by Sisyphus. Libba trod the measure as woodenly as she knew how, trod on his toes with considerably more passion, as she made comments on Milton and Greek mythology with the pedantry of a bluestocking. Surely that would be enough to convince him that his confederate was right, and that she was too unpleasant a matrimonial prospect for even the most desperate of impoverished earls to take on. But Lord Hardcastle was clearly made of sterner stuff.

"Our Libba seems to have made quite the conquest," Mama broke the ghastly news on the carriage ride home. "Lord Hardcastle has begged permission to call at our earliest convenience . . ."

"Oh, Mama! Please, no!"

Mama's eyes widened. "I don't see how we can politely refuse him. He's Cousin Cornelia's guest for the summer."

"But the man's a complete and utter bounder."

Mama shook her head. "Impossible. His title must be

quite in order. Cousin Cornelia would not receive him otherwise."

"Title or not, he's determined to carry off an heiress, even if he has to cross the Atlantic to do it. The only difference between him and his mad, bad father is locale."

She wished she could have the words back as soon as she had spoken them. For once again, that constrained silence seemed to have fallen between her parents.

It was Papa who broke it, saying quietly, "Then that's all the more reason to receive him. It would seem matters were far more amiss if we did not. Suggest some kind of scandal that made us leave England. Better by far to endure him, until he gets tired of his game."

Libba could only stare mutely at her parents, horrified at the predicament she now found herself in. She should have told them immediately about the encounter with Ransome. But, instead, she had chosen to avoid an awkward explanation. Well, more precisely, she had chosen to avoid Mama taking to her bed with a vial of *sels volatiles* while Papa seized one of the antique weapons that decorated the library in lieu of a horsewhip and ran out in search of the man or men who sought to accost his daughter. After all, Ransome had promised to handle matters, and she had thought it simplest to trust him to do just that.

But now an awkward explanation had rapidly devolved into an *exceedingly* awkward explanation, and Libba was ashamed to feel her eyes well with frustrated tears.

"There, now, miss, you're just tired," her father said, as his heavy hand closed over hers with surprising gentleness. "No need to settle this right now. Better not to say things you might wish unsaid. Why do we not leave this talk until morning?"

Fortunately, her father was an early riser. And was inclined to react less dramatically to awkward explanations than Mama. His features might be as granite as the quarries in which he had made his fortune, but Libba had always found him easier to talk to than her mother. He had always treated the delicate needs of the females in his household with exactly the same bluff no-nonsense that he approached any other business dealing. So, once the immediate instinct to seize a weapon to defend hearth and home was gone, he would consider the matter with that same canny common sense that had made him the richest quarryman in the Hudson Valley. He was even the sort of man who might take a secret pride in being called stubborn. For that was Papa.

"I'm not ashamed of what I am," he had snorted on more than one occasion, as he stuffed the battered pipe Mrs. Wadsworth deplored and retired to his study after dinner, instead of listening to Libba play the piano, which she did badly, or watching her embroider, which she did even more badly. "How does the old saying go? You can't make a silk purse out of a sow's ear."

No, Papa, of all people, would take this kind of thing well. Papa would know what to do, even if he had seemed somewhat troubled as of late, Libba reassured herself, as she tapped on the door of the library before breakfast the next morning.

"You're up early, and you're wearing your determined expression," Papa said. And if it took him a shade longer than usual to muster his familiar smile, Libba blamed it on last night's late hours. "Dare I hope you might be bought off with the promise of a new frock?"

"I have no need of another new frock," Libba said.

He raised an eyebrow, then waved her to a chair. "That's

fortunate for me, since your mother seems to be intent on bankrupting me." He peered balefully at a pile of bills. "Who or what is Madame Aulney?"

Libba winced. "She's a French *modiste* who ships gowns from Paris for the shops on the Ladies Mile to copy, then allows them to use her name as though it's some Paris atelier so they can triple their price in exchange for a share of the profits."

Her father shot her a sharp glance. "I thought a head for business was supposed to be unbecoming in a young lady. I believe your mother has waxed vehement on the subject."

"Then you'll have to forgive me if I descend to such iniquity in front of his Lordship. I'm afraid it takes all my wits to keep from spilling the tea when I pass it."

He tossed aside the bills. "So this is about this afternoon's visit?"

"Yes," Libba said. "Yes, it is. Papa, must I really go through with this?"

"Go through with what exactly? Showing your breeding by greeting a house guest courteously? Showing him the hospitality of Braddock House? Entertaining him with some music?"

"You and I both know my performance at the pianoforte is scarcely entertaining."

"Perhaps you'd be better off entertaining him with cards." Her father's eyes flashed briefly with humor, and then he looked puzzled. "That is, if it is acceptable for a gently bred young lady to play at whist? Is it?"

"I would have to ask Mama." Libba's shoulders slumped. "Oh, Papa, *must* I?"

"Must you what exactly?"

"Be offered up on the pyre of polite society, as helpless a sacrifice to avoiding scandal as the helpless Iphigenia being sacrificed for a favorable wind to sail to Troy."

Her father looked shocked. And then he laughed out loud. "That's quite some image." With some effort, he forced both his face and voice to sternness. "Have you been sneaking down to the circulating library to borrow novels again?"

Libba flushed. The circulating library was another bone of contention between her and Mama. For Braddock's Landing was fortunate enough to boast two libraries: The Subscription Library was a genteel, white pillared-building that held pride of place at the head of the village's precipitously twisting Main Street, right across from the Congregationalist Church and the Braddock Memorial. Its disreputable cousin, the circulating library, skulked in the railway station that also served as post and telegraph office, as well as a general store. It was a source of continual despair to Mama that Libba far preferred the cheap novels of lady scribblers from the circulating library to the edifying tomes carefully selected by a ladies committee headed by the Sappho of Braddock's Landing.

"Homer is scarcely a novel," Libba said primly. "Simply the evidence of a strong education grounded in the classics, which Mama says is not unbecoming in a young lady as long as she does not attempt to read them in Greek or Latin. An ability to converse in French is enough for any gently bred young lady, and perhaps an acquaintance with Corneille and Racine."

Instead of answering, her father flushed at his gaffe. And Libba was consumed by the memory of his awkward apologies in Tavistock.

Forcing a smile she didn't in the least feel, she added, "There's a fine leatherbound set of Mr. Evans' translations somewhere in this room."

"Purchased back in the day when your mother hadn't yet given up hope of improving me." His eyes went briefly to the bookshelves filled with leatherbound volumes of the *Gentleman's Magazine,* complete sets of Walter Scott, Shakespeare, and the classics, most of whose pages remained uncut. And then he looked at Libba, his usually keen blue eyes suddenly somber. "And because of that, I'm certain that your mother is the person who best knows how to handle this. If she says receiving him is the best way to avoid scandal, I trust her judgment. Hold your head high. And your suitor at arm's length. I know you can play the great lady as well as your mother."

"And you accuse me of novel-reading," Libba retorted.

She wished she could have the words back, as soon as she saw the pain that flashed across her father's face. But as quick as it was there, it was gone, and her father was once more the canny businessman. "Let us call it a bargain, instead, shall we, miss?" he said. "I am only asking you to follow your mother's lead in handling this with dignity. I give you my word it will never come to a marriage not to your taste. God knows, there's already been enough of that in this family already."

Chapter 7

It could happen to any man, the ticket master, who was also apparently the telegraph operator and post master in Braddock's Landing assured him. And Ransome was forced to concur: surely he could not have been the first to come to grief over the Three-bird's orchis. Triphora trianthophora was an elusive flower that bloomed only for a brief six or seven-hour span on a single day that had to be determined by careful calculation of a fortnight's worth of high and low temperatures. It was made all the more elusive by the fact that, no matter how many plants there were in the stand, all the flowers bloomed at once. After rumor reached him in Poughkeepsie that such a bloom was imminent, it was only common sense for Ransome to leave his belongings to be forwarded to Braddock's Landing in order to make a brief detour to catch the moment with his new photographic equipment.

And who could blame him? Any self-respecting orchid-hunter would have done the same. No one would even notice the slight delay before Ransome arrived to claim his luggage in the tiny Braddock's Landing railroad station where he had planned to quietly transform himself back to William Ransome, Earl of Hardcastle and Viscount Naughton, along with a few other miscellaneous titles that did nothing to add to the estate's coffers. After having been thus transformed, he would find the imposter and persuade him to leave Braddock's Landing as discreetly as possible. But instead of retrieving his luggage, he was greeted with a cacophony of shouted news that seemed to come straight from the tabloids everyone in this country seemed addicted to. *Tragic steamer fire on the Hudson River. Scores overcome by smoke. Miraculous survival of a young lady clutching her opened parasol as a life-buoy. Heroic rescue of beloved puppy.*

Ransome was better equipped to handle such moments than most, having had to sort through similarly tangled explanations when he had unknowingly violated a voodoo temple in search of the elusive Ghost orchid, or had spent two days treed by an outraged fakir near Bombay. Usually such matters were quickly reduced to a straightforward business matter: A guide renegotiating his price, for instance. But it still took Ransome at least three iterations of the story before he was completely certain he grasped all the ramifications of the postmaster's announcement that the traveling trunk he had left for forwarding at Poughkeepsie, where the rumor of Triphora trianthophora had reached him, had not yet arrived, and was, according to the man's stammered explanation—irritatingly interrupted by continuous exclamations of delight at his Lordship's narrow escape from death—not likely to do so any time in the future. This was largely because Ransome finally elicited, after a half-an-hour's pressing for a more systematic arrangement of details, the steamship to which Ransome had entrusted his baggage, the same steamship from which he had impulsively disembarked at Poughkeepsie, had suffered a disastrous fire from a boiler explosion somewhere in the vicinity of Hyde Park, and had only just recently been towed to shore a burned-out hulk.

Absently agreeing with the postmaster's babbled comments about God's Providence and a divinely-ordained escape from death, Ransome was already considering the not-inconsiderable problem that now faced him. He was scarcely a lady who could venture nowhere without a convoy of steamer trunks; indeed, he had traveled for months at a time with little more than the rucksack and gun now slung over one shoulder. And in fact, he felt more than a little distaste at the thought of actually donning the items in his lost trunk, many of which had been hastily altered from his cousin's wardrobe on the eve of his departure after a flurry of negotiations with the London tailor who had arrived on their doorstep with a mountain of already unpaid bills.

Ransome was hard-pressed to share his mother's conviction that an imposter could only be confronted in proper afternoon attire. But the difficulty presented by the loss of his letters of introduction, and the proofs of his title drawn up by the solicitor was clear even to him. By some kind of perverse irony—the kind of perverse irony that did so seem to haunt Ransome, his mother might gently point out—Ransome had decided such letters would be far safer on a steamship than in his rucksack as he scrambled through the undergrowth of the Hudson Valley woods. And so, at the last minute, he had tucked them into his trunk.

A mistake. And a very bad one. The kind of mistake that would have been fatal in his previous career. Good God, was this what an earldom was fated to do to a man?

Ransome had always prided himself on being a man who moved quickly and invisibly through his surroundings. But apparently the weight of a title slowed you down.

It was exactly why he had taken the time to settle that little matter in Borneo before claiming his title—and it was a good thing, at least in certain circles. Although he doubted the circle that included the two countesses and his mother would see it that way. In fact, although none of them would ever be so vulgar as to give voice to such a thing, it would be difficult not to yield to an unvoiced suspicion that he would be willing to fake his own death in order to be spared the Earldom of Hardcastle.

Well, that last could be settled by composing a cable immediately, in order to spare his mother not only the shock of the bad news, but the pain of thinking ill of her son, for she did genuinely love him, even when she despaired of ever civilizing him. But as he reached for the cable form, Ransome paused to cast a suspicious glance at the ticketmaster. Damned if the earldom wasn't slowing him down worse than he thought. He had no doubt that the steamer fire was real enough. But he only had this man's word that his trunks were on it. In fact, he had been relatively certain that he had arranged to send them ahead by rail, not steamship. And the disappearance of his papers made his hopes of forcing the imposter to leave with a minimum of fuss unlikely. A fortunate break for the ersatz Lord Hardcastle. A bit of luck for which a man might pay handsomely.

Well, he had other, more reliable means of communicating with England. And more immediate problems to face—chief among them the courtship of Miss Libba Wadsworth, hoyden and bluestocking. And while there was a certain unworthy part of Ransome that wondered if there were any circumstances under which it could be considered an understandable efficiency to allow another man to carry on and do just that—had not the Dowager Countess herself suggested that he might take up the task where his proxy left off?—he was forced to concede that the longer this farce continued, the harder it would be to put an end to it quickly and quietly. But the question remained: How?

Not by demanding a confrontation without either clothing or his bona fides. Ransome did not need to picture his mother's and the Dowager Countess' combined reactions to know that would hardly qualify as 'quietly'. A daytime call on the Wadsworths would be the far more discreet option. And although Ransome was certain his mother would deplore his showing up in his walking kit, delaying until he could wire for the funds necessary to purchase even the rudiments of a gentleman's wardrobe would cost several precious days—even if he could be certain that the ticket master would even send his cable. So he did what he could to make himself more presentable, paying the inn-keeper's wife to launder what clothes he had and summon the local barber, before he set out for Braddock House in the morning. He was the miraculous survivor of a steamship sinking, after all. Allowances would have to be made.

Unfortunately, the sight of the Folly as he drew near Braddock House, recalled to mind his unfortunate adventure with the botanzing tube, and the memory of that encounter brought with it, the unhappy realization that Miss Libba Wadsworth had not impressed him as a young lady given to making allowances. Of course, first impressions weren't everything, but this one had brought with it a sinking suspicion that Miss Wadsworth's anger might dwarf even that of the Dowager herself. Even in her most towering rages, the Dowager would resort to no more threatening an option than cutting a man down with a sharp glance and an acerbic speech, whereas Ransome was morally certain that if Miss Wadsworth cut anyone, it was likely to be with the sharp edge of a weapon far more dangerous than a botanizing tube.

So lost was Ransome in considering this new complication, that he barely noticed the noise of hooves and wheels behind him, until he was forced to jump aside as a closed carriage rattled past him and up the drive to the house. By the time Ransome had recovered his feet, the coachman had already leapt down and opened the carriage door.

The image of an English lord in an impeccably tailored traveling coat emerged. He paused briefly to brush an invisible speck of dust from his sleeve before removing his top hat and bowing ceremoniously to the elegant woman who stepped out onto the portico to greet him.

"You'll have to forgive our country manners," Mrs. Wadsworth apologized by a way of a greeting. "But we don't stand on the ceremony of announcing our guests at Braddock House."

"I am honored to be received on such an intimate footing." He bowed low over Mrs. Wadsworth's hand, before turning to the dark, rebellious presence that had emerged behind her. "And your lovely daughter ..."

He bowed toward her hand, only to find himself being forced to freeze awkwardly in mid-air, when the lovely daughter in question kept both hands planted firmly behind her back, looking as awkward and hoydenish as any woman could. Ransome snorted with laughter, but in another moment it was gone, as the imposter regrouped himself almost immediately to greet the tall spare figure who followed the ladies out of the house.

"Mr. Wadsworth, it was delightful to make your acquaintance at Mrs. Braddock's ball, but pray do allow me to present myself formally. I am William, the Earl of Hardcastle."

And Ransome's suspicions were confirmed as the man pulled out a letter case—Ransome's *own* letter case—and went on, "Of course, being introduced by Mrs. Braddock would be considered by most to be *entrée* enough into polite society, but please allow me to present some letters of introduction from my countrymen."

No, it was too much. Impossible. Ransome started up the drive to put an end to this farce for once and for all.

Only to feel a hand land on his elbow. "Trade entrance is around the back," a groundskeeper told him, the pitchfork he held in one hand leaving little room for argument.

Chapter 8

If Libba had not had such good cause to know otherwise, she would have been forced to admit Lord Hardcastle was a fine figure of a suitor. In fact, he could only be described as above reproach. He was young and handsome, with soft, fair hair, and possessed of an impeccable tailor. His manners were faultless; even when Libba deliberately and childishly refused him her hand, he merely murmured "A violet by a mossy stone, half hidden from the eye . . ."

"Wordsworth!" Mama breathed. "Oh, Libba does so love Wordsworth."

How could Mama do it? It was not just a matter of Libba loathing Wordsworth and every last one of his daffodils, violets, and lesser celandines, far preferring the daring and impetuous Lord Byron. It was the way Mama's smile never wavered as Lord Hardcastle took her approval as a cue to draw Libba aside in order to recite with excruciating accuracy what seemed like the entirety of *Lyrical Ballads*—all the while exhibiting a gentlemanly interest as Mama showed him her various collections, deferring to her knowledge for the most part, but interjecting an occasional thoughtful comment that let her know her expertise was falling on appreciative ears. He demonstrated similar connoisseurship in their stroll around the rose garden, sharing the latest news about the new French approaches to hybridization, and insisting that he would have two of Monsieur Pernet-Ducher's finest cultivars, 'Souvenir of Wootten,' and the exceedingly new, and quite exquisite, 'Madame Caroline Testout,' sent over from Paris immediately.

He was perfection itself at tea, pronouncing himself enchanted by the intimacy of having only Miss Eustachia Ripley and the local vicar to make up the numbers. The London gossip he shared struck just the right note: the faintest hint of scandal to make the ladies blush, but nothing harmful or actually libelous. He navigated his way effortlessly through Mama's enormous silver tea service, and deftly pretended not to hear when Miss Ripley had leaned closer to Mama, deliberately cutting out Papa—who looked desperate to retreat to his financial pages—and breathed, "I am just back from the telegraph office. Horrid place of course, even without that nasty circulating library. But on occasion, one must. The latest installation of my galleys was available from my publisher—"

"Of course," Mama murmured. "One cannot deny one's service to the muse."

"Exactly!" Miss Ripley agreed, then lowered her voice. "But the postmaster bid me consult you on the matter of a few old letters never delivered. One assumes nothing damaging of course, but he preferred to consult whether he decided to make an attempt to redeliver."

That last was offered with an unwarranted roguish smile at Libba. But before she could protest that she had never written a single untoward letter in her life, Papa demanded, "Libba! Perhaps you could entertain us with a few selections. God knows, I paid that music master enough."

And Libba had no choice but to allow herself to be led to the pianoforte as a lamb to the slaughter.

Libba's repertoire of ballads had begun as one of her rare triumphs over Mama's ongoing fears about the propriety of her daughter's literary inclinations. For, although anyone who actually listened to the old ballads would see that they were full of at least as much forbidden passion and mortal quarrels as the novels Mama deplored, she felt a daughter singing to her father the old songs of his lost Scots homeland was picturesque. What was more, the simple accompaniments to her singing were all that the distinctly unmusical Libba had the patience to master. Although "master" was an optimistic term.

"Mr. Wadsworth's family was from the Highlands," Mama whispered to Lord Hardcastle as he watched Libba finish "The Bonnie Earl O'Moray" with dreamy fascination. "Among the last of the Old Lairds, and loyal to the Young Pretender. They were forced to emigrate with the Highland Clearances, and they've had a hard life since then. Mr. Wadsworth will not speak of it, of course."

Libba nearly slammed her hands down on the keyboard. It was a fib—no, it was a lie. A far more outrageous story than any novel from the circulating library.

"And here I thought the Wadsworth name was Cornish," Lord Hardcastle said.

The silence that fell was as awkward as if the vicar had begun to speak in tongues. With a sudden sense of foreboding she didn't understand, Libba glanced over at Mama, but her polite smile conveyed nothing. Papa, on the other hand, had gone grey. But why? There was certainly no shame in being Cornish—at least no more shame than being American.

"Oh, how could you think such a thing?" Miss Ripley gasped. "The place is half civilized. All tin mining and smugglers."

She gave a tinkling laugh to make it clear she spoke in jest, but there was no mistaking the malice that gleamed in her eyes, and Libba rounded on her, pleased to have a target with whom she was at least evenly matched. "But is not Tintagel, Arthur's seat, also in Cornwall?" she retorted. "I believe you've penned a lovely ballad about it."

An unpleasant smile creased Miss Ripley's lips. "Ah, but before it was Arthur's seat, Tintagel was the fortress to which the unfortunate Duke Gorlois sought to hide his wife, the lovely Igraine, from the unwanted attentions of Uther Pendragon. But Uther prevailed, entering the castle in the guise of Gorlois and begetting Arthur upon Igraine even as her husband lay dying on the battlefield at Dimilioc, where he had waged war in a hopeless attempt to keep his beautiful wife safe. An unpleasant story, really, no matter how Lord Tennyson attempted to improve upon it."

No, it was clearly something more than an unpleasant story, to judge from the ugly triumph on Miss Ripley's face. And as for Papa . . . well, Papa looked genuinely ill. But how strange to see him mortified over a social insult—Papa who took pride in falling asleep at the opera.

Then again, perhaps it was simply concern for Mama and her hopes. For it was painful to watch the way Mama kept her face set in its polite mask, determined to endure all this for . . .

For what? For Libba's sake?

Surely, it was not for her own.

What did it matter? No one should be forced to undergo such torture, no matter what their crimes. And what crime had Mama ever committed other than wanting to see her daughter happily wed? It was beyond unfair. But Libba was helpless to do anything about it, beyond snatching up the closest piece of sheet music with shaking fingers, and launching into an angry and amateurish rendition of the "Minute Waltz."

Hours later, Libba stared glumly out her bedroom window as she considered her options. Or lack thereof. No matter how much effort she had put into convincing any sane man otherwise, Lord Hardcastle had proved determined to remain enchanted by her, and had proposed a carriage ride and a *fete champetre* for lunch tomorrow. Mama had, of course, politely accepted before Libba could give into the distinctly hoydenish urge to suggest she would prefer a quick gallop along the cliffs and a Ploughman's lunch at the hotel by the Braddock's Landing railway station. Uninvited, Miss Eustachia Ripley pronounced herself delighted to join the party, just as the cowardly vicar had begged off by pleading catechism class. Even Papa had beaten an ignominious retreat, claiming an important meeting with a man of business up from New York—leaving Libba to brave the inevitability of enduring more Wordsworth over cold chicken with no better reinforcements than Mama and Miss Ripley.

Her gloomy reverie was abruptly interrupted by the sound of pebbles raining against the glass. Throwing open the casement, her stomach rose with relief when she saw Ransome standing outside on the moonlit lawn. For it was only then that she realized that at least half of her had been certain that she had imagined him, or at the very least, both he and his promise of rescue had been nothing more than one of those strange tricks of enchantment Mama liked to insist the moonlight off the river played on the unwary, destined to vanish with the dawn into a pile of dried leaves and acorns just like Henry Hudson's men.

Which, frankly, would not have been so bad, if only Lord Hardcastle could be persuaded to vanish with him.

Not bothering to throw a wrap around her shoulders, Libba ran down to the terrace. "Did you find something?" she asked. "Can you put an end to this farce?"

"Not yet," he said flatly. "Unfortunately there has been a complication."

Her stomach sank, and she realized how much she had been putting her hopes in him. "You seem to be a man who rather *attracts* complications," she said tartly.

"It has been said of me," he allowed with a grin. But immediately his face sobered. "I saw Lord Hardcastle came to call today. Are your parents encouraging his addresses?"

To her surprise he sounded truly concerned.

"Encourage might be a bit of a strong word. But yes, he was our guest at tea today. And tomorrow he proposes a carriage ride and lunch al fresco."

"What do you mean that encourage is too strong a word? Are they or aren't they?"

She bridled at his inquisitorial tone. "It's complicated," she retorted.

"You do understand that you cannot encourage that man's attentions."

"I have encouraged no one. But frankly, he is proving extremely hard to discourage. And at the risk of being what my Mama would term *accusatory*, I would remind you that I was rather trusting in your assistance in that matter. As you yourself proposed."

"And still propose. Unfortunately, right now the only option open to me would be to challenge him to a duel. And that is not an option most people would describe as discreet."

Well, no, it wasn't. But right now she was ready to fetch the Renegade's pistol and fire it on him herself. "I am forced to point out that your sense of humor is, to say the least, ungentlemanly," she snapped.

For a moment, he looked flummoxed. Then infuriated. And then his face relaxed into a defeated grin. "My apologies. But I fear I have already proved to you that I am, in fact, no gentleman. To the despair of my poor mother."

"Then who exactly are you, Will Ransome?"

Her question hung in the night air. Then Ransome shrugged. "Why not the truth? They say it's simpler to remember."

"Indeed."

"The truth is, I'm—"

"Libba!" Mama's voice rang worriedly from the terrace windows. "Libba, what are you doing out there?"

Ransome muttered something undecipherable, but decidedly uncomplimentary, about mothers and marriage, before his jaw set and he started toward the house. "Enough. It's time to finish this farce for once and for all."

"Libba, are you in converse with a *man*?" Mama's voice ratcheted to a horrified shriek. "Mr. Wadsworth! Mr. Wadsworth! Come quickly, or I fear we are undone."

Her voice stopped Ransome in mid-stride. He wavered for an instant, before, with another muttered imprecation, he turned back from the terrace, changing his mind. "Better that I speak with your father first thing in the morning." He shot Libba a long look. "When he's in a little less of a mood to reach for his horsewhip first and ask questions later."

And he was gone, but not before Papa had caught enough of a glimpse of him to roar, "Come back here, ye blackguard. Dinna I warn ye what I'd do if I caught you skulking around my daughter's bedroom again?"

"Again?" Mama said faintly.

And suddenly Libba could see nothing but the utter and complete absurdity of the entire situation.

"Papa!" she cried. "Please be reasonable. If he had wanted to abduct me, he could have done it in Tavistock. No need to travel across an entire ocean just to ravish an heiress."

If she had thought about it, she had meant to defuse the situation. Instead, to Libba's everlasting dismay, Mama's self-control crumpled as it never had in the face of even the cruelest of Miss Ripley's barbs. "How could you?" she choked. "My own daughter."

And she turned and fled across the terrace to the bright lights of the house.

"I'm sorry . . . I didn't mean . . . Papa?" Libba turned to her father, only to see that his face was white with a fury that was clearly directed at her. "I don't understand. I promise you I didn't mean—"

"No," he said, controlling his anger with considerable effort. "No, I'll wager you didn't."

And that was enough to decide her. Whatever was going on here, trying to protect her family's feelings was only causing unnecessary complications. "Papa. I fear we must speak frankly."

He studied her, his gimlet eyes appraising. And then his shoulders slumped. "Yes," he said. "I fear we must. But not tonight. Not like this. Go upstairs. Make your apologies to your mother even if you don't understand why. Better to talk in the morning when we've all had a good night's rest."

Chapter 9

The morning only brought fresh evidence that Ransome's luck was destined to hold true to form. He had marked Lucius Wadsworth as an early riser, and had started the walk from the village to Braddock House as soon as the sun began to bathe the cliffs with a rosy glow. Last night's misunderstanding about an elopement meant it would be difficult enough to offer the girl's father an explanation, without any of the extraneous swooning and weeping women always seemed to feel a necessary accompaniment to such a discussion. So Ransome intended to seek Wadsworth out long before any of the women in the household could be expected to have finished their morning toilette. The end result might well be that Wadsworth would drive Ransome off with a horsewhip, but not before Ransome could put a flea in his ear about the putative Lord Hardcastle. Wadsworth would handle matters from there, leaving Ransome free to retreat to New York City with a clean conscience, in order to reassemble his missing wardrobe and the remains of his matrimonial career.

With the birds singing in the trees and the mist rising from the river, it was an unexpected moment of peace in what promised to be a most unpeaceful day, and Ransome took the time to savor it. But as he reached the grounds of Braddock House—prudently directing himself toward the tradesman's entrance this time—he saw a tall, spare figure mounted on a sturdy cob riding out through the front gates. And before Ransome could decide to give chase, he felt a familiar burly presence with a pitchfork materialize beside him.

"That's two days you've come skulking around, laddie," the groundskeeper said. "I think it's time for you to explain yourself. You looking for work in the quarries? If so, all you need to do is ask for a trial. Mr. Wadsworth will hire any man who's willing to save his drinking and whoring until after his work is done. Beyond that, he don't ask a lot of questions. Respects a man's privacy, Mr. Wadsworth does."

"Thank you, sir," Ransome said. "Very kind, sir. But no thank you. I mean, I'm not looking for a job."

"Too bad. He's a good man to work for, even though he's hardheaded and close with a dime. Pays fairly, sees to your education if you're inclined that way, don't take away a man's cottage when he's too old for quarrying. Instead, he tries to find him a position that suits. Of course, Mr. Wadsworth'll tell you keeping his workers happy is naught but sound business. But there's many a man who'd say they've not seen a decenter man in their life." The man's face darkened. "This about the girl then?"

Ransome eyed the pitchfork as he weighed his answer. He was thoroughly prepared to face a horsewhip, but the pitchfork's edges looked sharper than many rapiers he'd seen, and it was covered in something that looked unpleas-antly like manure. "I mean her no trouble."

"That's good," the groundskeeper said with a bark of laughter. "Because Miss Libba has a way of finding that all by herself. Still, you'd best talk to her mother first, and she won't be receiving until midmorning."

But Libba Wadsworth apparently kept less fashionable hours. Or maybe the groundsman was right, and she did have a knack for finding trouble all by herself. Ransome had no time to contemplate the issue.

"Mr. Ransome!" her voice rang out unexpectedly from a side terrace. How good of you to come! Did they have any of the rosebushes I mentioned in my note...?"

She flashed the old groundskeeper a quick, conspiratorial smile, as she hurried across the lawn to take Ransome's arm. "Papa has entrusted me with finding Mama some of those new hybrid teas from France as a birthday surprise, and Mr. Ransome is acting as my agent in the matter."

"Portlands and damasks should be good enough for any rosebed. Anything else is nothing but trouble," the groundskeeper snorted, favoring her with a long stare that informed her he bought none of it.

"Nonetheless, you know how passionate Papa is about pleasing Mama's whims," she said firmly, as she pulled Ransome back toward the relative privacy of the side terrace, where she had apparently been sipping her morning coffee.

So she was an early riser, too. Or perhaps she had been up all night, to judge from the smudges beneath her eyes.

"What are you doing here?" she hissed as soon as they were alone. "Are you *trying* to get me locked in my room with nothing but bread and water until I agree to marry the odious Hardcastle?"

"Dammit! You cannot marry that man!"

The words slipped out before he knew it. But the smudges under her eyes angered him obscurely. Eyes like hers didn't deserve to be dragged down by sleep and worry.

"I quite agree," she said. "You scarcely needed to pay a dawn visit to inform me."

Self-consciously, he lowered his voice—modulated his tone, as his mother would prefer to say. "I apologize for any impropriety. I came so early in hopes it would lend me a chance to speak plainly to your father, as I promised I would do, but unfortunately, he has already left on business."

"I know. I . . . had hoped to speak with him as well." Inscrutable emotion flashed across her face, to be replaced immediately by brisk practicality. "So I am afraid that leaves no other option than that you speak plainly to me instead."

He studied her as he considered the possibility. Speaking plainly to a woman without fear of tears or swooning? It seemed about as likely as watching the sun rise in the west. But everything about this . . . woman? girl? . . . everything about Miss Libba Wadsworth seemed to wrongfoot him, starting with the moment he had given into that ill-conceived desire to kiss her wrist. As well as other, more interesting parts of her, if he recalled correctly.

But following that particular train of thought, enticing as it was suddenly proving to be, was not likely to improve the situation. Recalling himself sharply, he drew a deep breath.

"I regret to inform you that Lord Hardcastle is not the man he claims to be."

Her face lit with weary humor. "On the contrary, I would argue that he is apparently exactly what he proposes to be: an impoverished nobleman willing to brave marrying even an American hoyden for the sake of his estate. He might as well have it engraved on his calling card for the ease of American Mamas."

And once again, Ransome found himself wrongfooted, at the very moment he had been steeled to blurt out the truth. His preference had always been for sensible women— well, honestly, he thought with a twinge of guilt, the words he actually tended to use were "honest whore"—but nonetheless, wasn't there something *cold-blooded* about her attitude? Or maybe it was the evident sadness beneath her laughter that abruptly made Ransome feel small. For while there might be some confusion over the person in which Lord Hardcastle did his heiress-hunting, there was no question that was exactly what Lord Hardcastle was—with or without engraved calling cards for the convenience of scheming Mamas. And suddenly Will Ransome couldn't bring himself to admit that was who he was. What he was. Not when he suddenly realized how remarkable Libba Wadsworth's eyes were when they were sparkling with humor.

"You overhead the same conversation I did," he said. "You know what he is."

She glanced at him sharply. "Yes, but it is much less clear to me what or who you are," she said. "So while we are speaking plainly, perhaps you could explain exactly what your quarrel is with Lord Hardcastle?"

Ransome had long ago learned that when you lied, it was always best to stick close to the truth. Although with one glaring omission, he spoke the absolute truth, when he said, "My quarrel is with him wedding you. I have no desire to have that disaster on my conscience for the rest of my life."

She cocked her head as she studied him. "And why should it be on your conscience? What are you to Lord Hardcastle?"

There it was. The moment to speak plainly. But somehow he could not utter the words "I am Lord Hardcastle." For as soon as he did, there would be no speaking plainly between them anymore. There would likely be no speaking at all.

"I am—was his batman," Ransome improvised in sudden inspiration. "His personal servant during the India and Burma campaigns, and I just sort of followed along with him when he . . . we left."

The way she eyed him made it clear that she was as taken in by that explanation as the groundskeeper had been by her talk of roses. "To be frank, you don't strike me as the servant type."

"It was more of a partnership," Ransome amended himself hastily. "Jaunting around together suited both of us when we were in the army, and so we just went on as we had started. But my loyalty to a partner does not preclude me warning you that he is the worst kind of adventurer. You would do well to be rid of him as expeditiously as possible."

"Why? What secret sins is he so guilty of? Has he a wife already? Unspeakable habits?"

Who knew? Who knew what the man was, beyond the fact that he was emphatically not Lord Hardcastle? And that was precisely the problem. "I fear to offend a gently-bred lady's ears," Ransome prevaricated.

"Then I'm afraid you leave me no choice but to guess." Her gaze grew speculative. "India and Burma. Are you insinuating that he's picked up . . . unnatural tastes from houris?"

For the love of God, she sounded frankly *interested*. But now did not seem to be the time to point out that houris were usually Persian or Arabic, not Indian. Not only might he inflame her imagination enough to press for details, she might, at some point, come to wonder exactly why he was so well informed.

And yet, the sparkle in her eyes that had replaced the tired humor certainly aroused in him an urge to further inflame something . . . for she really had the most remarkable eyes. So remarkable that, before he could think better of it, he was already leaning forward to demonstrate his earlier contention that there were much more interesting places for a man to kiss than a lady's hand—

God in heaven! What was he thinking?

"Even worse. I regret to inform you that the man's an orchid hunter," Ransome said, too stunned at the disaster he had narrowly avoided to think of any other answer. "He was the man I was seeking to meet on the unfortunate evening you happened to surprise me in your bedroom."

She looked considerably less impressed by that announcement than he had hoped. In fact, she looked more than a little disappointed. "And what scandal do I have to fear from that? Mama is absolutely *passionate* about orchids. She has some wax ones made by that clever Mr. Gibson, whose work is said to have fooled the wife of the Reverend Henry Ward Beecher into taking them up and breathing in their scent."

Wax orchids? In a churchwoman's parlor? Why not woo a waxwork woman? Orchids belonged where you found them, whether it was the lush, dense jungle, or the harsh cliffs of New Hampshire. The windswept deserts of America's far west, which he still longed to visit, or on the English moors, where he had first learned how to find and love them. Orchids were everywhere, if you knew how to look for them, and as infinite in their variety as Shakespeare had claimed Cleopatra was, but the one thing they had in common—every last one of them—was their unexpected beauty.

Rather like Miss Libba Wadsworth, so sensible in her walking skirt, with her hair tied up loosely and her tired eyes. But when she turned, and you saw her from an unexpected angle, she was startlingly beautiful. And not a waxwork flower from a parlor, but a creature as exotic as an houri.

But it was best to avoid thinking about houris right now, just as it was best to avoid Miss Libba Wadsworth's remarkable eyes.

"Orchid hunting," he said firmly, "has been the ruin of many a fine scientific mind. Your American Mr. Gibson. Frederick Sander, the King of Orchids, and his plant-hunter Roezl, who gave up an arm for his plants. The Duke of Devonshire spending his fortune on hothouses—complete with indoor waterfalls. Even Darwin himself. All of them, absolutely obsessed. It's an addiction, it is. The drooping sepals and soft lips of the flowers can lure a man to its perdition just as surely as they do the innocent pollinator that climbs through the honeyed gates, only to find itself trapped by the softest of bounds imaginable, leaving it no option but to thrust its way through and fertilize—"

"I beg your pardon, sir!"

He broke off, flushing. "Apologies. Although if you'd read Messrs. Darwin or Gibson on the subject, you'd consider my description veritably scientific."

"Then it is certainly fortunate I have read neither one." But from the interest that sparked in her eyes, it was clearly an omission that she intended to remedy at the first opportunity. And it was not helping matters that Ransome suddenly found himself desperately thinking of how he might manage to be the one to help her find just the right passages.

Instead, he forced himself to say, "I am trying to warn you that Lord Hardcastle is in the grip of a mania. One that has already driven him to the brink of ruin—"

"Oh, we already knew he had no money," she said with irritating practicality. "Otherwise he wouldn't want to wed me. So if his worst secret is that he's ruined himself over a flower."

"He has climbed mountains! He has violated the strictures of sacred precincts. He has brought the curses of a dozen different tribes in a dozen different languages down on his head. He has fought snakes. He has wrestled crocodiles. He has clung to a life vest in the South Seas, for nearly a week, only to be rescued and ransomed by pirates. He has been wounded by pygmy's blow darts. He has had to battle a dervish in Cairo. He has lain, bound as a sacrifice to the terrible cult of Kali, and all for what, I ask you? A flower."

Well, perhaps the last few were not entirely true, but he had felt any amount of embellishment justified his main point.

"'Tis a terrible thing, I tell you."

His words drifted off on the morning breeze, and for a moment, there was no sound beyond the songs of birds and the water lapping gently against the shore. Then she said softly, "On the contrary, I would argue that a man risking anything for a flower is the most romantic thing I've ever heard."

Romantic? No! No! She had it all wrong. Will Ransome was not a romantic man. Will Ransome had even less to offer in that department than Lord Hardcastle—who at least had the spurious glamour of an earldom.

So overcome was Ransome with horrified denial that she caught him completely by surprise when she went on with a suddenly speculative smile. "But I must ask, how do you know so much about this? Are you really Lord Hardcastle's batman, Mr. Ransome? Or are you an orchid-hunter, too? A rival, perhaps?"

Any man with common sense would say no. That is, if any man with common sense were not suddenly drowning in Libba Wadsworth's eyes, as her lips parted in a way that made him wonder if the simplest thing might be to settle this right now by telling her the truth, asking for her hand, and sealing the bargain with a kiss. The kind of kiss that would reduce Mr. Gibson's poetic account of the deflowering of the *Cypripedium acaule* to something between a waxwork and a dissection.

"I see." Her smile deepened as she answered her own question. "And is it also a mania with you? A forbidden passion?"

No. No, this was headed for disaster as certainly as a runaway team of horses plunging over one of the river's steep cliffs. He had to stop this while he still could reach for the reins. Talk with her father. Get things sorted out sensibly while there was still a chance.

"Strictly business for me, I hate to tell you," he said, rising to take his leave with an insouciance he did not in the least feel. "Orchid-mania is not what it once was now that Hooker and Devonshire are both gone, but collectors will still pay a pretty penny for specimens. So I'm in it strictly for the money, and must needs be unless I can find an heiress of my own to wed."

Chapter 10

It made no matter whether they were mocking, troubled, or outraged, Miss Libba Wadsworth's eyes were really most remarkable. So remarkable that Ransome found himself lost in hopeless speculation over whether the taste of her lips could possibly prove their equal as he made his way across the lawns and away from Braddock House. Even more consuming—and by far more troubling—was the thought that there was a perfectly simple way to answer to that question. At least, if you were Will Ransome, there was. But he was rapidly coming to the unwelcome realization that William, Lord Hardcastle was under far more constraints. If he wanted a taste of Libba Wadsworth's lips, the only decent thing to do was pay court to her. And despite the fact that there were some singular complications— including that someone was already apparently doing that on his behalf and that he had been banned by an angry father who he had no doubt had grown even angrier given last night's episode—he began to wonder what was wrong with that plan? His female relations had all but given their blessing to the project. Libba and her family would be saved from scandal. And he might have found a wife who loved him with all his unfortunate habits, rather than trying to cure him of them. A wife who maybe even would consider sailing to Guatemala during rainy season a more appropriate choice of honeymoon than Niagara Falls. Of course, the money facilitated matters enormously, but was it too much to hope that, instead of the disaster he was dreading to report to the female relations anxiously awaiting news at the Hardcastle estate, this uncomfortable issue might be resolved to the satisfaction of all parties?

So lost was he in such happy reflections, that he didn't notice another set of remarkable eyes until their gimlet gaze stopped him in his tracks, and he looked up to find a tall, spare figure blocking his way.

"I still have that horsewhip," Lucius Wadsworth said.

In his lifetime, Ransome had faced down everything from the Dowager Countess' disdain to an extremely large and irritable cobra. Right now, he was morally certain that, silver-haired though Wadsworth might be, he dwarfed either of those threats.

Ransome flushed. "Sir!" he said. "In regards to that unfortunate incident—I mean, either unfortunate incident—you must take my word that there was no question of elopement."

"Damned right," Wadsworth said. "Or I wouldn't stop at whipping you bloody."

Ransome took a wary step backward. "I don't doubt that, sir," he said sincerely.

"So, out with it. Why are you here?" Wadsworth demanded. "Are there orchids to smuggle in America, too?"

"Well, actually, yessir, there are . . ." Dammit, but what kind of lover was he, if the threat of horsewhips could make him so craven? Well, frankly, a sensible one. Drawing a deep breath, Ransome called on the memory of Miss Wadsworth's remarkable eyes to stiffen his resolve. "If I could speak frankly—"

"I've been told that there's no surer sign a man is about to lie to you, than he says that," Wadsworth snorted.

Well now, that was unjust. Ransome had every intention of telling him the absolute truth—albeit arguably in a somewhat circuitous manner. "I am making inquiries about this man who calls himself Lord Hardcastle on behalf of the Hardcastle family," he said.

If it was at all possible, Wadsworth's face got harder. "Confidential agent, rather than an orchid smuggler then?"

"Often both," Ransome said, utterly truthfully. "However, in this case I am operating in a strictly private capacity. And distressing and shocking as you might find the news, I fear I must warn you, Lord Hardcastle's claim to the title is not all it seems to be."

Again, those gimlet eyes studied him. "Shocking, no," he said. "Distressing remains to be seen."

"Exactly," Ransome said with some relief. "It is the Hardcastle family's hope to handle this matter as discreetly as possible—and I hope we are agreed it would be in your interest as well. I'll just have a few quiet words with the man."

"That," Wadsworth said, "could be a bit of a problem. Seeing as he has already left for a day-long sketching excursion with the ladies of my household. Along with the most notorious, mean-minded gossip in the Hudson Valley."

Libba and Hardcastle, together for an entire day? Ransome was shocked at the surge of anger that overwhelmed him. "Then there is no time to waste."

"Wadsworth!" Hooves clattered up the road and a man swung down from a hired hack and hurried over to them. "Where have you been? My friends arrived from Manhattan nearly an hour ago."

"Gaddis," Wadsworth said uninvitingly.

But Ransome had already recognized the contemptuous cadences from the conversation he had overheard on the cliff's edge.

"Rather early, aren't you?" Wadsworth asked. "The New York train only arrives this afternoon."

"They have a private railroad car, of course." Gaddis shook his head. "You seem to have no conception of the people you're dealing with. My friends are important men—not men you keep waiting. It's bad enough you've forced them to journey all the way up here."

"I don't see why they did," Wadsworth replied. "My answer hasn't changed. I care nothing about whether it is Tammany Hall or your friends that run City Hall. And I care not if they steam up here on private railroad cars or ride bareback. I'll not participate in any dealings that take the bread out of the mouths of laboring men, no matter how many ball invitations the Vanderbilts extend."

There was a moment's thunderous silence. Then Gaddis said, his voice soft with fury, "You're quick to spit on an invitation most people covet. Why? Because your daughter has made one conquest."

"You will be so good as to leave my family out of this discussion!"

With considerable effort, Gaddis changed his tone. "Wadsworth, listen to me. I am speaking as a friend here. You need to be careful about Hardcastle. I don't think that man is all he claims to be."

Wadsworth's eyes sharpened. "Is that so?" he said. He jerked his head toward Ransome. "Funny. You're not the first to raise the issue this morning."

If Gaddis was surprised, he hid it well. He studied Ransome from behind his steel glasses, taking in the hiking kit, the dusty boots. "And who exactly are you?"

Ransome very much wanted to ask the same of him. Who was this man that he instinctively knew was far more dangerous than the putative Lord Hardcastle could ever prove? Gaddis's eyes shifted in constant appraisal, like a cardsharp in search of any advantage he could find. Ransome had yet to understand exactly what game the man was playing. Or what the stakes were. All he was certain of was that the man would seize any opportunity to cheat anyone he could.

But Ransome had considerable experience dealing with cheaters, both at the card table and in far more dangerous situations. And right now he had at least one distinct advantage of his own. No point in squandering it. Now was not the time to reveal himself—as a confidential agent or Lord Hardcastle.

"Will Ransome. Lord Hardcastle's batman from his army days."

Wadsworth shot Ransome a withering look. Ransome ignored him. The lie came more easily the second time around. Another few times and he might begin to believe it himself. Already, he heard himself venturing an embellishment, "Now, I function more or less as his gentleman's gentleman."

"I see," Gaddis said, although he clearly believed Ransome's story no more than Wadsworth did. "Then perhaps you can explain the details of Lord Hardcastle's succession to the title. My informants in New York suggest that he claims to be the son of Sir Roderick Naughton, an old acquaintance of the family, but he seems to be remarkably short on details."

Ransome felt, rather than saw Wadsworth's face grow rigid.

Wadsworth brought the discussion to an abrupt close. "Acquaintances and connections are for polite society, not for me. And so before there can be any hint of a scandal about today's excursion, I have asked Mr. Ransome to act as my emissary. And I will join him, as soon as I have informed your friends from New York that they have wasted their private railroad car, as well as their time, because my answer remains unchanged."

Chapter 11

It was sickeningly inevitable that Libba found herself seated by Lord Hardcastle's side as he took the reins of the pony trap, and their little party of four set out on their expedition to the vista that the celebrated Mr. Carmiencke had immortalized in his famous *Hyde Park: View up the Hudson*. Mama had naturally been mortified that the hackney carriage they had hired for Mrs. Braddock's ball had been unavailable on such short notice, especially when Miss Ripley exclaimed on the quaintness of riding in something as rustic as a trap, but Lord Hardcastle quickly assured them that country ways were the best ways.

Libba had longed to suggest that perhaps Miss Ripley would prefer to stay at home, rather than endure such common pleasures, but the popular vista could only be approached through an estate owned by Mrs. Philipse Braddock's Vanderbilt connections, and while Cousin Cornelia could not be expected to condescend so far as to accompany them, her emissary, Miss Ripley, was needed to assure their permission to cross the Vanderbilt lands, just as she had assured their entrée into the few drawing rooms that would accept them ever since Libba's sixteenth birthday.

Lord Hardcastle was no more welcome a companion. Only a few moments watching him handle the reins had convinced Libba that it was a mercy a carriage had been unavailable, for Hardcastle was likely to have killed them all if he had attempted to drive anything more spirited than the phlegmatic cob that had served their family for years. Perhaps his inability to drive something as simple as a pony trap was not unusual in an earl who had always had coachmen at his service, but how was Libba expected to believe that he had navigated the cart paths of the Himalayas if he could barely manage the well-traveled road from Braddock's Landing to Hyde Park? Her eyes lingered unhappily on the man as she tried to envision him wearing his batman's sturdy boots and rough chambray shirt as he scythed his way through tropical jungles, in single-minded pursuit of a mad passion. It was impossible.

Even worse, he sensed her gaze and looked up, and she was too slow in lowering her eyes.

"I would know what you are thinking of," he said.

Flushing at his insinuating tone, Libba turned toward the back of the trap for help. But Miss Ripley had monopolized Mama, unblushingly offering her services as a go-between in the unfortunate matter of those misdirected letters as Mama repeatedly refused the kind offer with an increasingly rigid smile.

Turning back to Hardcastle, Libba offered him an equally insincere smile of her own. "I am afraid your batman has betrayed you."

"I . . . beg your pardon?" Lord Hardcastle jerked the reins, earning a reproachful glance from the cob. "My man?"

His confusion only confirmed what Libba had already surmised. Will Ransome was no more this man's servant than Hardcastle was a rough and ready orchid hunter. "Mr. Ransome. He claims to have served you in India and the Orient, as well as in your career as an orchid hunter."

The stilted conversation in the back of the trap had broken off, and Mama's face had fallen back into its customary worried lines as Miss Ripley leaned forward with a predatory smile. "An orchid hunter," she exclaimed. "Why how very exciting! You must have some singular tales to tell!"

An odd expression crossed Hardcastle's face before he managed to regroup. "Oh, hardly anything as dramatic as that," he said with a forced laugh. "Ransome is rather a singular old acquaintance with a taste for a tall tale. Picked it up seafaring. I guess old sailor's habits die hard."

"I thought you were in the army together," Libba said. "In India."

Lord Hardcastle's face stiffened, and Mama intervened hastily, "Come now, Libba. No gentleman enjoys being *interrogated.*"

"I'm sorry, my Lord," Libba said with a meekness she did not in the least feel. "I did not mean to contradict."

"No need to apologize at all. I find a natural curiosity is a most fetching quality in a young lady."

Mama would have been quick to disagree. She had scores of cautionary tales about curiosity in a young lady, ranging from Pandora to Psyche to Bluebeard's wife. Mama was not much given to myths and legends, but when it came to cautionary tales, she displayed a surprising erudition. More effective than any of those tales, however, was a very real concern about exacerbating Lord Hardcastle's already uncertain driving. The cob may not have ever been roused to a canter in Libba's living memory, but there was no point in testing its limits.

"Still," Lord Hardcastle said, "it might be desirable to hear precisely what tales my man is spreading behind my back. Ransome is a remarkable servant, but he does have a talent for stirring up mischief."

"Oh, I'd hardly call it mischief. He simply explained your singular taste for orchids to me," Libba hastened to say—her eyes nervously on the way the reins were slackening in his hands. But instead of bolting, the cob philosophically seized the opportunity to stop, emboldening her to go on. "He made it sound most stirring. Told me that I must beg you to recount the great adventures you have pursued in your magnificent obsession, how you have scaled mountainsides in a pursuit of a passion as great as any lovers, ensorcelled by the charms of the delicate blossoms—"

Hardcastle's choked exclamation was second only to Mama's.

"Why how wonderfully exotic." Miss Ripley overrode all of them, not bothering to disguise her triumph at how deliciously inappropriate the eminently suitable hobby of botanizing was turning out to be. "Although I'm not sure orchids are quite a *nice* taste. You *do* know the old legends, don't you? As my dear friend Mr. Folkard has explained in his magisterial *Plant Lore, Legends, and Lyrics*, Orchis was the headstrong son of a satyr and a nymph—never the best of families wouldn't you say, even if they hadn't been dedicates of Priapus. Blood will tell. That's what I will always say, and so it was inevitable that Orchis offended a priestess and the great Bacchus himself by laying violent hands on her—"

"*Please,*" Mama said. "I don't think—"

Miss Ripley's smile grew even more malicious. "Oh, I'm so sorry, my dear. I completely forgot."

Libba, keenly aware that Mama's face had gone white, spoke before she could stop herself. "Oh, do let me guess," she mimicked Miss Ripley's solicitous tone. "They tore him limb from limb. Just like they did in your stirring poem on the Maenads. All that intoxication and frenzy. I don't know how you could make it seem so real. A foolish reader would believe you were writing from personal experience."

Desperately, Lord Hardcastle gathered the reins and clucked the cob back to an amble.

"Libba," Mama said faintly, and Libba subsided, plunging them all into uncomfortable silence that lasted until they had reached their destination and the merciful distraction of unpacking the easels and watercolor boxes that had long been a source of torment to the spectacularly unartistic Libba. But Hardcastle's hand lingering on her elbow as he helped her down from the trap warned her that far worse tortures were possible.

"Miss Wadsworth," Hardcastle said, "I understand that there is a folly hidden from view just on the other side of the copse. Perhaps you and I should explore it, in order to ascertain whether it would be a suitable place to take our collation."

And Libba's already uncertain temper exploded. "Indeed, Lord Hardcastle, your taste for meetings in follies is well known!"

"I beg your pardon—"

"Do you not recall another meeting at a folly where you discussed your marital prospects with a . . . what were the words? Bluestocking and hoyden?"

"My, my!" Miss Ripley said brightly. "*That* certainly must be a tale worth hearing. Do tell, Lord Hardcastle."

"I must protest," Lord Hardcastle stammered. "I am uncertain as to what Miss Wadsworth is suggesting."

"Libba, please!" Mama said, in a voice that brooked no resistance, as she drew Miss Ripley to the other side of the trap with a firm suggestion that they inspect the luncheon foods.

But Lord Hardcastle had already regrouped, and a dangerous determination now lit his eyes. He took her elbow and guided her toward the Folly despite her objections.

"Miss Wadsworth, it is no secret that I came to Braddock's Landing in search of you," he said. "And so I would not waste time with trifles." He stopped and turned toward her. "I apologize for my precipitateness, but I have grown to admire you so much, even in this brief acquaintance, that I am already moved to ask, may I have cause to hope that you might do me the honor of becoming my bride?"

He might better well hope that she didn't give him cause to rename this particular stretch of cliff "Hardcastle's Leap" by shoving him straight over the edge. But her temper had gotten her in enough trouble already, and she had the sense to instead answer him with lowered eyes, just as Mama had taught her, "I cannot, of course, speak of my inclinations without my Father's permission."

"But perhaps you could offer me a token."

And then his lips moved toward her—and not toward her hand but toward her own lips. Appalled, she edged backward, only to find herself caught against a tree as the unpleasant length of Lord Hardcastle's body suddenly pressed uncomfortably close. Too close. Libba drew a deep breath to scream for help, only to stop, suddenly certain that was just what Lord Hardcastle intended her to do, so that Miss Ripley would come running to witness the scene with avaricious eyes, and the only hope of hushing up the resultant scandal would be to announce their betrothal.

Abruptly, Lord Hardcastle released her with a most ungentlemanly curse—as footsteps crashed into the copse. And both Libba and Hardcastle turned to stare with equal bewilderment at the specter that greeted them.

"Apologies. Damned clumsy of me to interrupt," Ransome said, sounding not in the least apologetic. "But you were quite right to send me ahead to scout out a suitable location for luncheon, for I must inform you that this one will never do. Why, it cannot be more than a half an hour since I saw a *snake*."

"A snake, sir!" Libba gratefully seized the excuse to slide a comfortable distance beyond Hardcastle's reach. "Why, I declare I am absolutely terrified of snakes."

"Well, then allow me to shield you!" Gallantly, Hardcastle reached for Libba once more, but Ransome was too quick for him.

"I also feel it incumbent on me to warn you, Hardcastle, there has been some question of your *bona fides*." Ransome spoke softly, but there was nothing soft about his grip on Hardcastle's arm. "Of course, I did my best to vouch for you as your batman, but Mr. Wadsworth is an . . . empirical sort of man. As well as quick with a horsewhip. I might suggest that it would be prudent to withdraw if your explanations are anything less than adequate."

Hardcastle glared at him. "I can assure you my explanations are more than adequate, and my *bona fides* authentic. If my word on the subject is not enough, I suggest you ask Mrs. Philipse Braddock." He turned to Libba. "In the meantime, shall we, Miss Wadsworth?"

But before Hardcastle could offer her an arm, Ransome objected, "Of course, as your loyal servant I would say nothing of the shocking scene I so nearly stumbled upon. Still, I think you ought to be aware that American manners are a trifle more prudish than those you have been accustomed to in England."

And taking Libba's arm himself, he drew her aside to lead her back toward the carriage, and hissed, "What happened? How could you allow yourself to be alone with him? You know what he is."

To her surprise, he sounded genuinely angry. As though this was somehow her fault, Libba thought irritably.

"Well, perhaps you had better make some progress in settling this matter as you promised," she snapped. "And I can only implore you to do it soon. For although I have yet to discover any of Lord Hardcastle's unnatural tastes, he certainly has exhibited an unfortunately *persistent* taste for me."

A moment's silence was her only warning. Then Ransome said in an odd voice, "Unnatural tastes? Fie, Miss Wadsworth. You are the most natural taste I can possibly imagine."

And as many times in as many minutes, Libba was thinking about kissing a man. But this time she was not thinking of houris and unnatural tastes. This time, she was thinking how very natural it might feel to be kissed by Will Ransome.

"Apologies." Ransome stopped himself with obvious regret. "Such things might be best kept for another time."

Another time. It was as much a promise as an apology, and a promise that Libba found herself suddenly intent on making sure he kept. She favored him with a mocking smile. "My, you are a rather *complete* servant," she said. "Is doing his Lordship's courting for him among your regular duties?"

Chapter 12

Mama had taken charge, and in no time they were laying out the collation. Miss Ripley was, predictably enough, gloating, as she spread the checkered tablecloth. Mama, on the other hand, was completely composed.

"I confess myself a little confused," she said to Lord Hardcastle, her pleasant smile never wavering. "Would you be so good as to introduce us to your . . . companion?"

She cast a sharp look at Ransome as she groped for a suitable word, and in that moment, Libba had never admired Mama so much. How did she manage to maintain that air of bland civility when her mind must be as teeming with questions as Libba's own? Questions such as, what was the relationship between Lord Hardcastle and Ransome? And why had Ransome followed him here? Had they known each other back in England?

"Name's Will Ransome," he answered Mama easily, "I'm his Lordship's batman. Gentleman's gentleman. Groom. And all around dogsbody. No point in mincing words."

Mama nodded uncertainly, as if no explanation struck her as less likely, but she was far too well bred to contradict a man to his face. And Libba could only agree. Batman indeed! Even more absurd to think Ransome some gentleman's gentleman. Certainly not to judge from the quavering valet Papa had inherited from Mama's father, who attacked Papa every morning with a shaving case full of soaps and brushes and the latest knowledge of how to tie a cravat.

If she needed any more evidence to give his story the lie, she had only to look at the way Lord Hardcastle's hands were trembling as he attacked the roasted chicken with a carving knife. Any worse, and he might discover himself inadvertently opening a vein—and Miss Ripley would lose no time in immortalizing the accident in a poem that recounted his despairing death at losing the affections of his intended. Perhaps she would even send him leaping over the edge of the Vanderbilts' celebrated vista, saving Libba the trouble of pushing him.

"Perhaps we should leave the luncheon preparations to Mr. Ransome," Mama suggested, with an anxious look at Hardcastle's hands. "As your batman, surely he has a knack for such things."

"Buttled no few dinners in the rough for his Lordship," Ransome agreed cheerfully, as he deftly extracted the knife from Hardcastle's fingers. "Everything from a five course dinner to thank the monks of Lhasa for their hospitality to—shall we say, a rather more intimate affair for an Aztec princess, complete with candlelight."

Lord Hardcastle shot Ransome an incredulous look, which threatened to send Libba into a fit of distinctly unladylike giggles. From the way Ransome's shoulders stiffened, he was struggling to control his laughter as well. But the two of them collapsing at some private joke—especially one that Libba, at least, only half understood, would be a disaster—even without Miss Ripley's eagle-eyed scrutiny. So as he contrived to carve the chicken, she carefully avoided meeting his gaze while she set out the remaining dishes and arranged Mama and Miss Ripley's voluminous skirts in order to find room securely between them—and out of range of Lord Hardcastle's attentions.

"My," Miss Ripley breathed with a rakish glance at his Lordship, who had been magically transformed into her luncheon companion. "I declare, I feel positively *ravished*. There is never a dull moment with the Wadsworths."

Mama's polite smile never varied, but Libba could see her mother's customary backboard-straight posture grow an inch stiffer. Once again, it was up to Ransome to salvage the situation.

"Mr. Wadsworth asked me to convey his apologies for sending me as a messenger, and would like me to assure you that he intends to join the party just as soon as he has wrapped up a small matter." His face grew studiedly neutral. "Involved a man named Gaddis. Are you acquainted with the man?"

"Some kind of business associate up from New York City," Mama said vaguely. Her face clouded. "I don't believe Mr. Wadsworth much cares for him. Something about Mr. Gaddis asking him whether he had no ambitions beyond being the richest quarryman in the Hudson Valley. I believe Mr. Wadsworth found the turn of phrase somewhat . . . insulting."

And if he found that somewhat insulting, what would Papa think about being termed a stubborn nobody? And his daughter a bluestocking and a hoyden. Libba flushed at the memory, and could only hope no one noticed—especially not the all-too-perceptive Will Ransome.

"He's not what I'd call a pleasant man," Miss Ripley broke off Mama's conversation with Lord Hardcastle to chime in unexpectedly. "Really a horrible, old gossip. You'd best stay clear of him, especially if you have any secrets to hide. The man has a positive *nose* for a lady's indiscreet letters."

For once, Mama couldn't manage to hide her emotions. Her careful mask slid ruthlessly away, leaving Mama looking . . . old. And afraid. Of course, Miss Ripley was not slow to notice. Eying Mama with a reptilian smile, she asked, "Why, my dear, are you quite all right? Perhaps it's just the heat, but you suddenly seem . . . peaked."

"How could she be otherwise after hearing such *harrowing* news about a snake?" Libba intervened sharply. Ransome had guided her back to the carriage with Hardcastle on their heels and news of the supposed snake sighting on his tongue. She turned to Lord Hardcastle, eyes wide. "I'm sure in your travels, you have encountered more than a few, but I must confess it makes me quite giddy."

Something about Ransome's sudden concentration on passing around a plate of biscuits warned her that perhaps she was being a bit too theatrical fanning herself to emphasize that giddiness, but as long as she was safely out of Hardcastle's reach, she was happy to prate on. "Then again, I suppose a poor reptile holds no terrors for a man who has staved off dervishes, pygmies, and pirates. And all in the service of a simple flower. I declare, it must be more than a quest. It must be a *calling*."

As Libba had hoped, the temptation was too much for Miss Ripley to resist. With a final speculative look at Mama, she turned her attention back to Hardcastle. "But orchids are scarcely a simple flower, now are they? I've heard they can be downright dangerous," she breathed. "Do tell, Lord Hardcastle. Were you acquainted with that poor explorer who was attempting to trace the route of two of his fellows who had disappeared, only to discover they had been devoured by *orchids?* There was nothing left of them but a single Orchis still chewing on the remains of the skull."

Like the painting in the rather shocking story by Mr. Wilde that Libba was not supposed to have read, as Mama's face began to regain its color, Lord Hardcastle's grew more sickly. "I can't say as I remember the tale. Do you happen to recall the chap's name?"

"Micholitz, of course," Ransome said casually. "You remember. Poor fellow worked for Sander, the orchid king. When *his* ship caught fire, destroying all the specimens he had collected, he cabled 'Ship burnt? What do?' 'Go back,' Sander replied. 'Too late,' Micholitz wrote. 'Rainy season.' 'Go back,' Sander said. And Micholitz did. Man's a regular tyrant. My good luck I never wound up working for him."

Ransome turned back to Miss Ripley with a smile every bit as unpleasant as one of her own. "As for your tales of man-eating orchids, I'm sorry to report that they were quite exaggerated. The plant in question was one of Micholitz' dendrobiums. I'm sure his Lordship recalls the details now. Skull and plant were both exhibited at one of Sander's sales along with an idol the natives insisted Micholitz bring back with him to protect him from the plants. Created quite the stir, although the bit about the devouring is arrant nonsense, as I'm sure Lord Hardcastle is too polite to say. Orchids are epiphytes, which means they grow on any organic, porous surface. A graveyard full of decaying bones, such as Micholitz discovered, is a perfect medium. I believe Lord Hardcastle made some modest experiments on reproducing the medium himself."

"I don't think," Hardcastle choked, "that perhaps the details are entirely appropriate for ladies' ears."

"Of course not," Mama concurred, her smile quite restored. "I had no idea that such a lovely flower could be so *improper*." But there was a gleam of interest in her eyes that suggested, to Libba's disbelief, that perhaps there was a tiny part of Mama that rather liked the idea.

"Well, there are always those who emphasize the orchid's exotic and unnatural aspects, but there are always people who will do that about anything, aren't there?" Ransome said, blandly ignoring the ugly flush that suddenly stained Miss Ripley's cheeks. "But since Sander also serves as Royal Orchid Grower to no less a personage than Her Majesty, the Queen, one would be hard-pressed to deem them improper. And even without Her Majesty's *imprimatur*, it doesn't take much delving into legend to find several improving stories nestled among them. The deep purple spots on the English *Orchis mascula* are said to be the stains of Our Saviour's blood as it flowed from his wounded body on the cross, at whose feet the Orchis was said to grow. And, of course, long before it was named for the wanton goddess of Cyprus, the Lady's Slipper orchid was said to have been created by the Infant Jesus so that his mother might be gently shod. Might still have been named for Our Lady, had not Linnaeus been too staunch a Protestant to stand for such papist nonsense. Pity the man was so sorely lacking the fundamentals of a good, classical education. Nonetheless, you do have to admire his capacity for organization."

As the words spilled casually from his lips, he continued to pass around food, seemingly oblivious to the stunned silence in which everyone was staring at him. Batman, indeed. He was clearly set on some deeper scheme, but what? What had he being doing in her bedroom in Tavistock? And why exactly had he followed them here?

The sound of rapidly approaching hoof beats forced Libba to set aside the question—at least for the moment—as Papa rode into the clearing, the placid cob's brother moving at a pace he had not achieved since he was a colt. Behind him rode another man, his face set with palpable anger.

"Gentlemen!" Mama exclaimed. "What an unexpected pleasure! Have you decided to join us for luncheon?"

The man cut Mama off. "I'm afraid I have no time for niceties. We need to put an end to this business for once and for all."

Libba sucked in an angry breath at the man's rudeness, even before she recognized his voice. Then her temper flared. It was too much. There was no reason to allow this farce to continue. Why not just fling the truth of that overheard conversation in the faces of the two men who were standing there, and a pox upon the resultant scandal—along with Cousin Cornelia's vaunted Vanderbilt connections? Miss Ripley might dine out on the scene, but as far as Libba was concerned, she was welcome to sing for her supper at any table other than the one at Braddock House.

But as the angry accusations sprang to her lips, Ransome stopped her with a sharp glance. Slowly, meaningfully, he shook his head. And although she couldn't have told you why she obeyed, she subsided into unwilling silence, as Papa turned on Gaddis, his face as stony as the quarries he owned. "You were the one who insisted on imposing your presence. So I will thank you to show some manners or withdraw yourself immediately."

Not even waiting for Gaddis's spluttered retort, Papa turned to Lord Hardcastle and went on. "Gaddis, here, claims there are certain . . . irregularities in your connection with Mrs. Philipse Braddock, as well as with the Hardcastle title. Your man volunteered to ride ahead to prevent there being any hint that you might be attempting to take advantage of the ladies until the matter is fully resolved."

Hardcastle cast Ransome a venomous glance. "Jolly decent of him."

"Oh, your Lordship knows I would do anything on your behalf." He turned to Papa and added confidingly, "We're regular blood brothers under the skin. Practically twins. Why at times, we've even been mistaken for one another."

"Loyal as my man is intent on proving himself, I am happy to offer my own explanations." Hardcastle cut him with a tight smile. "My father was Sir Roderick Naughton, of the cadet branch of the Hardcastle family. The family conspired to deprive me of my inheritance by dismissing me as his natural son. However, Mrs. Philipse Braddock, who was an especial friend of my father's, was good enough to help me prove my legitimacy."

Papa's face was granite. "She helped you find your parents' marriage lines?"

"No, but I have a witness to their wedding . . . oh, I'm not too proud to say the word, their elopement. A fellow named Tam Jenkins. Perhaps you've heard of him?"

Papa froze, and suddenly, Libba felt like she was looking at a stranger. She glanced over at Ransome, and her stomach sank as she saw that his face had darkened with concern as well. And Libba was suddenly very glad she had held her tongue. No point in squandering whatever small advantage she had over either Hardcastle or Gaddis. She was beginning to believe she might very well need it later.

"As I recall, half the people in Tavistock mentioned him," Papa said, his voice carefully level. "But only as a rumor. A legend."

"Oh, Tam Jenkins is real enough. And it is just my good fortune to have found him."

"And do you intend to produce him in order to cement your claim?" Papa asked.

"That," Lord Hardcastle said, "might be something better discussed in private."

If it were possible, Papa's face grew even stonier. "If a matter can't be discussed in public, then I prefer not to discuss it."

"Deuced hard talking with a rumor in most cases," Ransome cut in. "So I beg you return to the question of Lord Hardcastle's *bona fides*. I'm certain all questions of legitmacy could be set aside, if he simply produced his letters of introduction for everyone to inspect."

"I've heard enough. I intend to inform Mrs. Philipse Braddock that your claim is spurious immediately." Gaddis swung his horse around, throwing one last threat over his shoulder before he nudged it into a trot. "And as for you Wadsworth, you might care to reconsider my offer. My friends are powerful. And they are disposed to take your side in matters. I would suggest you do your best to keep things that way."

"I appreciate your concern," Papa said—his gratitude clearly about as sincere as Hardcastle's amorous advances. The he turned and saw Mama, who had grown more drawn and pale with every word of the discussion, and his face went dark with a desperate sadness Libba could only wish she had never seen. "My apologies, ladies, for subjecting you to this uncomfortable discussion," he said. "And I think it best to spare you anymore. Mr. Ransome, would you be so good as to exchange your horse with His Lordship and drive the ladies back to Braddock House? For I'm afraid I must insist that Lord Hardcastle is unwelcome at Braddock House until he is able to offer a somewhat more satisfactory explanation than he has thus far."

Chapter 13

Ransome was not a man given to poetic flights of fancy. And, honestly, a livery stable was not a place to inspire such poetic flights. But, as he helped the groom unharness the cob from the trap and settle it in a stall until Wadsworth's man arrived to retrieve it, Ransome found himself musing that Miss Libba Wadsworth's mouth was at least as remarkable as her eyes. Arguably even more so, for in her mouth was her very clever tongue, which was extraordinary for its ability to enable her to stand her ground with the likes of Miss Ripley. As for what other extraordinary things that clever tongue might be capable of . . .

He shook his head. What was he thinking? Any more, and he might find himself composing a sonnet on the cob nuzzling at his feed bag. But such reflections were strictly rhetorical. He knew exactly what he was thinking. He wanted to kiss Libba Wadsworth—and not only on her lips. On all those very interesting places that he would enjoy helping her explore. What's more, he was startled to realize he had every intention of doing that. In the privacy and leisure of their wedding night, and for a very long time after that.

In short, he thought with remarkable clear-sightedness, he wanted to marry Libba Wadsworth—as much as he had wanted anything in his life. And when Ransome wanted something—from the chance to photograph the Three Birds Orchis in full bloom, to samples of the rare blue vandaceous orchid—he generally got his way. But somehow, he sensed, this was likely to prove far more complicated than scaling the side of a rumbling volcano or swimming a raging rapid with a specimen clutched in his teeth. First, there was the matter of getting Libba Wadsworth to say yes. He could take refuge in the fact that she apparently preferred him to Hardcastle—it did make matters easier to think of him as such, for the title still did not sit easily on his own shoulders. An optimistic man might take that as evidence of his innate charm with ladies, although Ransome was certain his female relatives would scarcely concur. Taking their side of things, a pessimistic man might find himself somewhat deflated by the level-headedness with which Libba seemed to treat him. And an even more pessimistic man would sense that the lady's level-headedness might harden into something much more . . . intransigent when she discovered he was not a simple adventurer, but an earl who had apparently been playing her family and her for a fool.

Then there was the matter of convincing the Wadsworths. Just the thought made Ransome wince. Despite her delicate appearance, Mrs. Wadsworth, he was morally certain, could fly into a rage that would rival the Dowager Countess at her most towering. But surely a *bona fide* earldom would be enough to placate the lady in time.

Wadsworth was more of a challenge. Wadsworth would be infuriated at being lied to, no matter how Ransome tried to explain that he had simply seized an opportunity and had every intention of setting things straight as soon as he could. It wouldn't matter that Hardcastle was clearly no friend to Wadsworth—although most men would be swayed by that argument. Just as most men would probably welcome the news that their daughter was now being wooed by an earl, rather than a confidential agent cum orchid smuggler. But Ransome had rapidly come to the conclusion that Lucius Wadsworth was not most men.

Most pressing, however, was the question of Gaddis. Neither Hardcastle nor the threat of scandal was an insurmountable problem. Time—and Libba Wadsworth— were on Ransome's side in both those matters. But Gaddis was a far murkier adversary— and, Ransome was certain, a far more dangerous one.

Well, if the army—along with his subsequent somewhat chequered career—had taught Ransome one thing, it was that when in doubt, it was far better to take the fight to the enemy than to wait for the enemy to attack on his own terms. And right now, there was one piece of ground that Ransome knew how to control. Flipping a coin to the stable lad, he started out for the railway station. Disguising himself as a batman had outlived its usefulness. It was time to take back his name and titles. He had taken the precaution of cabling for his *bona fides* from the Rhinecliff train station, and it was possible a reply already awaited him there. If not, he would draft a second, far more urgent cable—one designed to elicit a reply within the day. And then he would devote all his persuasive abilities—which most agreed were not inconsiderable—to convincing the imposter to accept a healthy sum simply to vanish in the middle of the night, taking his tales of clandestine marriages with him. The only trick would be to make sure he didn't carry off the family silver as well.

But when Ransome reached the railway station, he saw Hardcastle emerge with the air of a man who had just negotiated a successful business transaction. Operating on years of instinct, Ransome fell into pace behind him as Hardcastle strolled up the village's twisting main street toward the prominence where the Braddock's Landing Subscription Library and the memorial to the eponymous Colonel Braddock held pride of place. But Hardcastle was heading toward neither of those; instead, he turned toward the white, clapboard church. With a wince, Ransome mouthed a silent prayer to whatever powers he might have offended back in Tavistock that the man was not seeking another registry office. He was not certain even he would have the strength to defend himself to the Dowager Countess over a second instance of desecration.

But instead of going into the church, Hardcastle slipped into the grassy graveyard where generations of Braddocks rested beneath weathered gravestones. Moving with long-honed reflexes, Ransome doubled back through the well-tended garden of the rectory, then hopped the iron fence and slipped behind a marble angel who wept over the fates of generations of deceased Ripleys, in order to listen.

"I would have this out once and for all between us," Gaddis snarled. "What game are you playing at?"

Hardcastle smiled unpleasantly. "Dear me," he said, "Was Mrs. Philipse Braddock less prostrated by your news than you hoped she might be? Did she perhaps even tell you to mind your own affairs—maybe even to remember your place?"

"You have her in your power. Some kind of hold over her."

"What? Do you hope to startle me into a confession?" Hardcastle asked. "Do you have several stout Pinkertons hidden behind one of these gravestones, ready to leap out and apprehend me?"

Bloody hell. Had inheriting a title already caused him to lose his touch? Had Hardcastle spotted him?

"Then again," Hardcastle mused, "such drama might play havoc with the shareholders in the various business ventures Mrs. Philipse Braddock holds in trust from her late husband. Perhaps they might even be skittish enough to demand a complete examination of the trust fund's books."

There was a moment's thunderous silence. And then Gaddis said, "If you have an accusation to make, come out and say it."

"You're robbing her blind, Mr. Gaddis. You and I both know it. The only question is, who else finds out."

"You want money."

"I will certainly give you an opportunity to name your price. After I see what price . . . other interested parties might offer. Old Wadsworth, for instance. It might be a suitable bride-price to offer my new father-in-law."

"That's extortion."

"I prefer to refer to it as negotiating terms," Hardcastle said. "Which is why I don't really believe there is a Pinkerton lurking behind a gravestone. Because if I'm arrested, I know enough to make sure you're arrested as well. And from everything I've heard, there are plenty of people down in Tammany Hall who would be delighted to see that happen."

There was a long moment's pause. And then Gaddis said, "You have no idea who you're dealing with. But you are about to find out."

And he spun on his heel and stalked out of the graveyard. Leaning back against a gravestone, Hardcastle whistled an aimless tune as he watched Gaddis go. And when Gaddis's angry footsteps at last died away, he called out, "Do come forth, my loyal servant. Am I to believe you were there to cover my back? Or is it more likely that was where you were going to shoot me?"

So he had been seen, Ransome thought with a surge of professional irritation. Just as well that he had never had any intention of returning to his original career. But that was scant consolation in the face of the problem now facing him, for it did not take a decade's hard-won expertise to recognize the glint of a pistol in Hardcastle's hand.

"For God's sake, put that thing away before you get yourself in more trouble than you're already in," Ransome sighed. "Killing a man in cold blood in a graveyard is not a way to avoid scandal. Or hanging for that matter. Either of which would solve Gaddis's problems admirably, by the way."

Hardcastle thought for a moment, then conceded the point with a nod and lowered his weapon. "Who are you?"

"I think you know."

"And what exactly is your interest in this affair?"

"Beyond the obvious?"

"Humor me. You know as well as I do that I pose no serious threat to either your titles or estates. So why should you concern yourself with the Wadsworths and this backwater? There are far wealthier drawing rooms in this country where your earldom would be welcome. Leave this one to me. You have my assurance that in fact, I'm doing you a tremendous favor. This is one marriage you'd find yourself well out of."

Ransome's fists clenched. "Are you casting aspersions on the character of Miss Libba Wadsworth?"

"Casting aspersions on my future wife? Now that would be ungentlemanly," Hardcastle said with a soft chuckle.

Ransome's temper exploded, and it was all he could do not to simply wrestle the man to the ground and then off to the local sheriff's office right then and there. But while the resulting scandal might not rise to the level of desecration in the Dowager Countess's view, he was certain it would result in the kind of unpleasant interview he was doing his utmost to avoid.

"Listen to me, you bloody fool," he hissed, struggling to contain his fury, "I am offering you a chance you don't deserve. So I bloody well suggest you take it. Instead of having you hauled off to jail where you belong, I simply want you to leave. Immediately. On the next available train. And leave it to me to explain away this case of mistaken identity with a minimum of scandal."

"And why should I do that?"

"Because you know as well as I do that you will never get away with this in the long run. And right now, I am willing to pay you handsomely to put an end to things while you still can."

Hardcastle's eyes narrowed. "Why?"

"That's none of your concern. What is your concern is I am offering you a way out of this mess. And you are likely to receive precious few such other offers."

Hardcastle studied him for a moment, then smiled. "The problem is, I need no such offers. Go ahead. Expose me for an imposter. Libba Wadsworth will still not refuse me."

"You would force a lady into giving you her hand?"

"From what I've seen of polite society, that's simply called courtship," Hardcastle said with a shrug. "But since you did me a fair enough turn with Gaddis, I'll offer you a chance to find out for yourself—in the spirit of a gentleman. Before you interfere any more in the affairs of the Wadsworths, I suggest you inquire into their recent precipitate departure from Tavistock—on the heels of a visit from the bailiff, it is said." Hardcastle raised an eyebrow. "Having spent all that time and effort into scraping an introduction into English society it seems difficult to imagine what would make a lady as determined as Mrs. Wadsworth abandon her glittering plans for her daughter. Or perhaps I should say, who."

"Roderick Naughton?"

"My late unlamented father is, alas, dead."

"Then this Tam Jenkins."

"Come now. You cannot expect me to do all your work for you. But I would most earnestly advise you to spare yourself the effort and concentrate instead on other drawing rooms where your title will be welcome. For, make no mistake about it, I will wed Miss Wadsworth—unless I receive a better offer from Gaddis and his friends. And it will not matter in the least whether I'm the Earl of Hardcastle or not. Libba Wadsworth will marry me—she will have no choice."

Ransome studied the imposter, the urge to simply haul off and hit him at war with appalled pity at the man's blatant stupidity. "You should take my offer," he said. "You're playing a very dangerous game, and not one I believe you're destined to win."

"Is that a threat?"

"That is a fact. One that you would do well to realize before it's too late. Because there is only one way to release oneself from the clutches of a blackmailer—and that's to remove the blackmailer. I am at least proposing to do so using money rather than a pistol. But I can think of several others in Braddock's Landing who would not scruple to do otherwise." Shaking his head, Ransome turned to go. "Think about my offer, Mr. Naughton. Consider it very seriously. Because it is the only possible way you will leave Braddock's Landing alive."

Chapter 14

At least, Libba thought as she tried to drift off to sleep that night, Ransome had been more adept than Hardcastle at driving, commanding the cob's grateful cooperation with a single flick of the reins. So the dispirited return to Braddock House was mercifully relieved of the shadow of imminent death. Dying for love was all well and good, Libba had to suppose, when it came to the tragic Lady Cora, but even the poetical Miss Ripley would have to agree that dying for nothing but an unwelcome suitor's sheer incompetence could be nothing other than an embarrassment.

But it was not the matter of horsemanship that had Libba tossing and turning into the night. It was the memory of that last hasty conversation, when Ransome had drawn her out of earshot with a quick glance at Mama, after he had handed down the other ladies. "This farce has gone on long enough. I promise you that I will find a way to put an end to it," he said quietly. "I will send you word, as soon as I can."

"I will wait for it eagerly."

Which sounded so terribly forward, even to her ears, that she found herself blushing. And suddenly, Ransome was flushing as well—and strangely loath to release her hand. "When we finally have matters resolved to everyone's satisfaction," he said, with an awkwardness she would not have suspected him capable of, "I would like to explain myself to your father directly . . . that is, if you would not find it objectionable."

Objectionable? Should she? Did she?

Before she could even answer that question in her own mind, Ransome had leapt back on the box and urged the pony off in a brisk trot. And as Libba turned for the house, her fingers trailing to her lips at the memory of that . . . singular interview with Ransome, she felt Mama's worried gaze— a clear warning that no matter what Libba's feelings about Ransome's advances, there were bound to be serious objections from almost every other corner—objections that she could not imagine how even the indefatigable Ransome proposed to surmount.

Yet she found herself curiously certain that he would find a way to surmount them—and even more curiously, eager to see him succeed. So when Mama came downstairs the next morning, hours earlier than usual, already attired in a walking dress and hat, a string of pearls around her neck, and proclaimed the weather so beautiful that she would join the gardener on his walk down to the village to retrieve the missing pony trap, Libba insisted on accompanying her, hoping to engineer a chance meeting with Ransome. Alas, they arrived so unfashionably early that the only people on the street were the farmers delivering milk and the few lads and lasses who helped out at the hotel and livery stable down at the Landing. There was no sign of life on what was known as the high end of the street—both figuratively and literally. And no sign of Ransome.

Perhaps because there was nowhere else to go, while the gardener conducted his business at the livery stable, Mama went unhesitatingly through the doors of the circulating library. Even more unexpectedly, she encouraged Libba to go explore the newly arrived volumes on the shelves in the back room, while she collected the mail from the post master at the front desk. Such was Libba's surprise, that she barely noticed the newly-arrived titles. Was this meant to be a treat from Mama? Some form of atonement for the disastrous *fete champetre*?

She could think of no other explanation, for once their business there was finished, Mama called for the pony trap and asked the gardener to drive them back to Braddock House. But when he handed them into the trap, Libba gasped, "Mama! You've lost your pearls."

Mama blinked back from the troubled reverie that had consumed her all morning.

"What pearls, dear?"

"The ones you were wearing when we left the house. They're gone."

"Oh, no. I'm sure you must be mistaken, dear."

"I'm not. I distinctly remember." She turned to the gardener. "You were with us! You saw them—"

"Please, Libba! Contentiousness is so unattractive."

"But . . ."

"Sorry, miss. Can't say as I'm a man to remember the details of ladies' clothing," the gardener said, making any further debate useless.

But as he pulled the trap to a halt and handed them down at the front door of Braddock House, Libba saw him study Mama with a canny gaze that reminded her very much of Papa.

In another moment, the incident was forgotten, shadowed beneath a new and even more unwelcome development. While they had been at the post office, another missive had arrived, and now lay on the silver salver where the post was normally delivered: a delicate nosegay of garden pinks and roses. Mama froze in her tracks.

"Is that a tussie mussie?"

"It would seem to be," Libba allowed, uncertain whether she should even admit knowing about such bouquets with messages coded in the secret language of flowers.

"Then burn it!" Mama commanded. "I will not have such a thing in my house."

Libba eyed her mother unhappily, as aware of the reasons that underlay Mama's unusual vehemence as she was aware she was not supposed to know anything about a scandal that dated back to when Miss Ripley cemented her shocking reputation as a New Woman and Lady Novelist by returning from a tour of the continent with a Bohemian instructor from the Art Students League in tow. Ostensibly, he was there to illustrate Miss Ripley's arch *Language of Flowers*, which was said to be as naughtily satirical as that of Mr. Wilde. But while they worked on the book, they openly shared Miss Ripley's cottage, drinking wine and smoking cigarillos (and some whispered opium). The artist's surprising willingness to also attempt to refine a ten-year-old Libba's nascent accomplishments had only been explained when the volume was at last published. His flowers all had the same face: Mama, as the sensuous tulip, the fleshy carnation, the queenly rose, the dangerous oleander, the beautiful orchid, and dozens more—each illustration exquisite, and carefully within the bounds of propriety, even as the curves his crayons had traced her figure with more intimacy than a husband's. Miss Ripley had of course blamed Mama, telling anyone who would listen that Mama had flung herself at the man, seeking solace for a loveless marriage. Libba thought the fact that the Bohemian instructor had last been heard of seducing nude models in Paris suggested that the blame for what happened—if, in fact, anything had happened—lay squarely at his easel.

"We should first determine what meaning it is meant to convey," Libba said.

"You would consult that vile book?" Mama gasped, forgetting the unspoken conspiracy not to recognize anything untoward in the affectionately inscribed volume Miss Ripley had presented to a humiliated Mama.

"I think the message is simple enough not to require a dictionary," Libba said hastily. "Pinks mean a proposal of marriage, do they not?"

She needn't have phrased it as a question. She knew full well that when a gentlemen presented a lady with a pink, she was expected to respond with another pink if she accepted, and a carnation, if she refused. It was knowledge she had gleaned from a work by one Louisa Anne Twamley, a poetess who shared Miss Ripley's taste for arch satire, in which tragedy ensued when the over-enthusiastic Lady Edith had mistakenly sent Lord Rupert a carnation instead of a pink, in an attempt to convey her delight at his proposal by sending the largest blossom she could find.

"And a full blown rose over two buds symbolizes secrecy," Mama said grimly. She turned on Libba, her mouth tight. "So this bouquet is meant to suggest a secret proposal. Can there be any doubt to that meaning?"

"No," Libba conceded unhappily. She shook her head. There was no card, but surely this could only be from Hardcastle. But how was she to believe the sheer, untrammeled *persistence* of the man?

"Mama," she said earnestly, "I give you my word that whatever Hardcastle is scheming, I have no part in it. Surely you must know that I would never stoop to such a thing as an elopement—"

"Stoop!" Mama hissed. "Just who exactly do you think you're talking to?"

Libba's eyes widened. "I . . . didn't . . . I only meant—"

"I will not have it! I will not have it, do you hear?" Mama cried over Libba's stammered objections. And snatching up the bouquet, she stormed toward the kitchen, calling for Cook to fetch her a box of lucifers immediately.

"Mama! Wait!" Libba cried, wondering when everything she had thought was safe and comfortable in her world had developed an alarming propensity to transform into a scene from a sensation novel. "Would not returning it convey a clearer message?"

"Perhaps."

Mama paused to consider the idea, eying Libba in a way that suggested she suspected some ulterior scheme. And Libba was coming up with at least the glimmerings of a plan. She must return the nosegay to Ransome and hope that if Hardcastle were rash enough to attempt to carry her off, Ransome could catch him in the act—and put paid to Hardcastle's pretensions once and for all. Ransome had said discretion was in all their interests, but Ransome was wrong. Discretion was solely in Lord Hardcastle's interest, for as long as they were all afraid to make a scene, all he had to do was threaten one to compel their cooperation. Mama would be appalled of course, and Braddock's Landing would gossip. But Mama would recover, and a new scandal would arise eventually. The time had come to make the most shocking scene she could.

Libba was later to reflect bitterly that some evil genie must have overheard her wish, for that very evening, her world exploded into one shocking scene, followed by another. The first—and by far the least shocking—came when Papa returned home well after dinner and locked himself in the library. Never in her lifetime had Libba dared to brave such a clear signal—especially when, as she hurried across the terrace toward the French windows that gave into the library, she smelled smoke. A fire was unseasonable by anyone's standards on such a mild evening, but it was particularly odd for Papa, who prided himself on having the constitution of a Highlander. Suddenly cautious, Libba peered inside before she took the bold step of tapping on the pane. And saw her father crouched by the fireplace, feeding a stack of yellowed papers into the fire.

Papa burning letters? It seemed about as likely as Mama running the quarry. Or Miss Ripley giving a penny to a beggar out of sheer charity.

"Papa, I would talk," Libba began, drawing closer to the window in sudden resolve. But a gentle tap on the library door forestalled her and she drew back and watched in silence as Papa slid the remaining papers into his strongbox before turning the lock on the door and opening it.

He seemed as startled as Libba to see Mama cross the threshold and turn the key in the lock behind her.

"Mr. Wadsworth," she said, twisting the fringe on the edge of her India-silk wrap, "I would beg the privilege of speaking privately. And frankly."

"If that is a right I extend to my workmen, I see not why it would not apply to my wife," he said. "I apologize if I ever gave you reason to think otherwise."

"No reason, Mr. Wadsworth. Of course not. I had no intention of insulting you." Mama flushed and she pulled her wrap tighter, as if girding herself in sudden resolve. And then she pulled out a string of pearls. *The* string of pearls. The one that had gone missing. "I seem to have lost these in the village this morning. Happily, they have been returned to my jewel case tonight."

"The postmaster found them. He would have returned them personally, but I saved him the trip."

Her mouth twisted into a smile that still somehow managed to remain beautiful. "I said I would speak frankly, and I mean to. I never should have sought to hide my fault from you, grievous as it was. I can only plead that your knowing of it is a punishment I can scarcely bear."

"Who spoke of punishment? Do you confuse me with a judge or schoolmistress? A priest perhaps?" His face darkened. "If there is any fault to tax you with, it is not coming to me in the first place. I would have given you the money without question. Lord knows, it has been yours from the start."

"You know that's not the case! You built this fortune."

A glint of humor crossed his face. "Mayhap that is true. But at the very least, I would have gotten the papers back from the blackguard."

Mama's shoulders slumped. "He said the pearls only bought me the right to bid. He said he had other interested parties."

"And so he would have kept saying until he'd bled you out of every jewel in your case. And then he would have

started on the silver and the housekeeping money. Begging
your pardon, Mrs. Wadsworth," he corrected himself hastily,
at her choked cry. "But you did ask me to speak frankly."

She drew a deep breath. "From that am I to believe you
were more successful in retrieving these misdirected letters
than I was?"

"I would have you believe that the matter is settled.
And I beg you put it from your mind. Now, was there
anything else, Mrs. Wadsworth?"

She made as if to go, then stopped, her shoulders
stiffening. "Yes, Mr. Wadsworth, there is. I would have you
know that I have never once failed in my wifely duty. No
matter what others may insinuate about my character."

There was a long moment's pause, during which Libba
caught a glimpse of her father's face reflected in the open
terrace door. She immediately wished she hadn't. And then
Papa said, "You wrong me, Mrs. Wadsworth. You do me the
worst kind of wrong."

Her eyes flared. "Luke . . . please. I didn't mean . . . I
never meant . . ." Mama stammered. "The fault is all mine,
as I am well aware . . ."

Mama awkward and at a loss for words. Papa distant
and sarcastic. Of course, Libba had been long aware that
they moved through their separate spheres like polite
strangers—but strangers who were comfortable with the
arrangement. This was different; the scene inside the library
didn't belong in Libba's home. It did not even belong in one
of Miss Ripley's poems. This was real and private pain—of
a kind Libba never hoped to know in her life.

She should go; she had no right to spy on her parents
like this. But before she could slip back into the comforting
darkness of the lawns, she watched her father's face slacken

in defeat, then harden into a careful mask. "Please forgive my vehemence," he said, his voice preternaturally polite, as he stalked to the library door and opened it for her. "Of course, there can be no question of fault or wrong. There never has been. I would simply beg you to consider the matter settled, Mrs. Wadsworth, and put it completely from your mind. Now, if you would excuse me, I have a late night ahead of me already."

Mama hesitated, as if she was thinking of refusing. But manners won out, and she inclined her head stiffly. "Then I shall keep you from your work no longer," she said. "Good night, Mr. Wadsworth."

"Good night, Mrs. Wadsworth," he said, closing the door behind her. And locking it again.

Chapter 15

Orchid hunting—as well as a few less reputable ventures—had given Ransome too much experience of Hardcastle's type for him to have any hope the man would heed his warning. Men like Hardcastle were always looking for the quick and easy way out, so tragically sure of their own cleverness that they inevitably found themselves hoist on their own petard. They were men who would do anything to best their rivals: bribing natives to draw false maps, sabotaging camps, laming horses in the dead of night, and even pissing on plants that they could not carry out with them in order to destroy them before others might find them. Such things were counted bad behavior even among the rough and tumble orchid hunters whom Ransome called friends and colleagues, and there would be many among them who would argue that Ransome should have just abandoned Hardcastle to his fate. After all, death was unremarkable in the world of orchid hunters.

One of the most famous of them, Leon Humboldt, had once observed that all six of the orchid hunters he had enjoyed a dinner with in Madagascar were dead within six years. But it seemed Ransome's newfound unwillingness to dedicate his life to a career he had always assumed would be the death of him also made him unwilling to see others die. Ransome wanted—no, needed—to be better than that, for Libba Wadsworth's husband needed to be better than that. In fact, he was appalled to realize, Miss Wadsworth seemed to have infected him with a near-fatal case of *noblesse oblige*. Not that he anticipated spending the rest of his life riding to hounds and seducing chambermaids to the despair of his female relations, as his cousin had insisted on doing. But sleeping alone with only a canvas tent to protect him from the drenching rains and the mosquitoes suddenly didn't seem quite as appealing as lying in a soft bed with Libba Wadsworth in his arms. Just as even the Three Bird's Orchid in full bloom didn't seem like half so precious a prize as. . . .

That train of thought was cut off—all for the better, his mother would most likely opine—as an all-too-familiar pony trap emerged to block Ransome's path back down the hill toward the cable office at the railway station. The gardener who had menaced Ransome with a pitchfork held the reins in one hand. Somewhat improbably, in his other hand, he clutched a bouquet. Even more improbably, he climbed out of the cart in order to present it to Ransome with a mocking flourish. "Miss Wadsworth sends her compliments, but she begs me to say that there is no way she can accept such an offering from you."

Ransome eyed the bouquet in disbelief. "She believes this nosegay to be from me?"

"Would ye be saying otherwise?"

"Well, of course I would . . ." Ransome stiffened, his professional pride offended. "I am an orchid hunter, as

Miss Wadsworth is well aware. Were I to send a token of my esteem, how could she think I would send any lesser bloom?"

"The young miss was adamant that you had," the groundsman said.

"The lady is of an adamant disposition," Ransome allowed. "But I assure you, it was not I who sent this bouquet."

The gardener's eyes glinted as he studied Ransome. "She gave me very specific instructions. Said that I was to return this to your hands alone, and to tell you that the message it contained was anathema to her."

"Message?" Ransome eyed the bouquet somewhat more interestedly. So this was meant to be some sort of missive, smuggled out to him from beneath her parents' watchful gaze? Was he to then assume that there was some kind of message concealed inside? But where? How? Had she concealed a tiny spool of parchment among the flowers? Or perhaps she had used lemon juice as invisible ink on the delicate tissue that contained the stems?

"Did Miss Wadsworth perhaps read out loud the specifics of the particular message that offended?" Ransome asked.

"I wouldna' listen even if she had. Don't mind saying that I thought we'd put paid to this language of flowers with that tutor fellow years ago," the gardener snorted. "Tearing up my beds to send luncheon invitations. Nothing but sheer nonsense. Why do they not simply write poems? It would at least spare the poor plants."

Language of flowers? Ransome eyed the nosegay. Was he to believe the flowers themselves were the message, then? Who had ever heard of such tripe? Of course, Ransome knew some flowers had meanings—he had had the Bard with his rosemary for remembrance pounded into his head by tutors like any boy. But surely there were more efficient ways to communicate.

More to the point, how on earth was he expected to decode such a thing? "Might Miss Wadsworth have even offered a hint as to a basic vocabulary?" he said hopefully.

"The young miss said Miss Ripley was dictionary enough, and you might as well go back to her," the gardener snorted. "Said an unlettered man like you could never have mastered such a delicate art as the language of flowers, and that you must have consulted her to create even such a simple bouquet."

Unlettered? Incapable of mastering the delicate art? Such words were a trifle harsh, were they not? But Ransome bowed his head meekly, doing his best to hide his grin from the gardener's all-too-canny gaze, as he said, "Please convey my most sincere apologies to Miss Wadsworth and inform her most specifically that my only desire is to rectify the wrong in whatever way my poor powers can."

With a harrumph that suggested Ransome's chastened capitulation had not been entirely convincing, the gardener climbed back into the cart, clucked to the cob, and drove away.

It cost him several minutes debate whether to catch the local train to Rhinebeck to check whether his *bona fides* had at last arrived, or to pursue Miss Wadsworth's unconventional summons. In an agony of self-improvement that would have left his mother slack-jawed in disbelief, he chose the simpler option—only to find himself unjustly rewarded with the news no cable had arrived. Feeling more than a little hard done by, he was forced to wait until the morning to take directions to Miss Ripley's cottage.

Between the dusty hiker's kit and his arguably un-gentlemanly corrections of her misconceptions about orchids during the ride in the pony trap, he was somewhat uncertain whether she would even receive him. But the odor of scandal proved too enticing to resist; her eyes widened when she saw the bouquet. "Ooh, a tussie-mussie," she breathed. "Dare I hope 'tis for me?"

She could—as much as Ransome dared hope that no one had thought to torture a bunch of innocent flowers with such a ridiculous name. "I am certain that this nosegay befits you far more than its intended recipient," he said, with a gallant smile that would have immediately occasioned a whispered reproach from his mother about his unfortunate tendency toward *irony*.

Miss Ripley frowned as she studied the flowers. "Although, in truth, my honor forces me to protest, 'tis really rather a *naughty* message, is it not?" she asked.

"Naughty?" he asked, kissing the hand she held out to him, before he added with an unctuousness that would have had his mother gasping in outrage, "Unfortunately, I'm afraid I'm entirely at your mercy in the matter. I am, alas, too unlettered to parse the delicate language of flowers."

She rapped his knuckles with a swift tap of her fan. "Now, you descend to flattery, Mr. Ransome. If I did not know you better, I would charge you with seeking to know the worst of the Wadsworth's secrets. But perhaps in fact, you already suspect. . . ?"

A talent for irony was much diminished, Ransome thought, when you were fighting down the urge to throttle your interlocutor. That is, if, contrary to all his dear mother's worst remonstrances, he had ever actually ever possessed said talent. Grimly, he pasted his smile back into place. "I suspect nothing. I would simply understand. . . ."

"Like mother, like daughter, of course," Miss Ripley said. "The apple doesn't fall far from the tree, to coin a phrase."

She spared a moment's consideration of the nosegay. "Pinks, a proposal of marriage. A full blown rose, over a pair of buds, a request for secrecy. If ever I've seen a summons to an elopement, this is it." She shook her head. "You would have thought the girl would have had more sense. But she is pert—entirely too pert for her own good. Oh, well. Pride goeth before a fall, and all that. Still you would have thought that she would have at least taken heed of Braddock House's . . . unfortunate history of such things."

"You mean the tale of the Renegade and his unfired pistol?" Ransome said. "I understand you've penned a lyric work on the subject."

"Oh, my trifling contribution to the Sapphic art is but a pittance. The widow's mite at best," Miss Ripley said. "Although I do so love such old legends. In fact, 'tis the reason I chose to settle here after all my . . . peregrinations. The Hudson Valley is positively *crawling* with such things, you know. Headless horsemen and white ladies, gnomes, Manitou, Henry Hudson and the Catskill Witch. Not to mention a veritable *army* of outlaws, brigands, and renegades—of which our own Renegade was the captain. His exploits before his fatal duel over Mrs. Braddock provide enough inspiration to pen an entire *library*."

Miss Ripley struck a rapturous, and presumably Sapphic, pose before lowering her voice. "But I was talking about a more recent tragedy. I do so hope our dear Libba is not destined to follow her mother's sad example in consenting to an elopement."

Ransome sighed as an unwanted piece of the puzzle fell into place, and he suddenly understood Mrs. Wadsworth's hunted, watchful air. It was not difficult, for it was not much different from that of his own mother, who had succeeded in making an unfortunate match, just as Mrs. Wadsworth had presumably failed in such an endeavor. And although his mother's unfortunate match had had the arguably happy consequence of procuring Ransome an earldom, he found himself unwilling to believe that Mrs. Wadsworth's secrets would prove equally fortunate. But Miss Ripley was not to be stopped.

"Of course, there were those at the time who said it was only the Curse claiming its next victim. All sorts of talk of pistol shots and portents. I believe there was even supposed to be a blood moon—along with a ghostly figure stalking the cliff, alight with weird energy and laughing maniacally on the night of the tragedy. And who knows? It might have been.

"But the truth of the matter—as much as anyone can sort out the truth from all the rumors that swirled at the time—was that the English lord that dear Lydia seemed destined to wed, in what everyone agreed was a brilliant match, was not, shall we say, all that he seemed to be. Driven to desperation by love, he risked all on attempting to carry her off before he could be exposed. No one knows who betrayed the lovers—or the truth of what happened that fateful evening. All that is certain is that the tragic events left poor Lydia's father cataleptic and Luke Watkins—I mean, of course, Lucius Wadsworth—in charge of the business. Of course, everyone was quick to blame the Curse. But one cannot help but ask the age-old question, *Cui bono,* to whose benefit, such a tragedy, now can one?"

To whose benefit indeed? More exactly, to *what* benefit? That was the question that troubled Ransome long after he had left Miss Ripley's cottage, tossing the tussie mussie beneath the Braddock Memorial in a gesture that he hoped would keep the town in legends for another generation. Who would benefit from Libba Wadsworth eloping? Certainly not the lady herself, or her already scandal-plagued family. But certainly not Lord Hardcastle—real or putative— either. So, viewed objectively, why would Hardcastle pursue such a dangerous path when other options lay open to him? What had made him suddenly change his plans and decide to carry off his intended? Surely even he couldn't be foolhardy enough to believe he could kidnap a resisting Libba Wadsworth without arousing all of Braddock House? So what had caused this change in heart?

The only answer Ransome was sure of was that the answer must lie somewhere at Braddock House. And while he was fairly certain the anathema pronounced on Hardcastle would extend to his manservant as well, he was prepared to risk Lucius Wadsworth's wrath—as well as the sharp end of the gardener's pitchfork—to ensure Libba Wadsworth's safety. And if that was true love, well then . . .

Ransome had just paused inside the front gate of Braddock House, in order to consider whether to use the trade entrance or stride directly to the front door, when a shot rang out, rupturing the peace of the summer afternoon. Moments later, a terrace door slammed open and a figure leapt out and raced away across the lawns. Operating on sheer reflex, Ransome took off in pursuit, only to slow in disbelief, as he saw the hooded cloak billowing about the fleeing figure, and the dark scarf masking the fleeing man's face. By the evidence of his own eyes, he had just been confronted with the Renegade's apparition.

Well, those footsteps didn't sound ghostly to Ransome. But now he hesitated, his fear for Libba's safety at war with the instincts honed by a decade's career. His concern for Libba won out, and he turned toward the house, plunging through the neatly trimmed boxwood with a heedlessness that he was certain would have the gardener grumbling, up onto the terrace and in through the open door. Where he slipped on something viscous that he just barely had time to identify as blood before he stumbled over a man's body, lying face down behind Lucius Wadsworth's desk, his limp hand stretching toward the display of weapons that had crashed down from the wall.

Even before he turned the body over and felt for the pulse, that one quick professional glance assured him he would not find, Ransome knew whose face would stare up at him, vacant-eyed. But even thus prepared, Ransome felt a weird chill at gazing on the scene of his own murder. His female dependents, he was certain, would be dismayed—and not merely because of their unvoiced suspicion that Ransome had gotten himself murdered solely to evade an earldom. Even he felt a certain discomfort at the manner of his own demise. Being shot from behind was frankly undignified. Being shot in a library filled with antique weapons seemed more than a little incompetent. And being shot by an apparition seemed downright vulgar.

But if he had not been shot by an apparition—which as

a matter of general principle Ransome was inclined to be-lieve—then by whom? The woman he had just proposed to abduct? Alas, knowing Libba, it seemed at least somewhat more likely than the ghost of the Renegade arising in order to protect the Braddock Brides. But what was Hardcastle doing in the library when he was planning an elopement? He should be at the casement of Libba Wadsworth's bed-chamber. Had Libba lured him there in order to consult a volume of Miss Ripley's poems? It made no sense.

And what was that piece of paper clutched in the dead man's hand? Clarification or a further complication? Carefully, Ransome plucked it from the dead man's fingers, and unfolded a terse note that read, "I will receive you at 2 p.m. punctually." It was signed "Lucius Wadsworth."

And Ransome found himself suddenly and unusually uncertain what to do next. He could not work up much sympathy for the dead imposter, but he found himself fighting down a sense of angry betrayal as he straightened away from the body. Had Lucius Wadsworth done this? And in such a dastardly fashion? It seemed impossible. Dammit, Ransome *liked* Lucius Wadsworth, and he usually had good reason to trust his own instincts. Not that he doubted Wadsworth was more than capable of killing a man who threatened his family. But luring a man to his home only to shoot him from behind was a despicable act of treachery Ransome would never have thought the old man capable of.

"Now, then, you'll turn around nice and slow, do you hear me? And then you'll tell me exactly what you're up to."

Wadsworth's voice was cold and deadly, leaving Ransome no doubt the only wise choice was to do exactly what he was told. Raising his hands carefully, he turned to find Wadsworth aiming a blunderbuss that looked all the more dangerous for the fact that it had clearly been seized from the display of arms that had tumbled from the wall. And Ransome drew a deep breath as he arrived at the unhappy realization that he had just been afforded the opportunity to discover what the old man was truly capable of first-hand.

Chapter 16

There had been no blood-curdling shriek. No pounding footsteps in the hallway. No masked figures fleeing across the lawns of Braddock House beneath a blood moon. And yet Libba had known disaster had descended upon Braddock House even before she and Mama converged on the library to find Papa aiming a blunderbuss at a sheepish-looking Ransome, and, according to the men who had positioned themselves by unspoken agreement between the ladies and the horror that lay behind the desk, her suitor dead, the victim of murder most foul.

Mama would have suggested that the only thing a gently-bred woman could do, given the circumstances, was faint—and did so accordingly. Libba felt a vague obligation to follow suit. Miss Ripley, she was certain, would have her go one step further by dying of grief on the spot, to be transformed into a blood-red flower or forever waft the halls of Braddock House in a nightdress stained with her Sweet William's blood, cursing any further Wadsworth brides in vengeance for the dashing of her fondest hopes. But honestly, Libba felt nothing beyond an unworthy sense of having just had a narrow escape. Unfortunately, whatever relief she felt was seriously offset by sheer exasperation with Ransome.

"*This* is what you consider handling matters discreetly?" she demanded, as she knelt to attend to Mama, her fury so complete that she risked bruising her mother's wrists as she chafed them. "Murdering Lord Hardcastle?"

"Might be simpler to start with the second question," Ransome told her. "Bit of a logical impossibility there. A man can't murder himself, you see? Well, actually, he can, but that would be suicide and I can assure you I am possessed of no such tendencies—no matter what the ladies of the Hardcastle family might say."

There was a moment's pause while Libba tried to make sense of what he was saying, but could come to no better answer than Ransome had finally taken leave of his already questionable senses. And then Papa's eyes sharpened. "You're saying this man is not Lord Hardcastle?"

"More precisely, was," Ransome said. "Alas, I can assure you that he is no more. But otherwise, yes, you are correct."

Papa's eyes narrowed. "And the man he purported to be is, in fact, yourself?"

"Yes, sir," Ransome said.

"You told me you were an inquiry agent."

"Well, technically, I told you I was inquiring after him on behalf of the Hardcastle family, which was nothing but the truth." An ominous glint in Papa's eyes, and Ransome hastily chose a less Jesuitical tack. "I apologize for lying to you. It was a serious miscalculation, and one I sincerely wish I could have back. All I can claim is that it seemed the most expedient way to determine what he was planning— seeing as he had stolen my papers along with my identity."

"And what exactly do you claim he was planning to do?" Papa asked.

"Courting your daughter under false pretenses, among other things," Ransome said.

Papa's gaze grew dangerous—so much so that Libba feared he might pull the trigger. "You knew this and yet you let it go on?"

"Miss Wadsworth was aware of the danger. Completely by happenstance, I must admit, but I can assure you I would never have proceeded had the circumstances been otherwise."

Papa turned on Libba. "Is that so, Miss?"

Her fist clenched around the smelling salts as she fought down the urge to fling them at Ransome. "Apparently, I was not aware of at least one salient detail," she spat.

"I told you I had reason to distrust the man. I simply didn't specify what that reason was," he protested, before turning back to Papa hurriedly. "I had every intention of presenting myself to you when I could establish my identity beyond a doubt. I was merely trying to avoid scandal in the interim."

"And may I compliment you on what an excellent job you did of that," Libba said.

"Everything else I told you is perfectly true," Ransome said. "I left the steamer at Poughkeepsie on the trail of an exceedingly rare bloom of orchids, and sent my luggage ahead. This man had already posed as Lord Hardcastle to cross the Atlantic, but he seized the opportunity that arose from my carelessness in order to suborn your station agent into stealing my letters of introduction."

Papa considered that for a moment. "Plausible enough story," he finally decided, and a trace of humor seemed to warm his eyes. "Could happen to any man, I suppose. Still, that doesn't exactly prove which man you are."

"I fear I have little else to offer, except, perhaps, this," Ransome said, and he reached for one of his pockets.

"Slowly!" Papa warned, steadying the gun.

"Slowly," Ransome agreed, pulling out a battered leatherbound memorandum book, and skirting the desk to hold it out in a funny little dance. A chill ran down Libba's spine as she realized the significance of the gesture. There was a body on the floor. An ugly, messy, *murdered* body . . .

"I may not be able to prove my title, but this would presumably prove my *bona fides* as an orchid hunter, as well as my story about the steamship," Ransome said. "I have yet to develop my photographic plates, but I did take a specimen of *Triphora trianthophora*, the Three Birds Orchis that caused my unfortunate—or perhaps I should say happy—departure from the steamship."

He held out the book, but Papa flushed and nodded at Libba. "Best you do this, Miss," he said. "Wouldn't want to get distracted from my aim."

She took the volume unwillingly, hating the way the way the touch of the soft, worn leather reminded her of the way Ransome's lips had brushed her skin. But she hated the thought of embarrassing her father even more. It was well known that Papa could run down a line of figures with breathtaking speed, but his taste for reading was confined to the newspaper's financial pages.

She opened the book and found a tiny flower pressed between two pages of neat handwriting, its pink petals staining the pages. Shaking her head, she glared up at Ransome. "*That* is an orchid?" she demanded. "Am I to believe that such is the root of—how did you term it?

A magnificent obsession that could lead a man to scale mountain peaks and seduce houris—"

"Well, perhaps I exaggerated about the houris," Ransome conceded hastily. "But, in answer to your question, that is exactly why I seized the opportunity so precipitately. The flower is really too delicate to survive pressing, so much so, that I even hesitated at taking one sample. But if you had seen an entire sea of them alive and blooming—it's a like a field of butterflies. And all for just one day . . ."

Briefly, his face was as transported as a poet's. But, Libba wondered, what kind of man—poet or otherwise—spoke of flowers when he just murdered a man on a lady's behalf?

"I think we'd best save the botany for another time," Papa echoed Libba's sentiments. "Even if you are who you say you are, that does nothing to prove you dinna shoot this man. I would argue that would give you every reason."

Ransome nodded thoughtfully, and his eyes went down to the flintlocks and muskets scattered on the floor. "Well, there is also the matter of the smoking gun."

"What smoking gun? I see no smoking gun."

"Exactly," Ransome agreed. "And yet you seem to have caught me red-handed. When and where would I have had time to conceal the murder weapon? Clearly, none of those have been fired in quite some time."

He glanced anxiously at the blunderbuss Papa still wielded. "Nor has that one. And I must really insist, sir, for all our sakes, that you lay it aside . . . *Gently*. For if you pull that trigger, you're likely to set the entire house on fire, if in fact, there is a bullet in that thing."

Papa grinned faintly, and he laid aside the gun. "Of course there's no bullet. Only a fool would hang a loaded gun on the wall . . ."

"Unfortunately, Mr. Ransome's credentials as a fool are far less uncertain than those as an earl," Libba hissed.

Mama's eyelids fluttered, the faintest whiff of impropriety resuscitating her in a way no smelling salts possibly could. "Libba, dear," she said. "That's no fit tone for a lady."

"No fit place for a lady either," Papa said, his face immediately taut with concern for his wife. "Miss, will you help your mother to the drawing room and ensure she is comfortable there. Mr. Ransome and I will follow as soon as we have secured this room, and we will attend the policemen there together."

Libba had no choice but to obey. But as she assisted Mama to her feet, her eyes went to the wall above the fallen weapons, and she finally registered the anomaly she should have noticed the moment she walked in the room. For while most of the collection had been casually hung wherever a place could be found on the wall, the Renegade's pistol, with its unspent bullet, had held pride of place in an inlaid shadowbox above the fireplace—a box that now gaped emptily from behind its shattered glass front. "But wait!" she gasped. "Look! Someone has taken the Renegade's pistol!"

The scene in the drawing room, if anything, could only be described as more uncomfortable. For the threat of scandal and putative English lords were such a powerful tonic that, by the time Papa had firmly locked the library doors and stationed a manservant in front of each one, Mama had recovered sufficiently to take thorough charge of the situation.

"Libba," she broached her inquisition once they were all perched on the drawing room chairs, sipping cups of restorative tea. "Am I to understand that you have been in *communication* with this man? For how long?"

"Since Lord Hardcastle's arrival. Mr. Ransome and I both overheard a rather unpleasant conversation about Lord Hardcastle's intentions. Mr. Ransome begged me to allow him to handle things, and I did so, believing it was the best way to avoid a scandal," Libba told her mother. She glared at Ransome before adding, "And while I admit I am appreciative of seeing an end to Lord Hardcastle's attentions, I am forced to point out that cold-blooded murder is scarcely what I would call *discreet*."

"I have as much desire to avoid scandal as you do," Ransome protested. "If you met the Dowager Countess in person, you'd not doubt me. Terrifying woman—more than capable of throwing me in a dungeon for nothing less than using a fish fork. You have to believe me."

Which took them back to the first point. The first, incredible point that Libba had yet to digest. But it was Mama who was brave enough to give voice to the issue that pressed upon all them. "Mr. Ransome. Am I correct in believing that you now claim to be the true Earl of Hardcastle? Or did I perhaps mishear?"

"Had the title for less than a year. Still doesn't sit easy, I know." He smiled ruefully as he gestured at his dusty clothing. "And the hiking kit doesn't improve matters. Alas, everything that might have proved my claim has been stolen by the imposter."

Conveniently, some might have said. At least that certainly must have been Mama's opinion as she leaned forward and pressed, "And am I further to believe that you have been conspiring with my daughter to unmask this man's identity?"

"'Conspire' is such a strong word. It might be more accurate to say that Miss Wadsworth and I suddenly discovered a shared mutual interest in determining whether the bounder had any more diabolical plans than simply courting your daughter under false pretenses." Ransome suddenly seemed to remember his manners—if, in fact, he had ever been possessed of such a thing in his life. "Which is hardly an excuse for my admittedly impulsive and ungracious decision to steal even a day from the pleasure of your company in order to pursue the beauties of your native orchids. All I can plead is that it happily spared me perishing in the disaster of the S.S. *Henry Hudson*."

"God moves," Papa said with grim irony, "in mysterious ways."

"Unfortunately, that decision also afforded this imposter the opportunity to steal my papers as well as my good name." Ransome ventured a glance at Libba. "Of course, there would be those who would say that was simple justice for me neglecting the native beauties offered by Braddock House. I can only apologize for my ignorance."

Dear God. Did the man think he was in Mrs. Astor's ballroom? Surely even Mama could not be taken in by such arrant nonsense?

"As I've said before, even if you can prove you are Hardcastle, it does nothing to prove you weren't the one to kill him," Papa pointed out.

"What reason would I have to do that? I've already cabled London," Ransome said. "My *bona fides* should be arriving any day. Why should I risk putting my head in a noose when I could simply prove the man a liar?"

Libba would not go so far as to say Mama was taken in by Ransome's arrant nonsense, but neither would she say that Mama was troubling to hide the fact that she was inspecting Ransome for signs of his lordship as some might inspect a horse. And to judge the worried frown that knit her brow, she was struggling to convince herself that the spavined nag in front of her was, in fact, descended from the Byerley Turk himself.

"At the risk of insulting his Lordship," Mama began.

"Honestly, I prefer Ransome," he said. "Name I was born with and all that. Frankly, the Lord Hardcastle I knew was a tightfisted philanderer who only seemed to be able to get girlchildren on his long suffering wife—all of whom I seem to suddenly find myself responsible for—on an orchid-hunter's salary. All in all, a thoroughly unpleasant chap. I've no desire to further the connection—is that how one would say it politely?"

"I'm sure I couldn't say," Mama replied faintly.

"If we can return to rather more pressing matters than correct titles and female dependents," Papa cut in, his eyes still canny as he studied Ransome, "there is still the point that there is a dead man in the library, who someone has killed."

"Must have been murder," Ransome agreed. "Can't shoot yourself in the back and run off with the pistol, now can you?"

Mama made a choked noise.

"Apologies," Ransome said. "But earl or not, I am a straightforward man. Some would even say rough."

Instinctively, Libba reached for the *sels volatiles*. But Mama showed no signs of fainting again. Instead, she seemed to remain focused on examining Ransome for evidence of noble blood, her scrutiny as exacting as if she were walking the paddock at Saratoga.

"What made you go into the library, if you didn't kill him?" she asked.

"I thought I saw the killer fleeing—although, obviously, I had no idea that a murder had taken place at the time. If I had, I would surely have given chase instead."

There was a moment's thunderous silence. And then Papa growled, "Why did you not say so right away? Did you know who he was? Can you describe him?"

"This is where it grows complicated," Ransome admitted.

"*Everything* with you is complicated," Libba snapped. "It seems to be a positive *mania* with you."

"Libba, dear," Mama murmured, a new, dangerous spark in her guileless blue eyes as she continued to appraise Ransome. "There's no point in being *accusatory*."

"I saw a man in a cloak and a tricorn hat pulled low to hide his face, racing away from the house toward the cliffs," Ransome said.

"The Renegade?" Libba snorted. "Come to lift the Curse of the Braddock's Bride by firing his own pistol?"

"I trust you see the difficulty," Ransome agreed.

"Quite the contrary, I see no reason why you would expect us to believe any part of this far-fetched tale," she snapped.

"I suppose that depends on what exactly you think I expect you to believe," Ransome answered, taking no umbrage. "If you're asking whether I think a ghost killed this man with the pistol he once wielded in life, of course not. If you're asking whether I saw a man in a cloak with his face hidden by his hat, I would be willing to swear to it in a court of law. Ingenious disguise, really. Hides the man's identity completely—if, in fact, it was a man. No reason it couldn't have been a woman. It doesn't take much strength to pull a trigger—only a ruthless enough constitution. And I have met many such women in my time. Present company excepted, of course," he added, flashing Libba a rather unfairly pointed look. "So if the murderer was unfortunate enough to be seen, not only would he or she be impossible to identify, but the witness's testimony would be dismissed as absurd—as you just did. You really must hand it to the murderer. It was an excellent idea, every bit as good as the rest of the plan."

Another long pause. And then Papa asked, "And what exactly was the rest of the plan? If you would be so good as to explain."

"Sending the tussie mussie that proposed a secret marriage. I could not fathom why the imposter would do such a thing when he had just told me that he had very different plans for Lib . . . Miss Wadsworth."

"He told you *what?*" Libba heard her voice ratchet upward. "Did you propose to negotiate my marriage settlement with him as well?"

"*Tone*, Libba, dear," Mama warned. "Never does to become *strident*."

"It was hardly anything of the type." Flushing, Ransome broke off and retreated to safer ground. "It made no sense that the imposter sent the tussie mussie. But the murderer sending it was nothing short of a stroke of genius. He lured the imposter here, in order to kill him in cold blood. But the tussie mussie suggested an entirely different motive altogether—especially given Braddock House's unfortunate history with elopements."

As he warmed to his theme, his voice grew increasingly animated, almost cheerful. But both Papa and Mama had suddenly gone deathly pale.

"That's quite an imaginative reconstruction," Papa said quietly. "So believable that one might be forgiven for being led to wonder whether the only way you could command such details would be as if you had been there yourself."

Ransome drew a deep breath, steadying himself against a danger Libba did not quite understand. Coming to a sudden decision, he pulled a piece of paper out of his pocket and handed it to Papa. "You have yet to ask how the imposter was lured to the scene," he said.

Papa was not a reader, but it did not take him long to take the note's meaning, to judge from the way his face froze as he read it. And then his expression grew thunderous, and he muttered some words that Libba had only ever heard among the ferrymen at the Braddock's Landing docks. But when he spoke to Ransome, his voice was preternaturally calm. "Do you propose to blackmail me, sir?"

"If I did, why would I give you back such a valuable thing? Go ahead. Tear it up. Toss it in the fire, if you care to."

Papa's eyes remained on Ransome, wary as he slowly slid the note into his fob pocket. "Then perhaps I should ask why you are so suddenly keen to advocate on my behalf? It would be more proper to hand such a thing over to the authorities."

A flush stained Ransome's cheeks as he glanced at Libba. "There might be a more appropriate time for such explanations."

Papa's gaze grew incredulous in a way that Libba might have found insulting under other circumstances. Even worse, Mama's eyes grew frankly speculative. She couldn't . . . She wouldn't . . . A murder had just taken place. It was unseemly. And yet Libba found herself grudgingly admiring her mother's ability to remain focused on her priorities, no matter what the situation.

Mercifully, they were interrupted by the sound of horses and carts clopping down the drive.

"Coroner's here. The rest can wait. Dead bodies first," Papa agreed, suddenly as businesslike as if he were making arrangements at the quarry. He glanced at Mama and Libba, his gimlet eyes brooking no objection. "Messy business, the lot of it. I must ask you two to withdraw."

Somehow, Libba was certain he was not speaking only of the dead body. Which simply served to redouble her fury as she gathered herself to her feet and swept to the door, pausing on the threshold to take her leave of Ransome.

"Pray do not trouble yourself over any further explanations. Your *Lordship's* position is perfectly clear to me, and I will be happy to explain any extraneous details to my parents."

She spat the title like an epithet. And gathering what shreds of dignity were left to her, she spun on her heel and slammed the door behind her, before she humiliated herself by bursting into tears.

Chapter 17

"So this," the coroner said, "is not you?"

Which was not as much a question, Ransome thought irritably, as a logic riddle. And a logic riddle that had grown increasingly tiresome, as the coroner had asked it for at least the third time, repeating himself suddenly and without warning, as if he was hoping to trap Ransome into admitting otherwise.

"I am William, the Earl of Hardcastle," Ransome said for at least the third time. "And no, that man is not."

And for at least the third time, the coroner's eyes narrowed in suspicion. And who honestly could blame him? For, if one viewed things objectively, one was compelled to admit that the body that lay on the block of ice was far closer to the picture of an English gentleman than Ransome had ever been. And while perhaps such a comparison was somewhat mitigated by the fact that Ransome, at least, was alive while the imposter was dead, it still gave rise to the unhappy—and given the circumstances, arguably inappropriate—question of how he expected to win Libba Wadsworth, when so much more presentable a specimen had failed?

It was not the sort of question Ransome was given to asking himself. In fact, Ransome was a man rarely given to either self-pity or self-doubt. But all he found himself thinking as he stared down at the slack corpse, was how much more confidence his female dependents might have had in sending this specimen as their emissary—even after his sudden and bloody demise. At least, he had put in an *effort*, Ransome's mother would point out reproachfully. And, the Dowager Countess would join in smartly, that he certainly had less of a tendency to argue.

Nor did it help matters that the coroner was also the barber who had trimmed Ransome's hair and shaved him, for the interest with which he was now comparing Ransome and the corpse seemed far more sartorial than scientific.

"Stole your papers, you say?" The coroner studied Ransome's clothing, which was increasingly in need of a fresh laundering. "Your garments, too?"

Ransome gazed unhappily at the bloodstained sack coat, wondering unhappily whether he recognized it from the bewildering array that his mother and the Dowager Countess had assembled with the attention of an army quartermaster from the remains of his cousin's closet, clustered around his trunks like the three Weird Sisters.

"I could not say with any assurance."

"So you have no need of them being returned?"

Ransome's nostrils flared in distaste. Not only was there the question of how the coroner thought he might remove the bloodstains, there was also the fact that much of his wardrobe had already been altered from his cousin's. Surely even a man as rough-hewn as Ransome could be assumed to balk at the thought of wearing clothes that had been taken off the backs of, not one, but two, dead men.

"I can assure you that if these are, in fact, my garments, I have no desire other than to burn them."

"Well, that eliminates one motive," the coroner allowed.

"Yes," Ransome was forced to agree. "It does seem to. However, I think we do need to examine the pockets of the coat. I believe you will find some papers there. My papers."

"Which you claim this man stole from you."

"Technically, I believe your station agent was the actual thief. This man's crime was more in the way of trafficking in stolen goods."

The coroner's eyes narrowed. "Still gives you a good reason to kill him, though."

Ransome was coming to the conclusion that he was rapidly developing as many reasons to kill the coroner. But he managed to keep his tone as carefully modulated as when he was taking tea with the Dowager Countess, as he said, "That may well be, but I offer you my assurance, I did not kill this man."

The coroner neither conceded nor argued the point. Instead, he turned to Wadsworth, who had said little ever since they had removed the body from the library to the ice house down by the river, where the coroner was conducting his investigation. The ice factory was a peculiarly American institution, a wooden warehouse painted white to reflect the sun, its walls insulated with straw and sawdust, where blocks of ice harvested from the Hudson in the winter were stored and shipped down the river and around the world. Usually, the steam driven conveyor belts would have been creaking down to the waiting barges, but they had been turned off in deference to the situation, and the body lay silently on a makeshift, slowly-melting bier.

"And as for you, sir—" The coroner broke off abruptly

as Wadsworth froze him with a glare. "Pure formality, of course. But you do understand that I must ask. May I also have your assurance you did not kill this man?"

"I can assure you that if I killed a man, I'd not muck about with an antique dueling pistol instead of a decent revolver," Wadsworth growled. "Criminal inefficiency. And I'd look a man in the eye when I killed him, if only for the pleasure of seeing him die, and be hanged for it if needs be. But I'll be damned if I'll be hanged for a scurvy attack like this one."

Ransome glanced at Wadsworth sharply. Surely it was a bit odd for a man to have such a complete philosophy of hanging. Almost as if he'd given it thorough consideration.

The coroner turned back to study the body. "This man was shot from behind," he opined. "There is no way the murderer looked him in the eye when he died. Unless of course, he caught him in his arms while he collapsed. But surely he would not have lowered him to the floor face first afterward, if that were the case."

"Perhaps," Ransome suggested, "instead of speculating, we could examine the body for evidence?"

"What kind of evidence?" the coroner demanded.

"At the risk of seeming insistent, I strongly suggest that you search the man's pockets for any papers he might be carrying," Ransome repeated himself patiently. "If you would prefer that I broach the task . . ."

"I'm not afraid of a little blood," the coroner said, a claim to which Ransome could attest after having been subjected to his barbering skills. And at last the man reached beneath the corpse's jacket and pulled out an all-too-familiar leather case. "Says this man is William, Lord

Hardcastle," he announced, after studying the papers inside. "You're saying that's you?"

"Unhappily," Ransome said. "Be more than happy to concede the claim, frankly. But one draws the line at stealing one's papers. Matter of principle, more than anything."

"Why not just murder you instead of going to all this bother with papers?"

"Have to do something like that on the Atlantic crossing. Easier to dispose of the body," Wadsworth interjected, with a sort of grim expertise that was frankly unnerving.

"I don't believe he set out with the intention of impersonating me, but rather to simply impose himself on Americans who have no reason to know differently. I believe seizing my papers was a spur of the moment choice, occasioned by . . . rather singular circumstances."

"And what circumstances would those be?"

Mercifully Ransome was spared the necessity of attempting to explain the enticements of *Triphora trianthophora* once more, by a yellowed sheet of paper that fell out of the leather case. And this was no letter of introduction—at least not unless the Earl of Hardcastle preferred to present himself as "Escaped from Her Majesty's Prison Hulks. Armed and Dangerous."

And preferred to use the name Tam Jenkins.

"What's this?" the coroner asked.

"A wanted poster," Ransome hastened to answer before Wadsworth might offer any untoward observations about prison breaks or armed and dangerous fugitives. "And I would argue strong evidence of how this man obtained my papers. Don't you Americans have them hanging in every train station and post office?"

The coroner nodded slowly. "Need to have a word with the station master."

"Not sure that will be possible," Wadsworth said grimly. "I already have."

Before either Ransome or the coroner could ask him what that meant, the door to the ice house slammed open, and Ransome seized the opportunity to scoop up the yellowed notice and pocket it.

"For the love of God, Wadsworth! What is going on?" Gaddis exploded. "Constables and deputies swarming all over the place. There's already talk of summoning the Detectives Bureau from New York. Are you deliberately trying to get yourself hanged?"

"A man could be forgiven for saying you almost sound like you'd like that to happen."

Gaddis cast him a long, appraising look. "Whatever my personal inclinations in this matter," he said, "it is time you came to realize who your friends really are."

"At the risk of offending," Ransome interjected, "perhaps he already has."

"Ah, yes, the tale-telling batman," Gaddis sighed. "Leave us. This is none of your affair."

"Well, I certainly hope so. But there's something about finding oneself murdered makes one feel interested. So, I'm afraid I must tell you that I have no intention of going anywhere until I am reassured this truly does have nothing to do with me."

"Why should it have anything to do with you?"

Ransome nodded toward the body. "Unfortunately, because that is not the Earl of Hardcastle. Arguably even more unfortunately, because I am."

"You are purporting to claim—"

"No purporting about it. My *bona fides* should arrive at the cable office in Rhinebeck on the morrow. In the meantime, I suggest we turn our attention to discovering why Mrs. Phillipse Braddock invited this man to Braddock's Landing." Ransome cast Gaddis a pointed glance as he recalled the overheard snatch of conversation in the graveyard. "And why she is so convinced of the legitimacy of his claim to have him as a house guest and sponsor his entrance into New York Society."

And leave the question of the armed and dangerous Tam Jenkins to another time—when the coroner and Gaddis were not around.

"I say we give the man a decent burial and have done with it," Wadsworth snapped. "Man proposed to carry off my daughter. What more questions do you need to ask? Surely that's reason enough to string him up."

"But we have already ascertained the man was shot, not hanged," the coroner said with a logic that made Ransome resolve never to allow this man to barber him again for fear Ransome would seize the razor and slit his own throat. "Perhaps it would be better to set aside such theoretical considerations in favor of a more practical one," he said.

"And what is that?" the coroner asked.

"I saw a man fleeing Braddock House just before I discovered the body."

His lofty intellectual castles in the air shattered, the coroner glared at Ransome. "Why did you not say so at once? Did you recognize him? Can you describe him?"

Ransome drew a deep breath. Even though he was telling the absolute truth, this was not a moment he had been looking forward to. "I saw a man in a cloak with a scarf muffling his face."

"The Renegade?" Gaddis snorted incredulously. "Do you propose to accuse a ghost?"

"Doesn't seem necessary to me," Ransome said. "Occam's razor and all that. A flesh and blood man can don a cloak and muffler as easily as a ghost, at least I would assume that was the case. I'm afraid I'm no believer in the spiritual world."

"Now that's where you're wrong," the coroner said. "I don't mind saying I've seen many things in the line of duty. Things I wouldn't care to repeat. But I can assure you that there are more things in heaven and earth, Horatio."

There was a long moment's pause during which Ransome, at least, did his very best not to try to imagine what sort of things the coroner might be referring to.

And then Gaddis snapped, "Oh, for God's sake, the man has already proved himself a congenital liar. He's simply spreading fairy tales to muddy the waters."

It was a judgment Ransome found more than a little harsh, even if he was forced to admit that it had been leveled at him more than once—in a regretful key by his mother, in a more accusing one by the Dowager Countess on the most recent occasion. "*Someone* certainly is spreading tales," Ransome said. "But I would argue that the killer has considerably more motive to do so than I do. And speaking of motives, what was the killer's motive? Surely not simply to prevent an elopement? It would be a rare man who would put his head in a noose over that, no matter what the lady's charms." He met Gaddis's eyes deliberately. "Darker crimes make more sense. Blackmail, perhaps?"

There was another long silence as Gaddis eyed Ransome with cold fury. Then he said softly, "I will assume, for your sake, that was a speculation, not an insinuation.

But consider yourself warned that I will not be so generous in the future. In fact, I would go so far as to further assure you that you would very much prefer to have me as a friend than an enemy. And even if your prospective father-in-law is too stubborn to heed my words, I strongly suggest you be more sensible than he."

It was not a pleasant note upon which to leave an inquest, no matter how informal. Nor were matters improved when Ransome found himself invited—more or less at blunderbuss point—to remain as a houseguest at Braddock House.

"Safer this way," Wadsworth explained. "The way I see it, you and I have equal reason to kill the bounder. Following that reasoning to its logical conclusion, one of us dying is the shortest trip to the hangman's noose there could be for the other. So it is in both our interests to keep each other alive."

"Prisoner's dilemma," Ransome said.

"All things considered, I prefer to see this as an exercise in keeping us both out of gaol," Wadsworth said.

"At the very least," Mrs. Wadsworth corrected her husband with careful diplomacy, "Braddock House might be more able than our local hotel to provide your Lordship with the amenities to which you are accustomed."

Alas, Ransome did not fully understand the dangerous ramifications of that last remark until he found himself abruptly trapped in the coat and starched collar that Wadsworth's man had perfidiously found for him to borrow against the deeply unwelcome promised manifestation of Wadsworth's personal tailor on the morrow. Even less comfortable were the glances Mrs. Wadsworth cast his way as they assembled after dinner in the drawing room—glances that suggested that, even properly attired, Ransome was still not proving a particularly convincing specimen of an English lord.

"But why go to so much effort? Why sail halfway around the world to Braddock's Landing simply to besmirch a lady's honor?" Mrs. Wadsworth objected at the conclusion of Ransome's carefully-edited version of the coroner's investigation.

Mr. Wadsworth snorted loudly. "Man's impersonating another man. Don't think he's likely to worry about honor, do ye?"

The look Mrs. Wadsworth cast her husband was the sort of look that had made Ransome flee into the army, and then pursue his travels. His adult life had manifestly been designed to escape the enticement of wedded bliss that had been held out to even a son of a disgraceful union of a second son, long before he had come into his unexpected and unwanted inheritance of an earldom. But, frankly, was the direction in which Ransome's thoughts were heading any more appropriate? Indeed, could they be described as anything less than unthinkable? Even he had been one to balk at taking the clothes off a dead man. Could taking a bride off a dead man be seen as anything better? And yet was what he was about to propose really anything less?

Ransome wished irritably that he could walk. He liked to walk. He thought better when he was in motion. And right now, he had a lot to think about. In fact, he found himself consumed by an idea that seemed so simple and obvious that he could see no flaw in it beyond the fact the Dowager Countess would loathe it. Which in his mind could only be the strongest recommendation possible. Still, he wished he could ramble along the cliffs of the Hudson, nearly all the way up to Rhinecliff and back again, mulling over the possibilities with all the ferocity he would normally dedicate to finding a particularly elusive species of bloom, before he heard himself saying, "As long as we're discussing the issue, exactly what objections are there to my going ahead and marrying Miss Wadsworth anyway?"

He addressed the question to Wadsworth, who he still deemed a sensible man, despite his rather ready philosophizing on the subjects of violence and murder. Somewhat disappointingly, the response was less than encouraging. Wadsworth frowned, studying Ransome with gimlet eyes.

"Is this a theoretical discussion? Or are you honestly proposing that you marry my daughter?"

Ransome flinched as he felt Mrs. Wadsworth's eyes on him, equally appraising. As for the outraged gasp that seemed to arise from Libba Wadsworth's direction, it was best not to think of it, but instead, to plunge further into the drink and make his case as best he could.

"I can see where you might find it unconventional. But think about things objectively. It could put a quiet end to the entire affair. Miss Wadsworth's already been linked with the Earl of Hardcastle. Granted, not this Earl of Hardcastle, but why waste the effort?" He flushed, unwilling to meet Libba's gaze, as he plowed ahead. "She and I have already become acquainted—informally, I must admit—but we get along well enough. And the title's as legitimate as you could want . . ."

Mr. Wadsworth's eyes went sharp with speculation. "More Mrs. Wadsworth who cares about that."

There was a pause that seemed to last an eternity, as they both waited for Mrs. Wadsworth to decide exactly how much she cared. Mercifully, if arguably predictably, the response came in an excited obbligato.

"I care about making our dear daughter happy, of course," Mrs. Wadsworth said. "But if your Lordship has found it in his heart . . ."

"Have to check the *bona fides* thoroughly this time, you understand," Mr. Wadsworth cut in over her. "One imposter we can explain away. But two would seem . . . irresponsible."

"Oh, his Lordship could not possibly be an imposter!" Mrs. Wadsworth opined. "Such magnanimity of heart is proof positive of his noble blood."

"We could say the . . . deceased me was my agent sent to negotiate on my behalf," Ransome said.

"A batman?" Wadsworth asked.

Ransome ignored the undisguised irony. "No need to offer specific explanations. Simply dismiss it as an unfortunate misunderstanding that he was taken for me."

"The society pages do have a way of getting such things confused," Mrs. Wadsworth fluted.

Another long, wary stare from Wadsworth, during which Ransome could only believe his future father-in-law was considering every possibility, including the one that Ransome had murdered the imposter solely to obtain Libba's hand. Which, Ransome realized, he would have been perfectly prepared to do if the circumstances had been otherwise.

"Well, there'd be no harm in at least considering the matter privately," Wadsworth finally conceded. "However you understand, there can be no commitments until we check your references thoroughly this time."

Mrs. Wadsworth clapped her hands. "But among us, why not consider it settled to everyone's satisfaction."

Ransome felt, rather than saw Libba's anger coalesce into a real and physical presence, like one of the vengeful ghosts haunting the family pile, which he assumed would be the sort of *bona fides* Mrs. Wadsworth would prefer to those sought by her husband. A presence that clearly evinced that *everyone* was not satisfied with the arrangement at which they had just so happily arrived. And while he had to admit that the anger swelling in Libba Wadsworth's dark eyes was nothing short of magnificent, he couldn't fight down a surge of irritation that things were clearly not going to work out so simply after all.

Chapter 18

Libba Wadsworth had a remarkable capacity for silence. Under ordinary circumstances, Ransome would have found that an admirable trait in a woman, or anyone else for that matter. He loathed making small talk almost as much as he loathed the stiff collar and boiled shirt front that Wadsworth's valet had conjured with such cruel efficiency. Under the present circumstances, however, the lady's silence was nothing short of infuriating. It was not, as he was rapidly growing weary of explaining to her rigid back, as if he had meant to deceive her. It was not as if he had sent another, more personable, man to trap her into marriage, just as the beautiful exterior of the orchid lured the hapless bee into its trap. For the love of God, were his own charms so minimal that she really believed he had to take lessons from a *plant*?

Libba would come round, Mrs. Wadsworth assured him. It was just a matter of tact and patience. Mr. Wadsworth muttered something best not understood about hastening matters by confining her to her room with nothing but broth and bread until she agreed, and privately Ransome thought that sounded like an excellent plan indeed. But he had had enough stern lectures from his own relatives about the indelicacy of his approach to the fair sex to understand that was a sentiment best kept to himself.

Instead, he could see no course but to continue to advance his case as they sat awkwardly on the terrace, trying to ignore the men heading in and out of the library. There was little else they could do. The constable had issued no formal cautions, but Mrs. Wadsworth had insisted with a certainty that suggested she had consulted a chapter in an etiquette book that had addressed precisely this situation, that it simply wouldn't do to be seen down in the village so soon after the tragic event. She was equally adamant that lawn amusements such as croquet or badminton would project an unfortunate air of levity, if not outright callousness. A stroll around the grounds might be permissible, but the fury in Libba Wadsworth's eyes as she handed around a tray of sugar cookies warned Ransome against venturing anywhere near a cliff's edge with her in her present humor. It was enough to worry whether she had gone so far as to sprinkle the cookies with arsenic, before she returned with furious concentration to punching a needle in and out of a tortured piece of embroidery that was rapidly taking on the appearance of a battlefield dressing.

"The title is real," he addressed himself to Mrs. Wadsworth by default. "If you believe the Dowager Countess, it goes all the way back to William the Conqueror—although I don't mind admitting, most feel it's degenerated over time, especially when they discovered the last scion is me. Bit of a blindside, I admit. Came to me when my cousin attempted to take a stone wall after taking a stirrup cup or six too many. Not what any of us would have chosen.

But the eponymous castle does exist—and by all accounts, it's hard enough that no one chooses to live there beyond a few spectral Cavaliers and a population of bats. But they're really no more terrifying than the female dependents. Place is positively crawling with them, new ones turning up daily it seems. Wouldn't be surprised if half a dozen more appeared by the time I brought Miss Wadsworth back as my bride."

Mrs. Wadsworth coughed, a gentle signal that perhaps Ransome was veering, yet again, from the most promising conversational tack, and he glanced up apologetically, in time to see Wadsworth studying him with sudden suspicion.

"Nothing untoward, of course," Ransome stammered. "No wronged women showing up with babes in arms—at least not fathered by me. The previous earl, that's a little bit more of a story of course . . ."

This time, his voice trailed off of its own accord, without any warning coughs from Mrs. Wadsworth. Dammit, why did they have to skirt around the issue? Libba Wadsworth suddenly found herself in desperate need of Lord Hardcastle pressing his suit—for Ransome could honestly see no other way the scandal could be minimized, if not actually averted. And the Hardcastle estate had almost as much interest in a wealthy American bride to swell its spavined coffers as it had in keeping the gossip surrounding the match to a minimum. So if Ransome was willing to solve all their problems in one happy matrimonial blow, why could the girl not be equally logical? Lord knew, she had been level-headed enough about his approaches before. Why was she now suddenly determined to complicate the issue in any way she could?

And what was he to make of this new and even worse complication in his own heart: the conviction that if he could not have Libba Wadsworth, he did not want any woman at all? He had been as blindsided by the feeling as he had been by his sudden accession to the earldom, but now it consumed him like a character out of one of Miss Ripley's poems. Unhappily, unlike one of Miss Ripley's characters, he had no hidden inclinations for either sonnets or dastardly plans. Nor did he share the Renegade's taste for dying for love. Which left him no choice but to wonder in furious bafflement how a man who actually had smuggled a *Vanda coerulea* out from under the noses of a score of angry Thuggees, could conceive of no better plan to address this unfortunate situation beyond simply giving in to believing Mrs. Wadsworth's anxious assurances that Libba was changeable, and she would eventually come around.

He felt a moment's optimism when his letters of introduction at last arrived, and Wadsworth insisted on riding down with him to the village to inspect them, instead of waiting for them to be delivered. But that optimism quickly turned to wary puzzlement as soon as they were out of earshot of Braddock House.

"Might as well get straight to the point," Wadsworth began without preamble. "I wanted a chance to talk privately, without the ladies complicating the discussion with titles and ghosts and Renegades and such. Now, an English title doesn't mean a damned thing to me—what did we fight the Revolution for anyway? But I do want to see my daughter happy, and although I'm still not completely convinced you didn't kill that bounder, I do believe that if you did it, you did it for her sake."

What was this? A confrontation out of a sensation novel? Did the man intend to pull a revolver and administer justice himself?

"Sir! I give you my word, I am no murderer," Ransome stammered. "The female dependents wouldn't countenance it. The Dowager Countess would strip away my earldom personally."

Wadsworth flashed him a sharp glance. "Well, there are worse things a man can do than kill a man, but it does make matters less complicated in this case. Harboring a criminal in the bosom of the family can be a tricky business."

"I couldn't say, sir."

"I could. And I would have if need be, although I'm just as happy there is no need. For I am convinced you are the man to make my daughter happy."

"I am, sir," Ransome was startled into answering. His mind was more than a little preoccupied with wondering whether his mother would suggest it was intrusive to request some elaboration on those two mysterious words, 'I could.' "At least, I intend to be—with Miss Wadsworth's consent, of course."

Wadsworth's eyes hardened. "Not sure we have the luxury of waiting for that any longer."

"Begging your pardon, but are you suggesting that I . . . carry her off?" Ransome asked, suddenly certain that the old man had taken leave of his senses.

"And risk Mrs. Wadsworth's wrath?" Wadsworth snorted. "There's a difference between taking precautions and putting our necks in a noose—figuratively or otherwise. What I do propose is getting the settlements finished immediately. I've asked my man of business to draw up the papers, and meet us at the quarry offices to sign them tomorrow. He'll give you a tour of the place while we're there, so you can see for yourself what you're getting into."

Ransome studied Wadsworth over his mount's ears. There was a strange note of finality in the proposed arrangements that sounded more like the old man was planning to draft a will rather than marriage settlements. And that made no sense. Wadsworth was in late middle age, not old age, his hair more silver than white. Late *vigorous* middle age. Why was he making plans to hand over the reins? Did he harbor some secret illness?

Or did he have reason to fear death from an entirely different source, such as the hangman?

"Do you have particular reason for such haste?"

"Obviously, earl or not, I'd not be taking your word that you are no murderer," Wadsworth said drily. "But you're owed the truth of the situation. That man Gaddis and his friends have been trying, for well over a year, to force my business in a direction I do not wish it to go.

"They have tried everything to gain control. Ball invitations for the family. Promised political offices. Bald-faced bribes." Wadsworth shook his head. "It is to such men I was referring when I said there is something far worse than a murderer. I've said no to them all. But whatever else Gaddis may be, he is no fool, and he can see as clearly as I can that the dead man in the library may give them the leverage they need. The only solution I can see is to settle the company completely on my daughter, for they hold no power over her."

Whereas clearly Wadsworth feared some kind of power they might hold over him. But, what kind of power? Had Wadsworth killed the imposter? Try as Ransome might, he could not imagine the man acting that treacherously. But how else to explain this sudden change of heart?

"Sir, I must confess I have no real expertise in running a business, let alone a quarry," he prevaricated.

"Not to worry. I have no more expectation of your doing that than I expect my daughter to. It is only a precaution, nothing more." Wadsworth's eyes grew distant. "But in the . . . unlikely event, I shall leave complete instructions. Including provisions for Mrs. Wadsworth and . . . a few others. You seem experienced with female dependents. You can take on a few more, can you not?"

Ransome could only nod, suddenly aware of how this man had gotten where he had in life. It was not just that he was canny. He was a force of nature, as overwhelming as one of those flash floods that constantly threatened to sweep a man away in the rainforest. And yet, Ransome was reasonably certain there was one sticking point that would prove resistant even to Wadsworth's inexorable determination. Still, a man could always hope.

"And as for gaining Miss Wadsworth's consent?" he ventured.

Humor glinted in Wadsworth's eyes. "I haven't the faintest idea. I rather thought I'd leave that part to you. Only fair that you shoulder some of the burden."

Damn the malicious humor in Wadsworth's eyes as he consigned Ransome to his fate. A gentleman might have at least offered a hint on how Ransome was expected to shoulder what he was given to argue was an unfair share of the burden.

Even less fair was the surge of unexpected hope that

buoyed Ransome when he returned to Braddock House and found that Libba had exchanged her abused embroidery for a volume entitled *The Romance of Nature*. Then she looked up to greet him with a sweet smile. Surely that had to mean . . . Mrs. Wadsworth had said she was a changeable girl, hadn't she? Ransome nearly fell over his own feet as he hurried to join her on the terrace.

"May I ask what you're reading?" he asked—almost as clumsily as he had hurried onto the terrace.

"Do you recall Miss Twambley's mournful tale of carnations and pinks? I have spent all afternoon looking it over. The final two stanzas are truly a delight, do you not think?" she asked, giving Ransome just enough time to realize that both title and smile were about to prove deeply and annoyingly misleading, before she began to recite,

> Now, Lady—when a Cavalier
> Presents a chequered PINK,
> 'Tis time to ascertain my dear,
> His rent-roll, you may think;
>
> And then—provided his estate
> Don't meet your approbation
> It cannot, be too late
> To cut—with a CARNATION.

Her smile vanished, and she slapped the book shut, a firm signal that her sole reaction to any further conversational gambits, as well as his polite offer of his arm for a stroll around the rose garden, would be nothing but the silent dignity of a queen being led to her execution. Still, Ransome persevered, enduring nearly half an hour's mute marching, during which he began to seriously consider researching the rumored ways of making a love amulet out of the tubers of any one of a dozen recommended orchid species, or burning the roots of *Ansellia africana* to spare Miss Wadsworth the dire fate of spinsterhood, before he lost his patience and drew her to a halt, determined to handle things the only way knew how—sensibly, leaving both love amulets and poetry to those more qualified than he.

"Be reasonable, won't you?" he asked. "You were perfectly reasonable when you thought you were talking to my batman. What has changed between us?"

Instead of answering, she turned her back and stalked away. Swallowing his ego, he hurried after her, adding, "I understand that as a courtship this scarcely qualifies as a young girl's dream. But it did give us a chance to get to know one another better than most couples do before they wed. And you must admit, we do seem to get on well enough."

She snorted in a most unladylike fashion. But at least she was answering him. That was a good sign, was it not? "And your father has pronounced himself perfectly satisfied with my *bona fides*," he added, scrambling to more secure argumentative ground. "So while perhaps I pale beside the lover you might have dreamed of, you have to admit I am at least a step up from your most recent prospect, for I feel impelled to point out that an earl with an estate, no matter how badly impoverished, would be considered by most as an improvement over an imposter and a bounder. And your father, at least, agrees. Enough so that he proposes to draw up the settlements in the morning."

At last she halted her furious progress. "Papa has already proposed to draw up the settlements?" she asked. "Without consulting me?"

There was an ominously strangled edge to her voice, but at least she had spoken.

"He was satisfied enough by my *bona fides* to leave securing your consent to me," Ransome said, wondering if it might be too forward to offer hands on the understanding like gentlemen. Only when she at last turned to him, her eyes flat with angry disappointment, did he realize how badly he had misstepped.

"Well, I suppose there's no point in keeping up any romantic pretenses, given that I seem to have no choice in the matter."

Her voice was as flat as her eyes.

And every bit as flat as the resignation in his own voice when he had finally found himself cornered into accepting a title he never wanted, along with all the responsibilities that came with it. Resignation had not come any easier to the new Earl of Hardcastle than it did to Miss Libba Wadsworth, and, indeed, resignation's darker side threatened them both.

"And do you not think I would prefer a wife who would choose me freely?" he asked, his anger suddenly matching hers. "As much as I would have a wife at all."

The words were out of Ransome's mouth before he could wish to have them back.

"As much as you would have a wife at all," she repeated. "Once again, I must thank you for your refreshing honesty. Now if you will excuse me."

With a sigh, he tried a gentler track. "I understand women love children and hearth and all that, and I admit I'm a sorry specimen when it comes to such things. And I promise you—I give you my word of honor—it shan't be all that bad. I'll give you complete control of that sphere—"

"I dislike children."

"As do I," Ransome was startled into agreeing. "But there's such a thing as nannies. And one sends them off to school eventually. In the meantime, surely at least one of my female dependents must love children. My mother, for example . . ."

"Well, then, that settles it," Libba spat with magnificent sarcasm. "We are a perfect match."

She spun on her heel, and he had to move swiftly to keep her from dashing off the terrace and down to the sanctuary of the rose beds. "Dammit, woman," he hissed. "Must you be *wooed*?"

"Apparently my father did not see fit to include that in the marriage contract," she retorted, but her voice cracked and the tears he had not seen her holding back suddenly swelled. And when her lips began to tremble, Ransome was overcome with the urge to stop their trembling with his— to kiss away the stupid words he had never meant to say. To kiss her into accepting him, even. For he had never claimed to have a way with words, but he flattered himself that there was more than one lady that would be willing to attest to the fact that Will Ransome could be quite convincing in other ways.

But Lord Hardcastle was bound by different rules than Will Ransome. And Lord Hardcastle knew, even if Will did not, that this problem did not bear in itself any such simple solution.

"Well, if woo you I must, then woo you I will," he snapped. "But we will be wed. I give you my word on it."

And when Will Ransome gave a man his word, Will Ransome made good on it, whether it meant scaling a Himalayan peak or fighting his way waist deep in the piranha-infested waters of the Amazon. But this was Lord Hardcastle, and this was a woman, which meant he had no earthly idea how to make good on his promise. Spinning on his heel, he stalked back into the house, wondering what suggestions the helpful Miss Twambley might have to offer.

Chapter 19

Papa had already arranged the settlements? Without Libba's consent? It was impossible! Had he not promised? Her sudden sense of numb betrayal was worse than anything else that had transpired. Far worse than an unwanted suitor—earl or imposter. Certainly worse than hearing herself being called a hoyden. Worse even than discovering a dead body.

Papa had betrayed her. It was as if her universe had swerved off its axis. When it came to the matter of handling her parents, Libba had long since learned—as everyone sooner or later seemed to do—that one had to make allowances for Mama. And such was the essential goodness of Mama's heart, that one simply didn't mind doing so. But Papa had always been her rock, his word as much his guarantee within the family as it was in his business dealings. And Papa had given her his word there would be no forced marriages. So what was different now? What had transformed him from the Papa she had always known and loved into a cruel father out of a sensation novel, willing to pack his daughter off to a ruined castle where she would be confined to a mad earl's harem, while he traipsed the globe in search of better adventures than wooing an American heiress as a bride?

Could the mad earl be holding something over him? Unwillingly, her mind went back to those papers she saw Papa burning late at night, that strange interview between Papa and Mama, and the wild desperation in both their faces whenever they heard the word "elopement." Clearly there was some secret between her parents, one that underlay the quiet constraint between them that Libba had taken as a matter of course as she had grown up. But was she seriously supposed to believe that it was a secret desperate enough that Papa would kill a man in order to preserve his daughter from a similar fate? And that the Mad Earl of Hardcastle had not only discovered it, but was using it to force Papa to deliver Libba into his harem of female dependents?

The only other possibility she could imagine was that Papa intended to murder Ransome—and was offering the promise of a settlement in order to lull him into complacency. But surely the deaths of two Lord Hardcastles would never be dismissed as a coincidence. Even if Papa were planning to make it look like an accident this time, suspicions would be raised.

Stop it! Ransome's madness must be contagious. How else to explain her even considering the possibility that the one person she had loved and trusted her entire life was not only a cold-blooded murderer, but was ruthlessly calculating how to get away with it again?

With an angry shake of her head, she went downstairs. There was no way to stop her ceaselessly revolving thoughts other than talking to Papa. Better to face the truth straight on, no matter how horrible it was.

To her relief, the library doors stood ajar, and there was no sign of the constables and workmen who had bustled back and forth, taking notes and measurements. When she stepped inside, she saw that order had been more or less restored. All the antique weapons, save the Renegade's pistol, had been returned to their places on the walls, and a large chunk of carpet had been excised, and covered with a rug brought down from the attic.

But the calm of the scene was abruptly disturbed by a rustle and thump near the fireplace—and Ransome emerged from where he had been kneeling behind a chair, somewhat improbably clutching a copy of Captain Marryat's *The Floral Telegraph.*

"What are you doing with that?" she demanded.

He raised an eyebrow. "Working on my wooing, of course. I am told ladies are quite mad for the language of flowers."

"Well, then you were told wrong. Any level-headed woman would never be charmed by such arrant nonsense."

His eyes gleamed dangerously. "Just as any *level-headed* woman would see the clear advantages of us announcing our betrothal without any further delay. 'Twas you that removed matters to another plane of discussion altogether. So I am doing my best to remedy my shortcomings as best I can. Unless," he added hopefully, "you are willing to return to the dictates of common sense?"

"Common sense would dictate that a man would not waste his time on an effort at which he is destined to fail."

"Alas, it is my abiding fault that, as I've already told you, I am a very determined man. Many would use the word 'stubborn'—my female dependents prominently among them." He turned back to the book with a flourish.

"So if you would still insist at holding me at arm's length, there is nothing for me but to follow in the footsteps of Sir Horace Honeycomb as he penetrates the walled garden and the secrets of the nymph Floribel, imprisoned there as punishment for her disastrous but well-meaning intervention in an arranged marriage, securing her release by mastering the language of flowers themselves."

"What tripe!" She laughed despite herself. "That makes no sense as either a story or a metaphor. Honestly, it makes Miss Ripley sound positively lucid."

"What can you expect of a Navy man," Ransome agreed with a grin. "But what's this about Miss Ripley? Did she pen a work on the subject as well? Perhaps we should compare? Shall we pit the naval captain *mano a mano*—or should I say *flor a flor*—against the poetess?"

No!" Libba snapped.

Surprise flashed across Ransome's face, only to be replaced by a quick, concerned frown. "I apologize for my levity," he said with careful formality. "My mother insists it is the worst of my many failings."

"Then let us speak no more of it," she said.

She tried, and failed miserably, to speak with her mother's cool formality. Instead, she found herself dangerously close to bursting into tears. And Ransome seemed to sense it, for he closed the book and laid it aside.

"Glad to know you find such nonsense as distasteful as I do," he said. "Even worse than the blossoms that every sentimental female feels impelled to crush between the pages of a book. Who could torment a flower by putting it to such foul purposes? I wouldn't believe it even of Linnaeus, despite the fact that by all accounts his wife was a shrew."

Linnaeus? Who was he? Had they ever been introduced in polite society?

"I am sure I have no answer," she said. "I can assure you that I have no taste for such practices—as any *level-headed* girl should."

Abruptly, his face grew serious. "Then what, pray tell, is your objection to simply marrying me?"

"I'm sure most would agree that it's simply a case of my being as much of a stubborn nobody as my father."

"There would be many to attest to the fact your father is stubborn. But it would be a very foolish man who dismissed him as a nobody. And I would argue the same about his daughter."

"And yet at least one Lord Hardcastle was foolish enough to believe that the Wadsworths were nobodies enough that all he had to do to capture the goose that lays the golden egg was to create such a scandal that would render us ripe for the plucking." She impaled him with a glare. "I suppose the real question is, were there two?"

In the silence that followed, she was greeted with the sight of Ransome looking profoundly shocked. "Mixed metaphors aside," he finally said slowly, "am I correct in inferring that you believe I might have *staged* this scandal to put you in a position where you had no choice but to accept my offer? Hired this imposter to press my suit? Then murdered him—all to force you into marrying me?"

"Well, murder in cold blood seems a little beyond even your pale," she conceded. "But you must admit the rest seems to bear your stamp. Perhaps the original scheme got out of hand or the imposter tried to blackmail you."

Or Mama.

Libba's shoulders slumped at the stark thought. But Ransome was laughing in pure delight. "Well, now, I won't say I'm not flattered that you think me capable of such a scheme. But I really must protest that the ruthlessness of your imagination exceeds even mine. Which happily suggests that we are admirably suited, Miss Wadsworth."

"Pray leave off! This may be a jape to you, but I can assure you . . ."

Her words choked off angrily, and Ransome was immediately contrite. "Forgive me. Cursed levity again. My mother would not be alone in pronouncing it my fatal failing." He drew a deep breath, steeled himself, then plunged ahead, "It would be far more fitting to beg you to accept my assurance, Miss Wadsworth, that my interest in you and your family's future happiness goes far beyond a desire to paper over an awkward situation or even a desire to make an advantageous match. And if there is something that troubles you, I can only implore you to trust me with your burden."

He flushed as he spoke, and Libba could only think how appealing he was when his cocky self-assurance slipped. Appealing enough that once she had wanted him to kiss her. Even appealing enough that she found herself wondering whether marrying Ransome really seemed like such a bad possibility. Even with his orchid madness, his crumbling castle, and his harem of female dependents.

She, too, drew a deep breath.

And saw the mess on the hearth. The ashes in the fireplace had been stirred and spilled in a way that would have had their housemaid sacked.

As if someone had been searching through them.

It took little effort to guess who—and the suspicious

ashy smudge of the cover of Captain Marryat's book confirmed it.

"You *liar*!" she said. "You were searching the fireplace."

His face set carefully. "And why would I do a thing like that?"

And Libba stopped, flummoxed. He had been looking for the papers she had seen Papa burning, those indiscreet letters that he had retrieved from the postmaster, of course. But how did he know? *Did* he know? Or was she about to blurt out the truth and give him even more to hold over the Wadsworth family's head?

Ransome studied her with a disconcertingly acute gaze, then smiled crookedly. "I don't suppose I can hope that it would be anything as mundane as an indiscreet missive that troubles you? Memories of an old love? A lost love you dare cling to still?"

As if love had ever been something she had desired to cling to. But Mama. . . ?

"You need have no fears on that account," she said. "I can assure you I am quite heart whole. As well as rapidly growing resigned to the fact that I have precious few options in this matter."

If it had been any other man, she would have said that Ransome looked . . . hurt.

"Then pray inform me," he asked quietly, "what concerns you so about the ashes in the fireplace?"

Why not just answer him? He was clearly half-mad, with a thorough-going penchant for disaster, but she trusted him instinctively.

As instinctively as she had trusted Papa?

Footsteps rattled down the hall, interrupting her whirling thoughts. The library doors flew open, and Gaddis strode in, followed by a hefty man in a dark suit and bowler derby.

"This is a murder scene," Gaddis said with a scowl. "What are you doing here?"

Ransome shrugged. "I could ask the same of you, and with far more reason, I might add. I am paying court to the woman I intend to marry. That much is no mystery. But as for you...?"

"I'm seeing that this case is properly investigated, which no one else around here seems to care about doing. The local constabulary is too inept to even keep a fox out of the henhouses. I've called in the Pinkertons. They've sent their best man." Gaddis acknowledged the man in the bowler hat, who glared around the library as if he suspected the shelves themselves of harboring miscreants. "Already, he has unearthed a significant development."

"Postmaster done a midnight flit," the Pinkerton announced with a heavy nod.

"What?" Libba gasped.

"It seems our local station master has absconded, leaving the station and post office closed until further notice. It seems likely that he was colluding with the imposter, and there was a falling out among thieves," Gaddis clarified.

"Blackmail is a dangerous business," the Pinkerton opined. "Mighty easy to get in over your head."

Blackmail. At last the ugly word no one wanted to speak was out. But while Libba would agree with pride that any man who went up against Papa was likely to find himself in over his head, she could not believe Papa ...

And yet there was the terse assurance he offered to Mama that the matter had been handled. What exactly had he meant by that?

"Sir, are you suggesting that this imposter was black-mailing the ladies of Braddock's Landing?" she asked, with all the haughtiness she could muster.

Gaddis shot her a very sharp glance. "No one said 'lady' in specific. Would you have reason to suspect that is the case?"

Curse her quick tongue.

"How did you come by this information?" Ransome cut in, mercifully covering her gaffe.

"Sources," the Pinkerton said.

"And what do you seek to discover here?"

"Well, to start with, the murder weapon," the Pinkerton said, heaving his considerable bulk straight toward Papa's desk. "So, if you would be so good as to excuse me . . ."

"You mean the missing pistol?" Ransome said, stepping smoothly in his way.

"Sheer incompetence no one's found it," Gaddis said.

"Maybe." Ransome appraised Gaddis. "Or maybe simply a rather good plan."

"I beg your pardon?"

"The pistol may have been the murder weapon," Ransome said, "but there's no way to know that for certain until it is examined against the bullet taken from the victim's body. Which I must point out is quite difficult to do when the pistol has disappeared."

The Pinkerton stopped for a moment, clearly baffled at being confronted by logic rather than fists. "Well, now, that's very clever, sir," he said with heavy-handed irony. "Very clever, indeed. But I suggest you leave this matter up to the professionals."

Once more, he made for the desk, as if he expected to triumphantly produce the missing pistol from a drawer.

"No!" This time it was Libba who stepped into his path, forcing him to bang a shin against one of the desk's heavy edges. She took an unworthy surge of pleasure at the angry pain that flashed across his face, but immediately masked it with the sweetest smile she could muster. "I beg your pardon, for the forcefulness of my tone. But I must be certain I understand you correctly. Are you in fact an agent of the Pinkerton Detective Agency?"

Despite his sore leg, the man in the bowler was not too tough to preen. "So you've heard of us?"

Oh, yes. Libba had heard of them. Mostly angry mutterings which a gently bred woman would feign not to hear, every time Papa read of a strike in the morning papers. But if one had been so hoydenish as to listen to his mutterings, the Pinkertons were nothing but spies and strikebreakers, murder squads as notorious as any Five Points Gang. The type of men that Papa would no more tolerate in his house than he had tolerated them at his quarry.

"In other words, you are a private detective, hired by private interests? Not some regular police officer?" she asked.

"We're the finest money can buy," he agreed. "Now, if you'll just step aside, I promise you we'll get to the bottom of this."

But Libba made no move to step aside. Instead, she planted herself even more firmly between the hefty man and her father's desk. "I am forced to apologize, but I shall do no such thing," she said. "In fact, I must ask you to leave immediately. You have no authority in this house."

Gaddis whirled on her, his gaze cold with menace. "Silence, girl. You have no idea what you're meddling with here."

"Her name is Miss Wadsworth," Ransome said. "And from what I've heard, it sounds like the lady has a very firm grasp of the situation."

"The lady is obstructing justice. And I am more than minded to call the local constable and see how a night in jail improves her manners."

"On the contrary. From what I have just heard, the lady is obstructing a private inquiry agent," Ransome said. "And as one who has sometimes served in such a role myself, I can assure you she's quite correct. Your man has no more authority than I do. So I can only urge you to call the authorities. In fact, I'm afraid I must insist. In the meantime, I believe it's in all our best interests that this room remain locked until either an officer of the law or Mr. Wadsworth gives the order to open it."

Scooping up Captain Marryat's book, he strode over to the oak double doors and threw them open, in a gesture that brooked no opposition. There was a moment's angry silence. And then the Pinkerton bowed to Libba with mocking courtesy. "Ladies first."

She swept out of the door, and he followed in her wake with the swagger of a defeated bully. Gaddis, on the other hand, paused on the threshold, a cold hard stare fastened on Ransome's face. "I told you once you did not want me for an enemy, and I repeat myself only as a courtesy to a foreigner who is apparently adrift in New York society. But you must believe me when I promise I will not warn you a third time."

"I appreciate your candor as much as I do your courtesy," Ransome said blandly.

Gaddis snorted and turned on Libba. "And as for you, missie. We'll see how your father thanks you when I return with an official presence. You have no more idea than he does, who your friends really are."

"So it is often said," she snapped. "At least among those who consider me a bluestocking and a hoyden."

His eyes narrowed with sudden suspicion, but she tossed her head and turned away before he could say anything more. Let him wonder.

But that momentary triumph was fleeting at best. As they stepped out into the hallway, the Pinkerton bumped Ransome's arm. Captain Marryat's book slipped, and while Ransome was quick enough to catch it, he could not prevent a slip of paper floating to the ground.

Gaddis's eyes sharpened. "Well, well, well. What have we here?"

"Might be evidence," the Pinkerton said, reaching for it.

But the detective was built for bullying, not speed. Ransome had already scooped up the slip and pocketed it. "Personal matter between me and Wadsworth," he said. "Man was gentleman enough to help me with a few temporary embarrassments."

The Pinkerton's fists balled. "Maybe you'd like to prove that by showing that paper to me?"

"Honestly, I would prefer not to." Ransome's voice grew confidential as he nodded toward Libba. "Miss Wadsworth has yet to honor me with her consent. Best not confront her with all my vices before she does."

Gaddis's nostrils flared as he drew a deep breath. Clearly he was thinking of demanding to see the scrap. But there was a certain coiled strength beneath Ransome's easy stance that made him think better of it. "So the old man bought himself a son-in-law over a few unpaid bills," he spat. "Wadsworth always did have a sharp eye for a bargain.

Still, I urge you to consider your loyalties carefully, sir. The going rate for an earldom is far more than a mess of pottage."

And he was gone, the front door closing behind him with a quiet snick that echoed through the suddenly silent foyer.

"Unpaid bills?" Libba turned to Ransome. "Mess of pottage?"

"Quickest lie I could come up with. Sometimes even my resources fail me."

"But what is it really?" Libba asked. "And what led you to search in the fireplace?"

"Well, as for the second, that's just common sense. As for the first, well, now there's the rub. Much as you'd expect from something you find in the fireplace, it's at least half burned. Could be a receipt, could be a bank draft, could be a pawn slip . . ."

"Pawn slip?" she said sharply. "What do you mean?"

"Come now," he said with a laugh. "Surely I need not explain such a thing to a woman who can stand down a Pinkerton. 'Tis a system of borrowing money often involving a lady and her jewels. My female dependents are positively addicted to it. Alas, the only known cure is a wealthy heiress."

Well, yes, of course she knew that—if only by reputation. What she did not understand was why it was here. Her acquaintance with ladies who frequented pawnshops had been gleaned strictly from the circulating library. It was a different thing altogether to think it might be her mother.

"All I can tell you for certain is that it involved the exchange of a sum of money. A not-inconsiderable sum of money. To whom and to what purpose I have no idea." His eyes held hers. "But perhaps you do?"

Only too good an idea, unfortunately. But there was no way she could describe that scene—or its unthinkable implications—to anyone. Even Papa.

"Mr. Ransome," Libba said in sudden decision, "I would take you into my confidence."

He raised an eyebrow. "Indeed, Madam, I have been longing for nothing less. May I hope to hear a happy confession—"

"No happy confession this. There was . . . an indiscretion. In the past."

He glanced at her sharply. "Indeed, Miss Wadsworth. Did you not just now give me to understand that you were heart whole?"

"Indeed I am. But once upon a time . . ."

"Once upon a time," he repeated.

"Oh, I know now, 'twas no true love that flourished. Only foolishness that Mama did well to put an end to quickly." Libba shook her head, searching the remembered pages of the circulating library for inspiration. "He was my tutor. He wrote me poems. They were very bad."

"Worse than Miss Ripley's?" Ransome inquired gravely.

"By far. Which is why I must beg you, Mr. Ransome, if you are not willing to defend a lady's honor, defend the honor of poetry itself, and please return that unfortunate reminder of my past folly directly."

He studied her, his eyes sharpening with concern as well as a glint of amusement. "I have entrusted you with the absolute truth," he said gently. "Can you not see your way to do the same?"

How she longed to. How she longed to have *anyone* to talk to about this mess. But this was not her secret to tell.

"I cannot."

He studied her for another moment, considering whether to press the issue. Then he conceded. "In that case I am forced to pursue my own investigations—until I can finally convince you that I am worthy of your confidence," he said. "In the meantime, Miss Wadsworth, can we at least consign this lost love of yours for once and for all to once upon a time? The recently murdered Lord Hardcastle is already more rival than any man should be forced to endure."

Chapter 20

Slumped on the window seat in her bedroom, Libba stared glumly out toward Cora's Leap. Her suspicion that Ransome had deliberately used the imposter to create a scandal that would force her to wed him was of course absurd. Even he could not come up with so convoluted a scheme. Yet try as she might, once she had considered the possibility, it was impossible to put it from her mind. In fact, the more she thought about it, the more it fit all the evidence. The Hardcastle family needed an heiress in haste. Cousin Cornelia had obliged her English connections with the daughter of a stubborn nobody who would not require a lengthy courtship. In fact, she thought back on Ransome's first, incredible appearance in her bedroom. Had no courtship been planned at all? Were the Hardcastles' needs so desperate that he had intended simply to sweep her off that night?

And when that scheme had failed—and the nobodies had proved too stubborn for even a polite courtship, had Cousin Cornelia suggested that the Wadsworths might prove more amenable to Hardcastle's charms at home in Braddock's Landing? Had the post master not been the only person to know of the skeletons in the Wadsworth family's closet? Had those not-inconsiderable sums been paid to someone else? Even more unlovely to contemplate, was Ransome now attempting to discover those skeletons himself so that he might hold them over her head if she continued to refuse him?

Well, unlovely or otherwise, explanations were what Libba needed right now. She rose to her feet in sudden decision and went down to the stables in order to send a lad down to the village with an urgent message. Then she settled herself to wait with no better companion than her own thoughts, making her way mechanically through dinner, then tossing and turning through a sleepless night, until the first hint of dawn at last broke through her windows, and she could throw back her tortured covers and don her most sensible walking skirt and boots to hurry outside.

Libba had assumed that beyond the kitchen staff and gardeners, who were both already busy with their responsibilities, Papa taking his habitual early morning pipe would be the worst obstacle she would have to avoid when she snuck out of the house. Certainly, she never suspected that Ransome might not prefer to sleep past dawn when he had the chance. So she was shocked when she stealthily descended the stairs to find him waiting by the silver salver on the reception table, unabashedly examining the yellowed card from the scandalous lady novelist wife of the mad Astor heir who had lived nearby at Rokeby that was the pinnacle of Mama's social climbing.

"Mr. Ransome," she said. "I must ask what you're doing downstairs at such an unconscionably early hour."

"Your father is a notoriously early riser," he said. "I wished to make a good impression, of course."

She raised an eyebrow. "Are you heading to the quarry, then? In order to complete the settlements with Papa?"

"I was," he said. "But I am certain your father will forgive me a delay if I yield to the temptation of accompanying you on your morning stroll. Indeed, it would seem positively mercenary to do otherwise."

"But you are mercenary," she pointed out. "Why should any of us waste time in pretending otherwise?"

She had intended nothing beyond discouraging his company before a meeting at which his presence could only be *de trop*, but Ransome went very, very still. "Do you honestly believe that of me?" he asked.

He had the audacity to sound sincerely distressed. "Well, of course you are," she retorted. "You fairly well announced it the moment you arrived. Or at least your surrogate did."

He drew a deep breath, clearly fighting down the hot words that sprang to his lips. "First impressions can be deceiving," he finally said with studied moderation. "I had hoped you had come to know me better than that."

"What more is there to know?" she demanded. "Does it really matter who said what? Would you honestly have me believe that your intentions are any different than your surrogate's? Or was he your confederate? Despite your assurances to the contrary, I still must confess myself more than a little confused on that issue."

If she had thought to put him off, she had miscalculated egregiously. "Alas, I see that it was too much to hope we were past the wooing," he sighed. "Very well, Miss Wadsworth. I simply must insist. May I have the pleasure of escorting you on your morning stroll around the gardens?"

He held out his arm courteously—but pointedly.

A battered wooden paint box that lay forgotten beneath the coat stand, among a tangle of walking sticks afforded her sudden inspiration. "Alas, I do not intend to stroll, but rather to sketch," she improvised. "It is said that at dawn one can witness the tragic story of the Renegade played out against the mists rising from the Hudson. I had only hoped to capture it in pastels."

His eyes lit with a malicious gleam. "Well, then, you simply must allow me to accompany you. 'Tis a central part of wooing to be fascinated by a lady's accomplishments, is it not? Especially if they can invoke a legend to rise wholesale from the mist."

"Oh, my poor accomplishments could be of no interest, let alone fascination," she stammered.

"On the contrary, I can only pronounce myself fascinated, since sketching is an especial passion of mine." He scooped up the paint box with a rather unseemly grin. "And being one with a passion for sketching myself, I completely understand that there is no such light to sketch by as the first light of morning, and the morning light waits for no man. And this is a glorious morning, Miss Wadsworth. I pray you brook no more delay."

She took his arm, along with the defeat, with what relative grace she could muster—contenting herself with signaling her displeasure by setting off across the lawns at a singularly unladylike pace. Ransome matched her stride with annoying ease, as she led him toward the Folly and the romantic vistas afforded by Cora's Leap—as far away from her real destination as possible.

"Would you have me set up your easel here?" he asked, when a stitch in her side finally forced her to a hot, humiliated halt.

She should have just conceded the point that she had no easel, nor any intention to paint, and allowed him to escort her back to the house. But there was something about that deepening glint of humor in his eyes that was too annoying to suffer, and so with a toss of her head, she opened the paint box and turned to the task of sketching the vista that had been the bane of her drawing lessons.

"I am certain I need no easel. A simple sketchbook will suffice. But I do fear I might bore you. For I must insist on complete silence, complete concentration while I work."

"A lady's wish is a gentleman's command," he said. Crossing his legs, he lay back against a nearby rock, pulling his hat down over his eyes, so she could not tell whether he was sleeping or watching her.

"Everyone speaks of this tragic story as if it were common village gossip," he said. "But as an outsider, I confess myself somewhat murky as to the details. Who is this Cora? And why did she leap?"

"Unrequited love," Libba snapped, as she tried furiously to remember how to capture the line by loosening her wrist so that her eyes could simply flow through to her hand, as Miss Ripley's Bohemian art instructor had attempted to teach her.

"For this Renegade? Why did she simply not run off with him?"

"Because he refused to dishonor her in such a way."

"An honorable Renegade then?"

"The Renegade had once been an English officer," she gritted. "Sworn to a fatal duel with Lord Braddock, only to walk away with his pistol unfired when the base coward fired on him early and missed. Instead of firing back, the Renegade saved his bullet—"

"For Lord Hardcastle?"

"For Lord Braddock, who grew to hate him all the more. For when war broke out between England and the Colonies, the Renegade proved to be the bane of the redcoats. And so Lord Braddock contrived a cruel plan to capture him. He let it be known he planned to seize Lady Cora, knowing that the Renegade would ride to save her honor. But when he arrived at Braddock's landing, he found, not the wronged lady, but a score of redcoats who captured him and hanged him from an oak in the nearby glen. And so the Renegade died, cursing the Braddock Brides with his last breath. And Cora leapt when she realized the part she had played in the tragedy. And now it is said the Renegade haunts these cliffs until the time is come for him to fire his pistol in defense of a Braddock Bride."

The pastel snapped as loudly as any pistol shot, scattering pale ochre dust all over her, and she emitted a most unladylike imprecation.

"Dear me. What language!" Ransome scrambled to his feet and had turned her sketch book to inspect it before she could object. "May I?"

He broke off and laughed out loud when he saw what she had drawn. "God in heaven, if that's your excuse for avoiding my company, I can only suggest that my conversation will prove far less torture than that seems to be," he snorted. "Pray, leave off, before you ruin every crayon in the box."

Dear Lord. Why had she seized on this of all excuses? Next to her sketching, she was positively proficient at the piano. "There's no need to mock me. I'm attempting to learn."

"Then, pray, Miss Wadsworth, allow me to assist you."

He took the pad and folded back a page. "Now, instead of starting with something as complicated as a river view, why don't we begin with something simpler?"

His eyes gleamed as he studied her, then began to sketch. It seemed to only be a matter of moments and a few deft lines, followed by a quick smudged shading with the edge of a crayon, before he presented her with a portrait that seemed to leap to life. To a girl who had been the despair of no fewer than three drawing masters, it was nothing short of magic. "How did you ever learn to draw so well?" she asked.

He shrugged. "One cannot always take a specimen of an orchid. As a matter of fact, it's damn . . . very difficult. Orchids don't transplant well, you see. I've carried them through shipwrecks wrapped in my own coat, and protected them from frost by placing them next to my heart, only to have them die in my arms when I reach England. 'Tis as heartbreaking an experience as a man can know." His face grew serious. "Which is why you must believe me when I assure you, Miss Wadsworth, I have no intention of having the same happening to my bride."

"Are you comparing me to a botanical specimen?" Libba demanded.

His lips quirked. "It might be more accurate to say that I know how hard it is to transplant an orchid. And I understand it might be equally difficult to ask you to uproot a life you have found congenial and replant it with mine." He met her eyes. "But I must assure you, Miss Wadsworth, I will do everything in my power to create a congenial environment for you, even if it means creating a glasshouse like Lord Chatsworth's ovens."

It was scarcely a declaration of passion out of a novel

from the circulating library, but there was no denying Ransome's sincerity.

But sincerity about what? His untrammeled passion? Her eyes went back to the sketch, which was as lifelike as a glance in the mirror—from the too-prominent bridge of her nose to the forceful set of her jaw and the unruly strands of hair that had escaped during her forced march across the lawns. "'Tis scarcely a flattering image."

"You need no flattering, Miss Wadsworth. I assure you."

"Why? Is a not inconsiderable sum of money not enticement enough?"

"You cannot believe for a moment that was really meant to cover my debts."

"You said so yourself."

"I had to say something. Surely, Miss Wadsworth, you would not accuse me of selling myself as cheaply as one hundred pounds."

"Was that the not-inconsiderable sum in question? I suppose I should consider it an improvement over a mess of pottage."

She glanced anxiously at the copse beyond the Folly, where the Renegade was said to have met his dreadful end. She was already late for her meeting there. She had to be rid of Ransome now. "'Tis the existence of the purchase, not the cost that concerns me," she told him icily. "So now that we have matters clear between us, would you be so good as to withdraw and allow me to contemplate my bride-price in private?"

Amusement warred with exasperation as Ransome studied her. Then coming to a sudden decision, he inclined his head and murmured, "As you wish."

Scooping up the paint box with a murmured comment

about rescuing them from further torture, he stalked back toward the house. As soon as he was out of sight, Libba hurried to the clearing, where the gnarled remains of the oak from which the Renegade had been hanged twisted picturesquely above a peaceful pool. But there was nothing picturesque or peaceful about the figure that awaited Libba beneath the blasted tree.

"Dear me," Miss Ripley greeted Libba with a kiss that neither of them savored. "A dawn meeting beneath the Renegade's Oak. How terribly dramatic. I must admit myself intrigued."

"I count that quite a compliment, coming as it does from the Sappho of Braddock's Landing."

Miss Ripley cocked her head to study Libba. "On the other hand, I am a little anxious at your insistence that your mother know nothing about our meeting. I hope you do not intend to propose something *untoward*. Involving a young man, perhaps?"

"I would scarcely insult you by assuming you would agree to assist in any such a thing," Libba said. "Your poems may explore . . . dramatic situations, but you personally have a reputation as the soul of propriety."

"Of course. But one runs the constant risk of a wayward chit taking my idle fancies *literally*," Miss Ripley riposted. "I know I may be guilty of the slightest bit of over-imagination on occasion, but I do feel my duty to youth most sternly. I would hate to think I had led more impressionable souls down such dangerous paths as my muse commands."

Libba drew a deep breath, as she steeled herself to turn the conversation to the matter of what had inspired Lord Hardcastle—or should she say the Lords Hardcastle— to travel across an ocean just to woo the daughter of a stubborn nobody. Now that she might find answers to her questions, she found herself uncertain whether she wanted them. No, to be honest, she was more than uncertain; she was frightened. So frightened, in fact, that she found herself wishing she had confided in Ransome and sought his advice before starting down this path. But she had not, and there was no going back now.

"Fortunately, unlike other impressionable souls, I have always had my mother's example to guide me. So perhaps we should cease to fence, Miss Ripley. I would like to know why you extended the invitation to introduce me to Cousin Cornelia's English connections?"

If Miss Ripley was caught by surprise, she recovered quickly. "Why because she asked me to, of course," she said. "How could I refuse a dear friend such a thing?"

"But why should she ask? She has never had the least concern for our family or my social advancement. In fact, I would argue she has positively gone out of her way to avoid us."

"Well, you certainly do not think I would *pry*! A friend simply serves without asking uncomfortable questions about debts at the card table or indiscreet letters . . ."

More indiscreet letters? Or was Miss Ripley referring to the same ones? How much more trouble were they destined to cause? Libba's mind went back to the painful scene she had witnessed, and a flush stained her face.

Miss Ripley's eyes widened. "Oh, dear. Have I let something slip?"

Libba drew a deep breath. "I believe the important question is into how many other ears you may have let such a secret slip."

Miss Ripley's face flattened. "I am not entirely certain what you mean."

"You once said Mr. Gaddis positively had a nose for ladies' unfortunate letters," Libba said, fighting to keep her voice steady. "One is given to wonder whether perhaps he had some assistance in finding this particular scent? Assistance from a lady who is well known to be a confidante of all the first families of Braddock's Landing."

There was an ominous pause before Miss Ripley forced a saccharine smile that caused Libba's heart to thump even more furiously in her chest. "You are still a child, Libba, no matter what you may think. So I will make allowances. But I must warn you that little girls who play with fire get their fingers burned."

Libba's breath was short now, and her pulse was pounding, but she had gone too far to stop. Steadying herself with a hard swallow that Mama would only dismiss as awkward, she said, "With all respect, Miss Ripley, I must be direct. Did Mr. Gaddis blackmail Cousin Cornelia into introducing us to Lord Hardcastle in order to advance his business interests with my father?"

A chill descended on the glen, so cold and abrupt that one could have been forgiven for believing the Renegade's ghost had just passed by them on the way to the gallows.

"You think you're a cleverboots," Miss Ripley at last said softly. "Well, perhaps if you were a little more clever, you would see that if Mr. Gaddis had any interest at all in seeing you wed, it would have to be to himself. So if you insist on pursuing this misguided search for whoever might have pressured Cousin Cornelia into finding you a suitor— which I can only warn you no one will thank you for, most particularly your mother—I would look for an Englishman as my villain—especially an Englishman in open need of money."

"Do you speak of Mr. Ransome?" Libba demanded.

"Mr. Ransome? Oh, yes, our new Lord Hardcastle. So hard to keep track. Imposters seem to be multiplying like barn cats these days."

"Are you suggesting Mr. Ransome is an imposter as well?"

"I am suggesting that Mr. Gaddis has recently dropped hints that your young man is not entirely what he seems. *Strong* hints." Her eyes glittering with malice, Miss Ripley tossed her head and smiled, before she made her exit. "Then again, what man is? Now, if you'll excuse me, my dear."

"No! Wait! How dare you. If you have an accusation to make—"

But to Libba's utter vexation, Ransome chose that moment to burst out of nowhere, crashing through the undergrowth and calling, "Miss Wadsworth! I have been looking for you everywhere. For there is the most remarkable effect of the morning light on the river I would help you capture."

And Miss Ripley slithered away, leaving Libba no choice but to turn to Ransome with a tight smile.

"Forgive me for being changeable," she said, "but I thought I had made it clear that I had tired of sketching."

Ransome raised an eyebrow after Miss Ripley's retreating figure. "I fear it is I that need to beg your forgiveness instead. I can only plead that a gentleman will be impetuous when he is about to hear his good name sullied."

Her temper flared—mostly in embarrassment at having been fooled so easily. "Were you eavesdropping?"

"Would a gentleman?" he retorted.

"Are you a gentleman?"

"Apparently not according to Miss Ripley. Although I would point out I discovered myself almost immediately."

"*Almost* immediately," Libba repeated. "I suppose it would be mean-minded of me to wonder why you were overcome by the dictates of honor at that precise moment?"

He didn't answer immediately, causing Libba to glance at him sharply. She had not thought Miss Ripley's insinuations were anything more than her habitual maliciousness. Surely, it could not be possible. . . ?

"Because you were going at it all wrong," Ransome said bluntly.

Her eyes widened. "Well, I do declare, Mr. Ransome, you seem to produce a new talent every moment. Am I to believe you are an expert in interrogation now?"

An odd look crossed Ransome's face, and then he drew a deep breath. "Please, Miss Wadsworth. Can we have done with this farce that benefits neither of us? I admit I followed you and eavesdropped—since it was perfectly clear you were prepared to fence indefinitely. In turn, will you be good enough to concede there remains no reason for us not to speak frankly? I will tell you the truth—at least as far as I know it."

He squared his shoulders—steeling himself, Libba thought cynically, against weaving a better tale.

"No one—least of all myself—expected my cousin to fail to produce an heir, and leave his estate in a shambles. And when he did, I admit a certain reluctance to take on the responsibilities of the position."

"As well as a certain reluctance to take on a wife?" she asked. "One that even a bank draft could not paper over?"

His jaw set. "I assure you, Miss Wadsworth, it would take far more than a bank draft to persuade me to take a wife that was not of my own choosing."

"Happily for you, this imposter was less selective," she said tightly.

And now there was no mistaking his anger. "Yes! Yes, happily for me! For I admit, I sailed after him only to prevent a scandal. But instead, I have been fortunate enough to find a lady I wish to make my wife—with or without her fortune." His anger faded as abruptly as it had flared, and he shook his head. "Why do you think so little of yourself, Miss Wadsworth, that you cannot believe that is the case?"

Why indeed? Was it the memory of the sad disappointment in Mama's eyes every time she looked at Libba, as if her daughter was nothing but a reminder of the loss of all her youthful hopes? Was it the fierce despair with which Papa tried not to embarrass her? But to speak of such things to Ransome would be a betrayal of the worst kind.

"Perhaps 'tis more a matter of thinking so little of the horrors of the marriage bed."

There was a moment's pause, and then his mouth quirked in frank humor. "Horrors, madam?"

"You needn't jest," she sighed. "I know it will be awful, and I shall lie back and think of England, just as Mama has informed me all the best society in England does."

"Your Mama seems to have a remarkable system of informants."

She was humiliated to feel the angry tears well in her eyes, even more humiliated to see the humor that lit his face. "There's no need to laugh at me! Mama won't speak of it, but everyone knows she keeps the communicating door between her and Papa's room locked."

Ignoring Ransome's stifled snort of protest, she plowed

ahead. "And you yourself made it sound terrible with your 'innocent pollinators.'"

"The science of botany is not exactly the same thing as the marriage bed."

"How exactly is it different? You yourself said those poor creatures are trapped! Terrified! Caught in a web of silken entanglement from which the only escape is pain and fear."

"I didn't mean—"He stared at her, his face momentarily a mask of confusion. Then a speculative gleam lit his eyes. "Frankly, when it comes to matters of the heart, I never had a way with words. I'm much better with scientific demonstration. So if such is the entire basis of your objection to marrying me, would you permit me, Miss Wadsworth, to attempt to allay your misgivings?"

He did not wait for permission, but Libba suddenly found herself disinclined to object. Much as she found herself completely unconcerned about the fate of trapped bumblebees or Mama's communicating doors. She had never known, she thought somewhat breathlessly, that science could be quite this . . . interesting. And, if this was what it felt like to be kissed by Will Ransome purely in the spirit of scientific inquiry, her unruly thoughts continued, how much more interesting might it be when driven by less pure motivations.

Nor was she inclined to raise any petty methodological objections, when he paused to murmur against her ear, "You are aware, Miss Wadsworth, that it is a principle of scientific investigation to repeat the experiment in order to replicate the results—over and over again, if need be, until a firm conclusion has been reached."

Chapter 21

Both his brief and far-from-illustrious career in Her Majesty's Army and his experience as an orchid hunter had honed Ransome's instinct to press an advantage the moment he recognized it. And from the moment his lips had closed over Libba Wadsworth's, Ransome knew he had the advantage. No, he knew he had won. There was no point in undue modesty about his persuasive abilities in that department. All he had to do was seize the moment and ask, and Libba Wadsworth would be his.

Yet, he did no such thing. Instead of falling to one knee and stammering out a proposal, or even—as would have admittedly been more instinctive—murmuring the question against her lips, demanding an answer in exchange for another kiss, he found himself docilely escorting her back to the house, chatting about no more personal matters than a comparison of the respective picturesque charms of Cora's Leap and the Renegade's Glen. Sheer perversity, the Dowager Countess would have snorted. A moment's panic at the prospect of relinquishing the comforts of his bachelor existence, his mother would have sighed, which no doubt even he could see upon reflection, bore the faintest taint of irresponsibility. They both would have been wrong. Nor was Ransome motivated by a gentlemanly impulse to clear up the matter of the half-burned scrap of paper before declaring himself, so that Miss Wadsworth would not feel herself under an obligation to accept him. He had every intention of wedding Libba Wadsworth by fair means or foul, if only to see the disbelief on the Dowager Countess's face at the news he had actually accomplished such a task. Eventually. But at the moment, he felt no desire to rush matters toward what he considered their inevitable conclusion. For right now, he was forced to admit the ghastly truth to himself: He found he was rather beginning to enjoy this thing they called wooing.

And, despite Miss Wadsworth's singularly alluring misapprehensions about the issue of silken entanglements, that, he reflected, was a decided difference between orchids and women. When hunting orchids, the chase was often difficult and dangerous, and almost always unpleasant and uncomfortable even when the worst threat one faced was swarms of mosquitoes. The discovery—of a flash of color high in the jungle canopy or tucked in beside a stream or even waving quietly and inconspicuously on the North York moors—was the only pleasure involved. On the other hand, when it came to wooing, the chase was proving at least as enticing as the range of interesting discoveries Ransome had every intention of savoring on his wedding night.

So he took his leave of Miss Wadsworth with nothing more than a decorous kiss on her hand, and strolled over to the stables to borrow a cob to ride down toward the village to see to the matter of the settlements, which had suddenly taken on a new and pleasurable urgency. Instead, a distinctly unwelcome shadow arose to accost him before he was barely out of sight of the house. In retrospect, he would have liked to have said he felt a shiver of ominous dread, as if the Renegade had bestirred himself to rise from his watery grave. But in fact, all he felt was a twinge of irritation as he recognized Gaddis.

"Mr. Ransome, apologies. Of course, I mean, Lord Hardcastle," Gaddis said, falling in alongside. "I understand congratulations are in order. For I have been given to understand that Mr. Wadsworth has pronounced himself satisfied with your *bona fides*. Indeed, it is said that he is so satisfied that he proposes to draw up the settlements—even before the lady has given her consent."

Ransome shot him a sharp look. "I scarcely think it appropriate to discuss the affairs of a lady's heart with anyone other than the lady."

"I am not interested in the affairs of Miss Wadsworth's heart. You have my word I am not your rival in that department," Gaddis said, with a laugh. "Frankly, I prefer a biddable woman. No, I'm happy to cede the honors of that field to you."

Ransome impaled the man with a glare the Dowager Countess would have been proud of. "Good of you."

"But my friends and I have a very real interest in Mr. Wadsworth's business plans. And if he has seen fit to confide in you about his arrangements, I would seek to confide in you as well, in the hopes that you will prove more sensible that your father-in-law has been."

"I'm not sure that sounds like the soundest footing to worm my way into the bosom of the family," Ransome said. "Especially when business has never been my forte."

A strange look crossed Gaddis' face. "No," he mused.

"No, I understand your strengths lie in a completely different direction."

"I beg your pardon?"

Gaddis just smiled. "Please, Lord Hardcastle. I propose to do nothing but explain the situation, and allow you to make up your own mind. Quarrying in the Hudson Valley is in danger—the entire quarrying industry is in danger. They have grown comfortable with New York City being an assured market for bluestone, not seeing that that is about to change. Cement, sir. Cement is what the city will make its sidewalks from. It's cheaper, and easier to use. Cement will replace bluestone completely within twenty-five years. So the time to look to the future is now. But your prospective father-in-law has no vision—"

Ransome frowned. "Of cement?"

"Of those who truly have his best interests at heart. He needs to make friends with the right people. The up and coming people. The people who make decisions about how New York City spends its money. The people who are determined to bring down Tammany Hall for once and for all next election."

"Tammany Hall?" Ransome shook his head. "Not sure I ever heard of them."

"A gang of corrupt, populist demagogues that currently profit off New York City and have been doing so for years." Another strange glance from Gaddis. "But somehow, Lord Hardcastle, I think you already knew that."

In retrospect, that should have been more than enough warning of what was about to come—although Ransome was damned if he could have told you what difference being forewarned might have made. Still, that was no excuse for losing sight of the basics of his tradecraft. Nor was his being blinded by love. In fact, in his line of work, that was the worst excuse there could be. "Apologies," he said with a shrug. "My interest is in American fortunes, not American politics."

"Of course. You are refreshingly candid for an Englishman—except, of course, when you are lying about who you are." Gaddis smirked. "But now that we know you are exactly who you claim to be, this time around, then let us be equally candid about the fortune you are about to marry into. My friends would like to do nothing but bolster that fortune. It is your future father-in-law who threatens it by refusing to cooperate with them."

"And who exactly are these friends?"

"Men who are determined to stop Tammany Hall and its corruption," Gaddis said. "Men who are determined to return morality to New York City. Men who will run New York City on strict business principles. Men who would ensure New York City sidewalks remain bluestone forever, in exchange for Mr. Wadsworth's cooperation with their cause."

"Sounds more like bribery than strict business principles to me," Ransome pointed out.

"Compromises are always made," Gaddis allowed with a wave of his hand. "But no one would question Mr. Vanderbilt's head for business. Nor would they question the social power his family wields. How else do you think they persuaded that upstart Straus with his clothing stores not to run for mayor on the Tammany Hall ticket? As if he were not skating on thin enough social ice already."

Frankly, Ransome hadn't the foggiest idea. But now didn't seem the most propitious time to admit such a thing. "And why exactly does Mr. Wadsworth object?" he asked instead.

"Some kind of nonsense about my friends' attempts at reform being nothing but an attempt to grab back power from the working classes. First thing would be to take the vote from the Irish poor. Then their wages. And finally their jobs. As if Tammany Hall didn't create public works to line their own pockets, not to create jobs for the poor." Gaddis shook his head in disgust. "If you listened to him long enough, you'd be ready to believe the man was a regular Fabian."

Ransome leaned back against the stable door. "Plenty of sound men and women are Fabians," he pointed out. "The playwright, Shaw. That Wells fellow with his time machine. Women, too—"

"Suffragists," Gaddis spat. "Ought to lock the lot of them up for a rest cure as far as I'm concerned. But the details of American politics are hardly an earl's concern. Even an earl with such a chequered career as yours."

This time, there was no missing the insinuation in Gaddis's tone. But that was impossible. He couldn't have discovered—

Instinctively, Ransome went on the offensive. "As long as we're speaking frankly, perhaps you might be so good as to explain what exactly your relationship was with the man who impersonated me? Beginning with why he felt you were robbing Mrs. Philipse Braddock blind."

He had hoped to catch Gaddis wrong-footed; instead he found himself neatly tripped up.

"So you have been spying on me, Lord Hardcastle?" Gaddis's lips curved into a cat-like smile. "Well, yes, of course you have. That is what you do, is it not?"

It took every ounce of Ransome's experience and training to confine his reaction to a quizzical frown. "If you have an accusation to make, I would prefer you come out and say it."

"Not an accusation. Information. Information discovered by my Pinkerton man when he found himself with some time on his hands after being so summarily dismissed by your intended. Being an industrious chap, as well as a fine detective, he used the time to discover that you have a few secrets of your own."

"Debts. Female dependents. I'm afraid my intended is already aware of my worst foibles and I flatter myself she is of a mind to forgive them. The persuasiveness of a title, mayhap."

"Let's not waste any more time fencing," Gaddis said. "I know exactly what you really are."

Ransome drew a deep breath that didn't seem to reach anywhere near his lungs. "I'm afraid you have it backwards. It's the other man who is the imposter, do you not recollect?"

"Oh, you may be who you say you are," Gaddis said. "William Ransome, briefly and ingloriously of her Majesty's army, cashiered out for reasons that remain carefully unspecified following Macaulay's botched mission to Sikkim and the Tibetan frontier."

Ransome shrugged. "There are worse things to desert for than a glimpse of the *Dendrobium pauciflorum*. However, my superior officers were not disposed to see things my way."

"As I said, I have no question *who* you are," Gaddis said, a trifle impatiently. "You are the disreputable Captain Ransome, whose sins seem to have been shriven by an earldom, at least here in America. The question is what you are."

"I'm not sure I'm following your meaning."

"Orchid hunter. Remittance man—"

"Without benefit of the remittance," Ransome interjected. "Hence the need for orchid hunting."

"And liar." Gaddis studied him from behind the wire-framed glasses, his eyes pale with appraisal. "A consummate liar. So good that I believe you lie even to yourself. You almost believe the tales you tell."

"I admit I've been known to spin the occasional yarn," Ransome said. "By all accounts the ladies find it attractive."

"I said, I was tired of fencing." Gaddis gestured toward Ransome's pocket with a small smile. "That paper you were so hasty to conceal from me outside Wadsworth's study. What was it really? Coded messages for your masters in England?"

Well, now, that was simply ridiculous. Did Americans really believe that the Crown's agents would be so ungentlemanly as to hide messages in a lady's pawn slip? Had circumstances been otherwise, it would have been enough to make Ransome laugh out loud. But there was nothing funny about this situation. "I must beg your pardon. Are you accusing me of sending secrets by tussie mussie?" he prevaricated. "For I can assure you, even we primitive English have Mr. Morse's telegraph now."

"Enough. You're a spy, Lord Hardcastle. Paying court to Miss Wadsworth was nothing but an excuse for you to snoop around the first families of New York. Unfortunately, you have been caught out. Awkward thing, that steamer fire. Even more awkward the postmaster stealing your papers. Without them no one would have ever known you were not aboard the boat at all—not in New York or Poughkeepsie. Instead, you were in Hyde Park and Oyster Bay, spying on the Roosevelts."

"Teddy Roosevelt is said to be an up-and-coming man," Ransome said. "Is it a surprise that an earl with hopes of marrying into New York Society might strive to scrape an acquaintance?"

"And whose acquaintance were you hoping to scrape in West Point?" Gaddis asked.

Ransome shrugged. "I climbed Storm King. I was told the view was spectacular."

"A view of troop maneuvers that I will find among your purported photographs of orchids? If, in fact, there are any photographs of orchids."

"Of course there are," Ransome said, nettled at last into honesty. "I'm very thorough. The orchids are real. As is, for the record, the earldom with its attendant female dependents. As well as the rather urgent need for an influx of American cash."

"You honestly want me to believe you came to America looking for a bride?"

"One does not exclude the other. How do you Americans put it? Killing two birds with one stone." Ransome rubbed his chin thoughtfully. "After all, an earldom rather puts paid to any career I might have had as a spy. Rather too visible. Attracts unwanted attention. A man should be allowed a last hurrah."

Gaddis smiled unpleasantly. "And now that a suitably desperate heiress has presented herself, you instead intend to seize the convenient opportunity to marry into New York Society and report back to your masters openly?"

"You will not speak of Miss Wadsworth that way!" Ransome felt his fists ball as he fought down the urge to lay the fool out with the swift efficiency that few people suspected he was capable of—at least until it was too late.

He had never killed a man in anger, but he was rapidly becoming willing to make an exception. Still, the spy in him knew he needed time to think, to examine all the options open to him. Maybe even find a way to make this an opportunity instead of a problem, although at the moment, he was damned if he could see how.

"Does any titled nobleman that moves in New York society do any differently?" he forced himself to sigh. "It's hardly spying. As a matter of fact, I'm fairly convinced I will never again hear a tidbit that your government does not expressly want the Crown to hear."

"Perhaps so. But most titled noblemen are not in the habit of setting steamer fires in order to manufacture a chance to slip away. Or murdering a man in cold blood when he is discovered."

"That is a damnable lie," Ransome snapped. "As you yourself just pointed out, both events made my situation decidedly awkward."

"Be that as it may. My friends could see you hanged for it before your embassy can even lodge a protest," Gaddis said. "Unless, of course, you are a sensible enough man to help me. Put all that tradecraft at which you reportedly excel at my disposal."

Ransome would sooner slit the man's throat. Or his own. But as his mother was always attempting to teach him, there was a time for every purpose under heaven. He forced himself to nod instead. "What do you want?"

"Answers. Answers to questions your Lordship might take a personal interest in as well. This man, Hardcastle—you, whoever he really is—imposed himself upon the society of Braddock's Landing on the strength of information he possessed. I would fain know what that information is."

"In order to turn it to your own advantage?" Ransome asked politely.

"Of course." Gaddis said shortly, as he began to enumerate. "So I believe it is in all our interest to ascertain, what is the truth behind the old scandal of Mrs. Wadsworth's rumored elopement? Why are the Wadsworths trying to cover matters up after all these many years? Why did Mrs. Philipse Braddock agree to introduce Miss Libba Wadsworth into London Society, when all agreed that the girl had already been on the shelf so long that she had no chance of making any decent sort of match? What happened in England that caused Lucius Wadsworth to snatch up his family and flee like a thief in the night? And above all, what do any of them have to do with an escaped convict named Tam Jenkins?"

"To what end? Am I to believe you would threaten Wadsworth's family with scandal in order to force him into a business decision?"

"The Vanderbilts believe that compromises are justified when it comes to serving the greater good. Social standing is only one of many such weapons in their arsenal."

And Ransome was insulted at the thought of passing messages in pawn slips. The Dowager Duchess was right. Americans were barbarians.

With the exception of one American whose interests he believed were very much his own. "And now that Hardcastle's death has unfortunately rendered him incapable of assisting you in your inquiries, you wish me to discover this information instead?"

"If you have a better means of persuasion at your disposal, by all means use it. But if not—" Gaddis held out his hand. "There is no need for us to be enemies. We're on the same side here. You are doing nothing but helping your father-in-law make a decision that can only be advantageous to all of us. So what do you say we shake hands on it like gentlemen?"

Ransome stopped him with a glare. "If I were ever to touch you, it would be to snap your neck. Which I am more than capable of doing, as well as being safely over the border to Canada before your friends are even aware you have been murdered. Make no mistake of it. However, I will concede you have the advantage of me. For in answer to your rather indelicate question about my motives, regardless of how secondary a goal finding a bride might have been when I arrived in America, I have found one. And so I am your man," he said with a calm he certainly did not feel. "You have bought my loyalty, at least for now. Because I love Libba Wadsworth. I want her. And I will do whatever it takes to win her. For now. But I swear to you, one day I will find a way to destroy you."

"On the strength of your honor as a gentleman?" Gaddis asked.

Ransome smiled at Gaddis. It was not a nice smile. "On the strength of abilities that you had best hope you never have a chance to discover," he said. "But trust me, I will be delighted to give you a first-hand demonstration if the opportunity arises—as I will make sure it will."

Chapter 22

Despite Mr. Ransome's rather convincing advocacy for the importance of the scientific method, Libba had suddenly developed a distressing—and extremely distracting—tendency to think in a manner that could only be described as having stepped straight out of the circulating library. Her rational mind could point out that, not only had Ransome proved his case, but that the experiment had been convincingly repeated. All that remained was for her to inform Papa of her consent. And yet, she found herself longing for something more *poetic* than a simple interview across Papa's oak desk. Maybe not a moonlit scene in the rosebeds, but was it too much to hope for some kind of . . . *declaration*, before Mr. Ransome repeated his very interesting experiment once more?

But what was Mr. Ransome likely to say that he had not already said in somewhat disappointingly forthright fashion? And did words really matter when the demonstration had been so . . . complete? Squaring her shoulders against another rush of missish imagining, Libba started downstairs to talk to Papa. But she was barely halfway down the stairs, when the front doors banged open and her father's quarry manager hurried inside, with little more than a muttered apology at not using the trade entrance. Suddenly the poetry—or lack thereof—of Mr. Ransome's conversation seemed like the least important problem in the world.

Carefully, she slid back up to the landing, making a meaningless adjustment in the flower arrangement in a Chinese urn as an excuse to eavesdrop.

"There's trouble at the quarry," the manager told Papa.

"What kind of trouble?"

"Man found dead down on the Rondout. Word is he was the station master here in Braddock's Ridge."

"Damn him!" Papa went on in the same vein with a series of expressions that would never have stood the test of Mama's drawing room, culminating in, "I *warned* him."

"Don't doubt you did, sir. But according to the stories that are going around, he might have already gotten in too far. Involved himself with a brigand named Tam Jenkins, who, the way they told it, had fled Five Points in order to establish a foothold here in Ulster County. Some say he has already established his base of operations at the quarry, and so they're sending the detectives to search it."

"Pinkertons?"

"Worse," the manager said. "The Detective Bureau. Byrnes's boys."

"The famous Inspector Byrnes?" Papa spoke the name as if it were a bad taste.

"A disgrace to Irishmen everywhere," the manager's brogue suddenly broadened. "If he can't pay someone to lie against you, he's happy to beat the confession out of you. The third degree, that's what they call it."

"But the New York City Police have no authority up here."

"Advisory capacity. They say they're simply helping the county sheriff in his inquiries, but it's clear enough someone's paid them to make trouble." The manager shook his head. "Now, you know as well as I do that they'll not find such a man among our workmen. But some of them may have pasts that won't stand up to such a search."

"As does many a man," Papa allowed. An odd shadow fleeted across his face and then was gone. "How much time do we have? Have they already arrived?"

"No. We've got a day's lead. Word is they'll be arriving by train from the city tomorrow." The manager's face relaxed into an honest grin. "It's supposed to be a surprise raid, but there are plenty that don't like Byrne any more than we have a cause to—that Roosevelt fellow among them. Wouldn't even put it past him to have sent the little birdie that warned me."

"Then we need to talk to the men, see if some of them needs be sent out of town for a couple of days," Papa said with a nod. "There's a cement works over in Rosendale that's looking for investors. Might be good to have some working men's opinion of the operation. And it's at least twenty miles away."

He started for the door, but the manager hesitated. "With respect, sir," he said, "Could be sensible for you to go with them."

Papa froze him with a glare. "I'll not have it said that I abandoned my men or my household out of fear for my own neck."

"Of course, sir. I never meant, sir . . ."

Ignoring the manager's stammered protests, Papa was

already out the door and heading for the stables, shouting orders for his cob to be saddled immediately—leaving Libba alone with only one thought whirling in her head. Why should her father fear for his neck? Papa had not shot a man in the back inside his own home; it was as much an article of faith with Libba as any she had been taught in Sunday School. So why had both he and his quarry manager spoken of the possibility as if it were commonplace? What could it mean—unless Papa had some other secret to protect?

Or was it a person Papa sought to protect? Once more, her mind went back to that horrible scene she had witnessed in the library. And Papa burning Mama's indiscreet letters—only to be interrupted when he had barely started the task.

Had he managed to finish it? Or might the letters remain in his strongbox, where the odious Mr. Gaddis and his equally odious Pinkerton still might discover them—especially if the proposed raid at the quarry were nothing but an excuse to divert attention, so that they could search the library while Papa was preoccupied.

And if that were truly the case, Libba realized with perfect, scientific clarity, only one simple choice remained to her. Sometimes it helped to have a reputation as a hoyden and a bluestocking. Mr. Gaddis might be triply infuriated at her; the Pinkerton might roar about jail. The constable and coroner would mutter uncomfortably about no one being above the law. But no one would seek to punish a rebellious daughter burning letters intercepted from an unsuitable suitor—and who would be able to prove otherwise once they were safely reduced to ash in the fireplace?

Would they?

No point in distracting herself with pictures of a grimy pallet in the Tombs, any more than wasting time dwelling on whether Mr. Ransome would consider a jailhouse visit to release him from any further obligations to poetical declarations. The best solution was simply not to get caught, she told herself briskly, as she slipped around to the terrace and into the library through the French door with the lock that hadn't worked for as long as she could remember.

It took her only a moment to find Papa's strong box where he had pushed it out of sight what seemed like a lifetime ago. With shaking fingers, she sought to wrench the iron hasp from the metal lid. Only to feel her shoulders slump in defeat as she realized she should have at least considered how she might do that before she committed herself to this path. She supposed she needed some kind of sharp tool—a paper knife or letter opener. There must be one somewhere on Papa's desk. His paper knife, with which he opened the mail every morning?

She reached for it, only to feel, rather than see, a shadow rear behind her.

"No point in leaving fingerprints. Bertillon has made cowards of us all."

She choked back a shriek that would have done the circulating library proud, as Ransome stepped between her and the desk, proffering a pressed white handkerchief embroidered with what she had to assume was the Hardcastle coat of arms.

"Pray allow me to assist," he said, reaching for the box.

Shock warred with humiliation as she struggled to regain what little dignity she might have possessed. "I beg your pardon! Do you propose to break into my father's lockbox?"

"It seems that you were the one to propose the course of action. I am merely suggesting that you allow me to do the honors."

His voice was calm. Reasonable. As if they were not speaking of fingerprints and burglary and destroying evidence—concepts that were as foreign to her as any houri had ever been.

"Why?" was all she could think to ask.

"Because frankly, I am certain that I will do a better job of it," he told her with the same annoying confidence he had accused her of making a hash of questioning Miss Ripley. "To begin with, I would strongly suggest that breaking the hasp is not the best way to go about matters. Better to leave as little evidence as possible of a break-in, and let me pick the lock instead."

He spoke as politely as if he were recommending the lemonade over the strawberry ice after a particularly strenuous quadrille.

"Of course," was all that was left for her to say.

"Then with your permission . . ." He reached into his pocket and pulled out a remarkably professional-looking set of what Libba could only assume were lock-picks— to judge from the swift efficiency with which he had the padlock opened. Throwing the lid back with a flourish, he placed both the picks and the padlock in his coat pocket.

"People may suspect it's been opened, but they will not be able to prove it," he said conversationally. His eyes sharpened as he studied her. "Except your father, obviously. And I don't think he is the one you are attempting to deceive?"

It was clearly a question—and clearly a question to which he deserved an answer. But it was not just bewilderment than made Libba shake her head and counter his question with one of her own. "How did you know how to do that?" For surely collecting orchids required no such talents. Where—and more importantly *why*—on earth had he learned to do something like that?

"More to me than meets the eye. One day I'll convince you of that," he said with a grin, as he began to examine the contents of the box.

"No!" Hastily she tried to intervene in a most unladylike way, only to find herself entangled with him in a way that could only be described as even more unladylike—and, much to her irritation, distinctly distracting.

Arguably even more irritating was Ransome's undisguised amusement as he took his time disentangling them. "Please, Miss Wadsworth. Do not force me to stoop to eavesdropping or searching the fireplace again. How much more damage could a few more pawn slips do?"

With a sigh, Libba conceded the point. "Is that what's in there? More pawn slips?"

Ransome's face darkened as he studied the contents of the lock box. "No."

And he pulled out a packet of letters, all yellowed and all addressed to Sir Roderick Naughton in what Libba could only describe as an all-too-familiar hand.

"Now this complicates matters," he said.

"Roderick Naughton," she said. "The Wicked Viscount. Not the by-blow."

A flash of humor lit Ransome's eye at her choice of vocabulary, before he continued, "Who snatched an American heiress off to Gretna Green—"

"It's impossible!" Libba said flatly. "Mama had never been to England before this year."

Ransome's eyes narrowed as he continued to study the letters. "We can only hope these will verify that story. But even if they do ..."

He shook his head with a frown, as Libba studied the packet of envelopes. Story? *What* story? An abducted American heiress. A missing witness—who arguably Papa was paying to remain missing. It was completely absurd. *Mama*, who was always the soul of discretion?

Or were these letters the grim explanation of her insistence on observing the proprieties? It made a horrid sense.

"May I read them first?" she asked. "And only summarize the relevant parts to you?"

"Sounds like a reasonable enough proposition," Ransome agreed.

But when Libba turned over the envelope, she saw the sealing wax was intact. Swiftly, she thumbed through the rest of them. "None of these have been opened."

For a moment, Ransome looked startled. And then he grinned. "Of course not," he said. "No self-respecting gentleman would read a lady's indiscreet letters. Especially not his wife's."

"But the postmaster was no gentleman."

Ransome nodded, considering the point. "No he was not. And therein lies the puzzle."

"What are you saying? This was never a case of Mama's letters? Then what? Your mysterious pawn slip?"

"That remains to be discovered. And discover it, I shall." Ransome turned back toward the terrace window. "In the meantime, I suggest we follow your father's example and return these letters to their rightful owner unread. And I am morally certain that you would make a more welcome choice of messenger than I."

Roderick Naughton. The Wicked Viscount. Letter after letter addressed to him in Mama's hand. Libba wasn't sure of the significance of what she had discovered—for all Hardcastle's claims of an abducted American heiress making him the rightful heir. But how else explain her parents' horrified reaction to any mention of the word elopement? And why else would Mama pawn her jewels to hide the very existence of these letters?

And how could Libba, of all people, be expected to determine how to handle the unfortunate situation? Her head reeling against the enormity of possibilities she could only half conceive, Libba retreated to the only safety she could be secure in truly knowing—that of her bed chamber.

But when she stepped into her room, she found Mama seated on the bedside chair, calmly searching beneath Libba's bed.

Libba could have been no more stunned if the Renegade himself had been waiting to snatch her away to her ghostly doom. "So you always knew where I hid my novels," was all she could think to say.

"Of course," Mama said. "I am not as stupid as people would believe."

"I never—"

Mama cut off Libba's protest with a careless wave of her hand. "I simply find it more convenient for people to think so. Many women do. Perhaps after you wed, you will come to find that for yourself. Although I believe yours will be a different path. It remains to be seen which one will be easier."

Ignoring Libba's stammered protest, she turned her attention to the packet Libba clutched. "I assume those are the letters your father managed to retrieve from that odious postmaster. Letters addressed to Sir Roderick Naughton?"

Numbly, Libba gave them to her mother. "You saw us in the library?"

"Overheard you, actually. You left the terrace door open." A moment's hesitation, and then Mama met her eyes. "Did you read them?"

"I couldn't," Libba said. "They were sealed."

There was a long pause, and then Mama said softly, "You mean, your father never opened them?"

"How could you think otherwise?" Libba snapped. "What gentleman would?"

She wished she could have the words back as soon as she spoke them, for Mama's face fell in mortification. "You are quite right, of course. Once again, I have wronged your father. I seem to have rather a gift for it."

For a moment, she simply gazed into the distance, then went on, "I confess, I had hoped you would never see this moment. But now I admit myself glad you have. For you can have no truer proof of your father's kind heart." Her jaw set, as she slid the letters up her sleeve. "As for the venality of my own, I'm afraid I must beg you to follow your father's example and turn a blind eye to my many failings."

It was scarcely a surprise, and yet Libba still felt a sudden lurch of disbelief. "An indiscreet letter is hardly a failing."

Mama laughed gently. "It was at the very least a grievous mistake. I wish you had never learned of it, but since you have, all I can do is assure you that it is my mistake. I will not allow it to harm my daughter." Once more, she met Libba's eyes, her gaze forthright and somewhat sad. "Which is why I must ask you to tell me the truth. Does

Lord Hardcastle seek to hold this over your head, in order to force you to marry him?"

The world was rapidly growing madder; easier far for Libba to believe that the Renegade had been invoked in a Spiritualist ritual by Miss Ripley to murder the false Lord Hardcastle out of sheer spite, than that she was truly engaging in this conversation with Mama. "I thought you wished me to marry him."

"I admit, I would see you wed him. But only if it is your own free choice. If he seeks to threaten you—"

"He has done no such thing! He did discover these letters along with me, but he made no conditions upon their return."

"As a gentleman should." The tension drained from Mama's face, but she made no move to return the packet to Libba. Instead, she folded her sleeves across her chest. "Nonetheless, best to remove any doubt in the matter. Lead us not into temptation, as our dear vicar would say."

Who was this woman in her bedroom—so grave, so knowing, so *ironic*? Surely not Mama. "I . . . I'm afraid I do not completely understand," Libba stammered.

Mama cast her a long look. "There is only one thing you need to understand. I have only ever wanted to see you happy, Libba. Not married. Happy. But I honestly think you will be happier married. Most women are." Mama shook her head with a sad smile. "For what other options do you see? Would you prefer to follow Miss Ripley's pitiful example?"

Libba's eyes widened. "You cannot convince me you feel *sorry* for that witch?"

"Language," Mama cautioned.

"But she has never done anything but torment you!"

"Perhaps she feels she has cause," Mama said. "And perhaps she is right. Still, I would not trade my life for hers. Nor would I see my daughter so reduced and disappointed either. You are a beautiful girl, Libba, even if you refuse to realize such a thing. You should be destined to blossom and flourish. Alas, for most women, the only soil conducive to such things is that of a marriage."

Just like Mr. Ransome's glasshouses, Libba thought. But, if that were the case, the question rose to her lips rebelliously, what was she to make of the locked communicating door, the uncomfortably proffered advice to lie back and think of England?

Or should she simply yield to this insistent instinct to trust Mr. Ransome's ... somewhat unconventional taste for scientific experimentation instead? Could she?

"Whatever you decide, know that I will not have you forced," Mama said as she turned to go. She strove, and failed, to keep a note of bitterness out of her voice as she added, "After all, many might argue that Society is all too good at that already."

Chapter 23

Ransome was well aware that no one would like him for what he was about to do. In fact, he was certain that if he was discovered, it might well undo all the progress his scientifically persuasive abilities had made with Miss Wadsworth. No matter how logically he might argue that he had promised *only* to not open her mother's letters, he had most certainly not promised to not seek the truth behind them. While confronting a lady with her indiscreet letters seemed no more gentlemanly than using her pawn slips to pass messages to England, Ransome was forced to plead that there were two possible logical inferences to be drawn from the name he had recognized on the half-burned receipt he'd fished from the fireplace, and neither of them were particularly conducive to his future happiness. Unless he took immediate action. But first he had to discover which one was the truth.

In the meantime, he was well aware that the clock was ruthlessly counting down the hours and minutes before Gaddis would seek to put a noose around Wadsworth's neck. Unless, of course, Lucius Wadsworth was miraculously inspired to change his mind, which, in Ransome's vaguely formed Church of England understanding, would have been less likely than the miracles supposed to have been wrought by the ghostly nuns whose lands the first, bad Lord Hardcastle had seized. In other words, he could not afford to wait for a miracle.

So he bided his time until Mrs. Wadsworth was safely distracted in the kitchen, going over the week's orders with Cook, and slipped upstairs to her bedchamber. It was a desperate move. If Ransome was caught, that was likely enough to be all the scandal Gaddis could desire—regardless of whether Ransome was taken for a jewel thief or a seducer—but he could see no other option.

Quickly, he opened Mrs. Wadsworth's jewel case. His hand moved expertly, testing the quality of a string of opera pearls and a diamond bracelet, even though they were not what he sought.

"They are not paste," Mrs. Wadsworth said quietly behind him.

Ransome closed the box and turned to face her. "So these letters have only recently surfaced?" he forced himself to ask with equal detachment. "The postmaster has not been bleeding you for years?"

"Scarcely gentlemanly questions," Mrs. Wadsworth pointed out.

"It has been said of me before," Ransome allowed. As he had been searching, his mind had been spinning with excuses to offer if he got caught. But even as his imagination sorted rapidfire through stories of cursed rubies in the Raj and the hereditary Hardcastle diamonds that had long ago been hocked to secure the safe passage of King Charles from his oak at Boscobel, he realized that he had never really looked at Libba's mother before—at least beyond dismissing her as an extraordinarily beautiful woman who was little more than a decoration. And as soon as he read the calm intelligence in her eyes—Libba's calm intelligence—he knew that the best decision was simply tell her the truth.

"Gaddis seeks anything he can hold over your husband's head in order to influence his business decisions," he said. "And clearly both Hardcastle and the postmaster believed they had such information. Now that they are gone, I have promised your daughter that I will find those secrets before Gaddis does. And—my apologies for speaking frankly—I don't think a failed elopement two decades ago is much of a scandal despite Miss Ripley's assurances to the contrary. So I must beg you to be forthright and describe to me the contents of those letters, so I can be certain they are not the secret Hardcastle sought to hold over your family."

She nodded, considering his words. Then her face blossomed with humor—and in that moment, she was truly enchanting. "Shall we speak in the rose garden?" she suggested, retrieving a delicate wrap from where it was tossed over a chair. "No point in courting further scandal by having me discovered *in flagrante* with my future son-in-law."

The last sentence was as much a question as a statement. Ransome grinned as he offered her his arm. "I have reason to believe that your daughter is already persuaded to accept my suit," he said—trying to keep the satisfaction out of his voice and not quite succeeding. "Which is why I feel a certain personal interest in clearing up this matter of Gaddis."

She nodded her acquiescence, then fell silent until they had reached the privacy of the rose garden. Only when they were alone, beyond the reach of any eavesdroppers, did she ask with an irony he would not have thought her capable of, "Do you need a full recapitulation of the family scandal, or may I trust that Eustachia has already seized the opportunity to fill you in on the most salient details?"

"At the risk of introducing an unwelcome subject of conversation, I would prefer to hear the story without the particular salience that Miss Ripley seems to feel she must introduce into every tale," he said.

Mrs. Wadsworth's shoulders lifted beneath the gauze of the wrap. "It is, alas, a salacious tale. All I can ask is that you in no way allow it to reflect on Libba."

"If the prospect of having been murdered can't lessen my determination to wed your daughter, I cannot see how a long-ago scandal would make a difference."

She laughed, then sobered immediately. "It was long ago, and the details are well known. I was destined to make a brilliant match. Not an earl, of course. I must concede the honors there to my daughter. A mere viscount, from the cadet branch of the Hardcastle family—that is if his story was to be believed."

"Oh, that much of Naughton's story was true," Ransome said. "Thorn in the family's side for years, before we could finally ship him off to America."

She raised an eyebrow. "Your loss was not entirely our gain."

"Apologies. I simply meant to emphasize the fact that there was no question of his legitimacy, just his morals. Unlike the man who sought to present himself as Naughton's son."

Her lips twisted. "One is sometimes given to wonder whether there really could be such a thing as a curse on our brides. Certainly the family seems to have a knack for attracting men who are not exactly what they seem to be."

Ransome fought down an unhappy surge of guilt. "Surely we all have our secrets. But some secrets bear overlooking more than others?"

She cast him a glance that was at least as penetrating as her daughter's before she went on, "He came to me, desperate, the evening before the party to celebrate our betrothal. Told me enemies were spreading lies about him, and he sought . . . to carry me off by force." She drew a quick breath and corrected herself. "He begged me to elope. And to this day, I could not tell you whether I went with him of my own free will or not. But it makes no difference. We were betrayed. My father and Lu . . . Mr. Wadsworth followed us. There was a struggle, and my father was stricken by an apoplectic fit from which he never recovered. It was nothing but an accident, of course, but my titled suitor fled nonetheless."

Ransome frowned. It was an unfortunate tale, pure grist for Miss Ripley's poisonous mill. But it did nothing to explain why a woman would pawn her jewels. Or the unhappiness that creased his prospective mother-in-law's face now. "As scandals go, I'd argue that's practically respectable," Ransome protested, "tasteful even. Every family worth its salt has at least one elopement gone wrong rattling around the family pile. Why even the Dowager Duchess—"

"I see I have much to learn about English standards of taste," she cut him off with a small smile. "But leaving aside the issue of the gaps in my education, you are correct. It was an old story, over long ago. And so it would have remained, had I not been foolish enough to accept Cousin

Cornelia's introduction to the Hardcastle family." She shook her head. "In truth, and with all respect to your relatives, I was dead set against it. I had no desire to relive that old story. It was Mr. Wadsworth who insisted. Some sentimental attachment to tin mines . . . I admit I never could follow that part of the tale. Cousin Cornelia insisted that there would be no question of being exposed to the Naughton side of the family, and asked me whether my foolish pride would prevent my daughter from winning an earl as a husband."

"And I can offer you my solemn word that I have every intention of being just that," Ransome said. "Unfortunately, in order to do so, I fear I must press you for the details of what happened with those letters."

"Soon after Lord Hardcastle arrived in Braddock's Landing, I received a demand for money from the local postmaster."

"In exchange for those letters?"

"In exchange for information that cast an interesting light on my marriage. Or even more correctly in exchange for not selling the information to the man who presented himself as Lord Hardcastle, who was also an interested buyer."

Ransome nodded, steeling himself for what he had to ask next. "At the risk of intruding myself in matters we would all prefer were left private, when exactly did you write these letters?"

Mrs. Wadsworth stiffened. "After the unfortunate denouement of my elopement, I would confess, I remained angry and disappointed about . . . many things." She drew a deep breath, forcing herself to go on. "Why put too fine a point on it? I was angry and disappointed at having been forced to marry my father's quarry manager before the ink had dried on the newspapers pronouncing me the Flower of the Hudson and the Debutante of the Year. I was dissatisfied with a quiet life in Braddock's Landing, when I had been destined for greater things, so I . . . I wrote to Naughton. Desperate letters. Indiscreet letters. Begging him to carry me away." Mrs. Wadsworth raised a shoulder beneath the gauzy wrap. "He never replied. Now I know why. Those letters never got further than the Braddock's Landing Post Office."

"But that makes no sense," Ransome objected. "You would have me believe they lay there all that time, only to surface now? Why so long? Why after all these years?"

She raised an eyebrow. "Is an expertise in dealing with blackmailers among your many skills, Mr. Ransome?"

"Actually—" He cut himself off abruptly, reminding himself that such expertise might be a talent best left behind with his career as a spy and an orchid hunter, and returned to the matter at hand. "Could Hardcastle have brought them with him? Did he seek to use them to press his claim?"

"It was the postmaster, not Har . . . the other Lord Hardcastle that approached me," she objected.

"But how would he know they were of any value if he never opened them?" Ransome continued to muse. "And how did the postmaster obtain them? Surely Hardcastle would not have mailed them to himself."

"I am sure I cannot tell you. All I do know is that the matter is closed." Her smile deepened, and her eyes were suddenly far away. "Mr. Wadsworth found out—I believe our gardener may have told him. By that evening, my pearls were on my dressing table, and the postmaster had left town, without my being forced to exchange the diamonds in Lady Cora's tiara for paste."

"That's glad news," Ransome said. "Because I will most likely find myself in the embarrassing position of being forced to request the loan of the tiara for the Happy Day. Most of the Hardcastle family jewels have gone the way your jewels have so narrowly avoided—and the thought of wrenching the sole remaining coronet from the Dowager Countess's coiffure would give pause to a much stronger man than I."

She eyed him levelly. "I am beginning to believe that my daughter has found a husband with much more to offer her than a title."

"And I believe I have found a wife with much more to offer than an American fortune," he agreed. "Although, as a token of good faith between us, I will tell you in confidence that I'm not sure I shall apprise my mother of such a thing. She's likely to think the less of me if I am genuinely happy in my intended—and would be if she had not a penny to her name or a countess' coronet to wear at her wedding. A true gentleman sacrifices himself on the altar of matrimony and all that."

Alas, the spy in him pointed out, there might not be any altar of matrimony, sacrificial or otherwise, if he did not discover a way to handle the difficulty at hand. Ransome drew a deep breath, unwilling to press the issue and yet knowing he must. "I must say, a pearl necklace seems a heavy price to pay for a decade-old indiscretion that came to naught."

Her gaze sharpened in a way that reminded him irresistibly of Libba. "My husband is a decent man. A good man. And those letters have the potential of hurting him irreparably. What price would I not pay to prevent that?"

What price indeed? Unhappily, Ransome's thoughts

flashed to Libba's unthinking revelation about the communicating door between her parents' rooms. He had already intruded far enough on their private pain. It could only be more mean-minded to put those letters to use himself. And yet if Mrs. Wadsworth was telling him the truth, these letters could not possibly be what Hardcastle sought to hold over the family's head. Embarrassing. Indiscreet. Hurtful even. But in their essence no more harmful than Miss Ripley's acid tongue. Which left only one other interpretation of the contents of Wadsworth's strong box.

Uncomfortable as this conversation was, he had to make sure before he could act. "Forgive me for pressing, and please accept my assurance I would never do so were it not important, but I must be direct. The letters with which he sought to threaten you were merely indiscreet. They offered no actual evidence of wrong-doing?"

She drew herself up. "I never wronged my husband. I have always obeyed my wifely duty. But I was unthinking and unkind. Mocking my husband for his lack of manners. For being uncouth."

Ransome grinned disarmingly even as his mind kept calculating. "Well, if that is all there is to it, I can assure you that Mr. Wadsworth's manners will pass muster in even the Dowager Countess's drawing room," he told her. "As a matter of fact, I am certain that his will seem an improvement on my own. At least in his tolerance for starched collars."

A flash of humor lit her eyes as she glanced at Ransome's collar, which had drifted askew some five minutes after Mr. Wadsworth's valet had attempted to adjust it for him, and had stubbornly stayed that way ever since. "I quite agree," she said. "And over the years I have come to respect and admire my husband greatly. But I still would not have him see those letters."

Ransome nodded slowly. There was something wrong. An indiscreet letter written a decade ago did not explain the putative Lord Hardcastle's arrogance.

"At the risk of sounding inquisitorial, I must ask you plainly. You never succeeded in eloping with Naughton? Your marriage was never prevented by the smuggler Tam Jenkins? You are not the American heiress Naughton's son would claim as a mother?"

For a moment she looked thunderstruck. And then she said, "I have never been to England before this year's abortive visit. If you do not wish to accept my word on it, you could verify that with the passport office."

"That will hardly be necessary." He shook his head. There was something he was missing. Something that he should be seeing plainly. Curse the title. Curse him growing soft and slow. "But why you? Why Braddock's Landing? Are there any other American heiresses knocking about?"

The ghost of smile traced across her face. "Is that how you would speak of the first families of New York?"

"Yankee upstarts, every last one of them," he dismissed them, as he got to his feet, his mind still churning. "Thank you for your time, Mrs. Wadsworth. And your candor. I understand the situation, now. I understand it completely."

"I'm not sure there's anything to understand beyond the fact that I have been a very silly, very stupid woman, and Mr. Wadsworth deserves far, far better."

And Mrs. Wadsworth deserved not to endure any more of this interrogation. He raised her hand to his lips. "And I can only give you my assurance I believe you are neither." He paused, for a moment, then added, "And maybe it is the anticipation of my own happiness that leads me to be overly forward. But true wedded happiness is not a matter of what one deserves, any more than it is a matter of sacrificial altars. You have my words as a member of my unfortunate sex that it does not matter to a man in the least what he deserves in a wife. It matters to him who he wants for a wife. And Mr. Wadsworth strikes me as a man who knows what he wants every bit as much I do."

Chapter 24

Nothing had changed, and yet everything was different about Mama. Libba found herself watching her mother as if she were watching a stranger. For although it was the Mama she had always known who wafted along the house's halls, smiling apologetically beneath the servants' affectionate disapproval, Libba could scarcely understand why she had never noticed the fiber of steely determination that ran beneath everything Mama did. How could Libba never have understood the resolve that stiffened Mama's spine, when she called for the pony trap and said, "I would that you accompany me to the village this afternoon. I have several volumes I need to return to the Subscription Library."

Several volumes? Mama might patronize the Subscription Library, but she read no more of its books than those of its ink-stained and furtive half-brother at the opposite end of the street. To her, the library was—like the Reformed Church and the Braddock Memorial—just one more of the genteel, white-pillared institutions among which the more refined of Braddock's Landing society moved. So why should Libba find herself completely unsurprised when Mama managed to manifest a slender volume of poetry and a three-decker novel of Mr. Trollope's when she presented herself at the circulation desk in the library's hushed lobby?

A troubled expression darkened the cheerful former governess who was volunteering that day, and she hurried into the reading room with a murmured excuse. Moments later, a familiar jaundiced presence manifested.

"Oh, my dear, this is terribly brave of you," Miss Ripley breathed. "Stiff upper lip and all that. But do you really feel your approach is entirely *wise*?"

Mama froze Miss Ripley with a glare worthy of Mrs. Philipse Braddock. "Why should it not be?"

"The Ladies' Committee is meeting in the reading room," Miss Ripley said. "Perhaps you were not aware."

To judge from Mama's expression, she was more than well aware of that fact, and, Libba suspected with unwilling admiration, that had been the reason for this otherwise inexplicable excursion. But Mama's expression was bland and mannerly as she informed Miss Ripley, "As I am a member of that Committee, I find it strange I was not informed."

"It is a special session. In order to consider the . . . events up at Braddock House."

Mama raised an eyebrow. "And why is that? Does the Ladies Committee propose to solve the case?"

Mama, ironic? Even Miss Ripley paused, flat-footed, before she said, "Come now, Lydia, be reasonable. Cornelia is furious, naturally, but I think the majority of the committee are disposed to allow this to blow over in time, if you allow it. But you're scarcely advancing your cause by bearding the lioness in her den, if you will."

"Seeing that it was my husband's money that paid for the entire refurbishment of the reading room last year, as well as his workers who performed the labor, I would argue that if this den belongs to any lioness, it belongs to me," Mama said, as she threw open the door to the reading room.

"Now, Lydia, there's no call to be vulgar," Miss Ripley protested, scuttling after her.

"She cannot help it. Breeding will tell." Mrs. Philipse Braddock rose from her seat at the head of the long reading table, around which were clustered the pastor's wife, the schoolmistress, and several other women who passed as Braddock's Landing society. "Lydia has never been capable of anything else in her life. But honestly a murder? It's beyond the pale. I am shocked and ashamed to have ever received you in my house."

"But this is not your house. This is an institution that has been supported by little beyond my husband's generosity," Mama said. She turned on the ladies. "By all means, cut your ties with me. But know that when you do, you cut your ties with my family's support as well."

"You speak in haste," the pastor's wife said.

"Perhaps. But at least, I speak to your face," Mama said. "Unlike those who convened this meeting so hastily behind my back."

"Be reasonable," the school mistress said. "One simply cannot ignore a dead body in the library."

"Better a dead body in the library than skeletons in the closet." Mama glanced pointedly at Miss Ripley as she spoke, but it was Mrs. Philipse Braddock who reacted, spitting, "You presume too far. I may have been forced to receive you once, but if you think to press your way into the first circles of society through blackmail, I will see you thrown in prison. We'll see how much your English earl enjoys visiting his relations in the Tombs. Ladies, if you will . . ."

She swept out, and, after a moment's uncertain hesitation, the rest of the Ladies Committee followed, leaving Mama and Libba alone with Miss Ripley, who hastened to explain with catlike commiseration, "Oh, dear. I feel I should have warned you. There was a certain . . . *pressure* behind your invitation to visit Tavistock, an insult that dear Cornelia still seems to take sorely. I suppose I should have informed you at the time, but one does not like to *gossip.*"

Mama raised an eyebrow. "Well, I do so hate to press you into something so obviously uncongenial, but seeing as I have just been threatened with prosecution, I'm afraid I must prevail on you to disclose who seeks so assiduously to advance my daughter's social career."

"Well, I'm sure I couldn't say. But you might consult Mr. Gaddis, of course. He seems to have taken a *particular* interest in the situation."

"Because he seeks to further his business interests with my husband?" Mama asked. Her voice was calm, but Libba could see her knuckles whiten around her reticule.

"I'm afraid you would have to ask him yourself," Miss Ripley said with an airy wave of her fan. "Some kind of Vanderbilt interest down in New York City. Politics and corruption. I find pursuing the details corrupts my poetical mind, so all I can tell you for certain is they are *sordid.*"

"Then we can only thank you for you kind advice," Mama said. "Come, Libba. I seem to recall your father is engaged to meet Mr. Gaddis at the hotel when he returns from the quarry. I think we need to secure a private interview before that."

Seemed to recall, Libba thought in bewilderment as she followed Mama down the Main Street toward the hotel whose graceful verandas overlooked both the ferry landing and the spectacular cliffs on the opposite side of the Hudson. Having witnessed this new side of Mama, Libba wouldn't be surprised if Mama checked Papa's engagement book nightly—and had been doing so for years. She certainly seemed to know where she was heading as she swept into the hotel's lobby and strode straight over to Gaddis, who was engaged with a dispatch case full of papers at a desk in an alcove.

"Mr. Gaddis," she accosted him, "I so hate to trouble you, but Libba and I find ourselves stranded. I had hoped to take tea in the hotel while we attended Mr. Wadsworth, but it would be scarcely proper for two ladies to take even tea alone. Could I prevail on you to join us? For propriety's sake?"

Gaddis looked like there was nothing he would care for less. But short of pleading an urgent trip back down to New York City, there was little he could do but offer her his arm and escort her into the hotel's restaurant, which was empty save for a chattering collection of visitors from New York, determined to take in the delights of the Hudson Valley.

Mama made charming but idle chit chat, until the sturdy farm girl, whose family supplied both Braddock House and the hotel with milk and butter, brought them a plate of cucumber sandwiches and a steaming teapot. Then Mama dropped all pretense, and, ignoring the food, said, "Mr. Gaddis, I will be direct. I would understand the matter that lies between you and my husband."

Gaddis shook his head. "I would not involve you in matters that are not your concern."

"But my daughter's dowry is my concern, every bit as much as it is my husband's," Mama said. "And since you have talked about such things with her intended, I would that you talk to me. For I am not silly enough to deny that my daughter's fortune is her principle charm. So I would know if it is threatened in any way, and if there is something I might do to rescue it."

Gaddis glanced at her warily, as if a talking mynah bird had started to give him advice. "With all respect, Mrs. Wadsworth, you are beginning to sound like a woman of advanced ideas."

"A suffragist you mean?" Mama dismissed the question with an exquisite shrug. "I am interested in the affairs of this world only when they touch me directly. I am perfectly happy to leave the affairs of state to the men who are interested in them."

"Sensible attitude," Gaddis allowed. "Half of them are spiritualists, the other half are hysterics in need of a husband's firm hand. As if we don't already have enough problems controlling the rabble from Five Points and Jones Wood, and now even the emancipated slaves in Harlem. Bread and circuses, that's all they want, and those scoundrels in Tammany Hall have understood that for years. The rabble love them because they give them jobs—jobs in public works that also serve to line Tammany Hall's own pockets quite nicely."

"Public works that often use bluestone from my husband's quarries?" Mama asked.

He cast her a long, appraising look, before conceding the point with a curt nod, and informing her, "They won't for long. Not with the developments in Portland cements. Now that the first concrete street has been built in Bellefontaine,

Ohio, but it won't be long before all cities pave in cement rather than bluestone. The quarrying industry as we know it will be dead within a quarter-century."

"And so you came here to interest my husband in investing in concrete?"

"I came here to offer him an opportunity! He can invest in concrete or retire with you to England for all I care. All I want him to do is to refuse to sell bluestone to . . . certain public works."

"Public works financed by Tammany Hall?" Mama guessed.

"Several of the city's first families are determined to take this matter in hand and take down Tammany Hall for good. J.P. Morgan, Cornelius Vanderbilt, Elihu Root—just to offer you the most prominent names—are determined to return morality and strong business principles to the running of this city. Very prominent names. The kind of social circle in which everyone might aspire to move."

Something set in Mama's face. "Social circles that might include an invitation to Mrs. Philipse Braddock's Midsummer's Ball?"

"Mrs. Philipse Braddock has claims to being a Vanderbilt."

"By marriage," Mama said, her voice only briefly cutting before she frowned with beguiling bewilderment and asked, "Nonetheless, I am still hard-pressed to understand why my husband objects to Cousin Cornelia's family's plans."

"As is any sane man! He spouted some nonsense about being more worried about men who were trying to feed their families than morality or strong business principles," Gaddis snorted. "Sheer Fabianism, if you ask me."

Libba wasn't certain what Fabianism was, but she did

know it was so like Papa to put a worker's wages ahead of social advancement. He had always been mindful of his workers, paying them fairly, schooling their children, pensioning them off with cottages when the time came. Of course, she had heard the nasty whispers that this was just one more proof of his workingman's roots, but here in America it was no shame to be a self-made man. And if these were the first social circles Mama dreamed of moving in, she wanted no part of them.

Mama smiled at Mr. Gaddis. "My husband is wont to indulge me," she said sweetly. "Especially if I can convince him that our daughter's future happiness is at stake. I would beg you give me a chance to speak of him of these matters before you take any further action."

He didn't answer immediately, and Libba worried Mama had gone too far. But she should have had more faith in these abilities she had newly discovered about her mother. "Perhaps a woman's touch is needed to make him see his error," Gaddis admitted. "He's been offered a tremendous opportunity, one that few men see in a lifetime. I pray you can make him understand that. For time is running very short—and not just for the quarrying industry."

As if punctuating his words, horns and bells sounded, indicating the ferry's arrival. With pained courtesy, Mr. Gaddis offered Mama his arm. "It seems as if your husband has returned. Shall we?"

He escorted them back out into the lobby, just as Papa strode through the front door, his face set with fury. "Leave," he informed Gaddis. "You go too far when you venture to disturb my family."

"It would be ungentlemanly for me to point out it was your wife who suggested this meeting," Gaddis said. "But it matters not. You cannot hide behind the ladies' skirts forever. Sooner or later my investors will have their answer."

Papa's face went cold. "Accuse me of hiding behind a lady again, and I will whip you rawer than a mule with a load of stone," he said. "And you may tell your investors that I have already given them my answer. Now, if you will excuse me, I must see to my family."

He waited until Gaddis was gone, then turned to Mama, his face granite. "I apologize for forcing you to witness such vulgarity. I will remain until the trap is brought round, and then burden you no further."

He moved to withdraw himself, but Mama stopped him with a hand on his arm. "Unfortunately, Mr. Wadsworth," she said, "I must beg the favor of your driving us back to Braddock House yourself. There is a matter of some urgency I must discuss with you."

Papa's jaw set, and Libba was certain he was going to refuse. But then he inclined his head, and said, "I'll have them bring the trap around."

The uncomfortable silence that fell remained until they were out of the village and ambling back toward Braddock House. Only when the easy clop of the cob's hooves had relaxed them all did Papa finally ask, "And what exactly is this matter of pressing urgency you would care to discuss?"

"I would like to talk to you about Portland cement," Mama said.

It was well the placid cob knew his way home and was beating a determined path toward his well-deserved bran mash, for Papa literally dropped the reins. He took his time regaining them—along with his wits, before he managed to find voice to ask, "Would ye, now, Mrs. Wadsworth? And what exactly would ye like to know about such a thing?"

"Mr. Gaddis is correct. I did solicit his company for tea. And during the course of what I can only describe as an encounter I would prefer not to be forced to repeat, Mr. Gaddis informed me that the quarrying industry as we know it will be extinct within two decades, and all the cities will move toward paving with cement and concrete. Along with a host of other things I confess I did not truly follow. Something about Tammany Hall. And labor agitators. Suffragists. And Fabians." Mama waved a hand in front of her face delicately. "I swear Mr. Gaddis's plots are more convoluted than Miss Ripley's. If I follow him correctly, which I sincerely doubt my poor woman's brain is capable of, he would force New York City to use an inferior material and stay the course of progress, all to gain your support in a war against a political rival."

Papa busied himself for a moment gathering the reins. When he finally recovered them, he said, "Poor woman's brain or not, Mrs. Wadsworth, I believe you have summarized the situation admirably."

"Horrid man," Mama ruminated. "He made it very clear he would stop at nothing. Even social invitations are apparently to be put in the service of this vendetta."

Libba glanced at Mama sharply, uncertain how Mama might have ever learned such a word. Papa's gaze was more unfathomable.

"And so, what exactly is the purpose of this conversation? Do you seek for me to explain Gaddis's plots to you?" he asked. "Or perhaps even defend them?"

"Oh, please, no. Trying to follow his plotting simply makes my head swim. But I must needs ask, would it not be far simpler to investigate investing in the cement industry yourself, instead of putting yourself in the power of this schemer?" Mama's face darkened only briefly, before she added, "And I am sorry if that means the Vanderbilts will cut us, and we will no longer be moving in the first circles. But I think Libba is going to have to be contented with catching an earl instead."

There was a thunderous silence, equal to the one that had clouded their departure from the village. And then Papa's eyes gleamed with humor, as he clucked at the cob who had seized the opportunity to graze on a choice patch of clover by the side of the road. "By happy coincidence, Mrs. Wadsworth, I am inclined to see matters that way myself. So much so, that I've already looked toward purchasing a cement factory over in Rosendale."

"Have you really?" Now, it was Mama's turn to look dumbfounded. Then she shook her head. "Why of course you have. Why, if even a fool like me can see the extent of Gaddis's folly . . ."

"Nae worries, Libba's dowry is safe. Safe enough to catch an earl, if that's what she decides. For I'm nae a fool, no matter what Gaddis may say." Papa's face broke into something that could only be described as a jaunty smile. His eyes lingered on Mama, as he pulled to the door of Braddock House and helped Libba and Mama out. "Nor did I ever wed one—for all my sins. I'd truly be a fool if I thought that. Now, if you'll excuse me, ladies. I have a cement company to bid on."

Chapter 25

Ransome would always remember that last dinner at Braddock House as the moment he was initiated into the mysteries of Portland cement. The entire family seemed fixated on the topic, speaking about it in some private language that only he didn't understand. Mrs. Wadsworth blushed like a new bride every time the words were mentioned. Even more inexplicably, she and her daughter seemed to have exchanged roles: Mrs. Wadsworth seemingly uninterested in anxiously parsing every word exchanged between Ransome and her daughter, while Libba supervised her mother with the beaming approbation of a chaperone. And as for Lucius Wadsworth, suffice it to say something had changed. Something that had him alternating between presiding over the table like a genial uncle and casting covert looks at his wife that Ransome was certain would scandalize both the Dowager Countess and his mother, both of whom shared a firm belief in the sacrificial, not sacramental, nature of matrimony.

But when Ransome found Wadsworth saddling his cob at the crack of dawn the next morning, his prospective father-in-law's face was all business—set with the same kind of grim determination that Ransome was more used to from his less savory professional acquaintances. And Wadsworth's expression only grew more granite when he heard Ransome call for another horse to be saddled.

"I have as much interest in seeing those settlements signed as you do," Wadsworth said, holding up a hand to stop the stable lad. "Still, today might not be the best day to see to it. Word is, there may be a spot of trouble at the quarry today."

"So I may have heard," Ransome allowed. "Rumor's gone round that the local postmaster turned up dead on the other side of the Hudson."

"And no more than he deserves. Man was nothing but a thief and blackmailer." Wadsworth shot Ransome a sharp look. "As I'm sure you're aware."

"I trust you're not insinuating that I had something to do with it."

"No more than you should believe I did. But someone's sent Byrnes's boys up from New York with some kind of cock and bull story about a gang of spies being run by the legendary Tam Jenkins." Another sharp look. "You have heard of Inspector Thomas Byrnes?"

Indeed, Ransome's understanding of the man in question far exceeded that expected of your average Peer of the Realm—but he was not ready to enter into awkward explanations about that topic quite yet. "All I can really gather is he's not someone your acquaintance Gaddis much likes," Ransome said with a shrug. "Which ordinarily would be endorsement enough as far as I'm concerned. But you must admit it is a bit strange that your business suddenly seems to be under assault from both sides, if you will."

"It's their own damned quarrel," Wadsworth said, giving vent to a sudden burst of frustration. "Thugs, the lot of them. Only difference is, one side has better manners than the other. Me, I don't give a damn about manners, any more than I care about the moral fiber of New York City politics. But I'll be damned if I'll let my family or my workmen be used as a pawn in some political quarrel that has nothing to do with them, or me."

Years spent in the spy business could only make Ransome concur. "Then you will allow me the opportunity to join in your defense—or if you prefer, in defense of my future wife's interests?"

Wadsworth's eyes narrowed. "With respect, these boys might be a shade different than what an earl is used to dealing with."

"And with equal respect, I've been an earl for less than a year, and an orchid hunter and inquiry agent for a decade and a half before that," Ransome said. "Given the earldom, I assume the day is destined to come when I've forgotten my way around a dockside brawl, but that day hasn't come quite yet."

Wadsworth shot him a last, appraising look, before conceding, "Might be useful to have you along. Just in case."

He seemed disinclined to specify in case of what and Ransome was frankly disinclined to enquire. He took it as a matter of faith that Wadsworth had not killed either Hardcastle or the postmaster, but he was not of a mind to have his faith put too severely to the test. So, once the horses were saddled, they ambled down to the ferry landing in a silence that, if it could not be described as companionable, could at least be describe as understanding.

The landing was half obscured by the mists rising off the river in a way that could make even a level-headed Englishman like Ransome think of Catskill witches hurling storms down from a gourd and gnomes playing at ninepins among the peaks. But all the unnatural creatures to emerge from Mr. Irving's imagination were nothing compared to the vessel that awaited them at the ferry dock. Ransome had expected some kind of sailing vessel, a sloop maybe, or even a tug. Instead, he found himself confronted with a peculiar wooden craft whose stern consisted of a pair of sheds. Two horses were harnessed on a pair of treadmills that were connected to the vessel's massive paddlewheels, while, as best Ransome could tell, the low, flat front of the vessel was intended for passengers.

"Is that meant to be a boat?" Ransome demanded.

"Untoward, innit?" Wadsworth said with a grin. "Most mornings, Caleb would have sailed the periauger, but the fog is low and the wind is up and an old riverman like Caleb doesn't like to take chances. The horseboat is slow and clumsy, for sure, but it's solid enough, for all I told Caleb that no true sailor would be able to show his face in port if it was known he had set foot in such a thing."

Ransome glanced at Wadsworth. "You a Navy man, then?"

Wadsworth's face darkened. "I said a true sailor. Won't find many of those in that damned cesspool. Every last one of those ships was built on the backs of convicts and conscripts. I'd take an honest slaver over Her Majesty's Navy—no offense meant."

"And none taken," Ransome assured him. In fact, his experience of Her Majesty's Army had been little different and had led to the unconventional career that had landed him in his current difficulties. Still, his prospective father-in-law's reaction was just one more piece of evidence to support the theory he had been formulating over the last several days. It was a theory that Ransome had to admit explained everything—but it also brought in its wake several serious complications.

He fought down the urge to study Wadsworth, fitting him against his theory much as a wife's dressmaker might try a bolt of cloth against a woman. Instead, he made a point of examining the two horses with which the ferryman proposed to propel them across the water. Ransome had used more than his share of odd methods of transportation—everything from a Chinese junk to a spitting and resentful camel. But his experience of horses was that it could be the devil itself to persuade them to cross a running brook. And this man proposed to take them across a river deep and broad enough ships could navigate it? But in the event, the horses took their work as a matter of course, plodding on their treadmills with the same indifference as a hackney would draw his cab along the streets of London. Ransome could only wish that his musings during the choppy voyage would be as smooth.

Wadsworth's quarry manager was waiting for them at the quay in a wagon drawn by a hulking draft horse, and Ransome disembarked not without some sense of relief at seeing horses back in their accustomed place between the traces with their hooves firmly planted on the ground. But the quarryman stopped him with a mutinous frown. "What's his interest in all this?"

"I should think that would be obvious," Ransome said, swinging himself into the back of the wagon, and settling onto one of the plank benches that lined the side.

The quarryman ignored him and looked to Wadsworth. "This mean you're going to let him handle matters while you go to Rosendale with your men?"

"Going to Rosendale's a coward's trick, and I'll have none of it," Wadsworth growled, as he climbed up to sit next to the quarryman.

"With respect, sir, the boys won't care all that much whether you're a coward or not. They will care if you're no longer the man running the quarry."

"You have my word, I have no intention of allowing that to happen," Wadsworth said, with a pointed glance back at Ransome. "And I'll thank you not to trouble my future son-in-law by continuing to press the issue."

With a snort, the quarryman clucked the horse into a lumbering trot, and Ransome slouched back in his seat, pretending to watch the passing scenery as if he were just another holiday maker up from New York City to enjoy the Catskills' renowned picturesque views. The journey was a study in contrasts. The bustling riverside docks quickly gave way to alluvial farmlands that could put the greenest pastures in England to shame. But the farms grew more hardscrabble as they headed up toward the cliffs that brooded down over the landscape, and soon gave way to inns and livery stables that serviced the holiday makers on their way up to the great hotels at the tops of the mountains.

Wadsworth's quarries were located on the flanks of one such mountain. Its hotel was smaller than the legendary Catskill Mountain House, but it did boast of surviving a memorable visit from President Ulysses S. Grant, the suddenly garrulous quarryman informed Ransome.

"Drunk as a skunk the whole time. I knew the man that drove him, and the way he tells it, it took a pint of whiskey to get Grant into town, and another to get him up the mountain. And there's another man over toward Kingston who still introduces himself by saying 'You're shaking the hand that held General Grant's horse while the General was having a quick one inside.'"

"All of it a pack of lies," Wadsworth snorted. "Pure political mudslinging spread by the teetotalers and vegetarians in Greeley's camp. You might as well believe Twaddell's tale about Grant riding Scott, the horse, until the clean mountain air began to make the President look younger and younger. 'Twaddell,' Grant said, pulling Scott up short. 'I'll be in trouble if I get any younger. The Constitution says that the President must be above thirty-five. I'm having trouble with Congress. They'll impeach me and throw me out of the White House.' 'Make for the stables, Mr. President,' Twaddell shouted, 'and give Scott his head. If any horse on this earth can get you back in time, it's Scott.'"

The men's burst of shared laughter was undermined by the unspoken knowledge that the situation they were facing was mired as deeply in similar political mudslinging. And their mood only darkened when they finally arrived at the quarry village: a tidy settlement of clapboard cottages, a general store, a smithy and stable, and an office tucked at the foot of the narrow path that led up to the quarries among the cliffs. It was a little world risen out of the Catskill mists as magically as Brigadoon. And right now, it was as empty as the hollow husk of the *Half Moon* after it had been abandoned by Henry Hudson's men. No sound of pickaxes rang down from the cliffs overhead. No children laughed or quarreled on the dirt streets. No women gossiped on the porch of the general store. The only sound beyond the steady clop of the horse's hooves was the rustling leaves and the birdsong.

"Sent the families down to Rosendale with the men. Made it a company holiday and picnic." The quarryman shot Wadsworth a pointed look. "At your expense. So it might be appropriate if you were there to make a speech so they could show their appreciation, you think?"

"Best leave the speechifying to those who can do it," Wadsworth said shortly. His eyes grew calculating as the quarryman pulled the wagon to a halt in front of the office. "Any idea how long we have?"

"Got word that they changed horses at New Paltz when I met you at the Rondout," the quarryman said. "They'll be here within the quarter hour."

"And we'll be ready for them," Wadsworth said.

The quarryman conceded with a grudging nod, and Ransome added his absent assent, for his mind was engaged with formulating the last elements of a plan whose outlines he had sketched while he had been pretending to sightsee during the wagon ride. It was an idea that he had no intention of sharing with anyone—especially Wadsworth. For, although he had grown to like and trust his prospective father-in-law, one was forced to admit that he had a stubborn streak to rival his daughter's—as well as a sense of honor that might force him to object to Ransome's admitted flexibility with the truth. And while there was much to admire about that part of Wadsworth's stern character, it could only be a hindrance now.

But before Ransome could do anything, he had to be certain that he had correctly estimated Byrnes's men—as well as the antipathy that lay between them and Gaddis and his friends. So he volunteered to stand watch on the office porch while Wadsworth and his quarryman went inside, his deliberately lazy posture hiding the grim appraisal with which he studied the road.

They arrived in an open wagon much like the one the

quarryman had driven, except that it was painted dark blue and had "New York City Police" stenciled on its side. There were at least a dozen of them, seated on slatted benches along each side, making a show of the shotguns and billy clubs they carried. Even after traveling nearly a hundred miles up from the city, their uniforms were still stiffly correct. But there was no doubt they were the blood brothers of a score of such dangerous characters he had faced down in his career—just with a different grudge to bear. It was exactly what Ransome had hoped for.

"Gentlemen!" Ransome called, his accent suddenly growing far more British, his aspect far more lordly, as he stepped down from the office porch. "A word, if you will. On behalf of Her Majesty, the Queen of England."

He ignored the bewildered mutter that burst forth in the office behind him. He was already well aware that there was a distinct possibility that, instead of answering, these American Irishmen might simply seize the chance to satisfy a few justifiable quarrels with England by beating one of Her Majesty's representatives—especially an earl—unconscious. He needed to talk fast. And be as convincing as he had ever been in his life.

"And what's Her Majesty want with us?" The police sergeant took charge. He was fat and mean, the coarse-cropped hair beneath his helmet looking like nothing so much as boar's bristles. "Going to invite us to Buckingham Palace for tea?"

He guffawed at his own joke, and his thugs obligingly laughed along with him.

"I understand you are here in pursuit of a dangerous criminal named Tam Jenkins," Ransome said. "And I am here to offer you Her Majesty's full cooperation in the matter."

"You expect me to believe Her Majesty the Queen wants to assist the New York City Detectives Bureau?" the sergeant snorted. "Maybe she'd like to leave a calling card at the Mulberry Street Morning Parade? Contribute a portrait to the Rogues Gallery?"

"Her Majesty's Government has no interest in common criminals," Ransome dismissed the man's japes loftily. The tension in the office behind him was palpable, and he heard what he knew with professional certainty was the sound of a gun being loaded. It was not an unexpected development, but it was an unwelcome one. He plowed ahead, raising his voice to make sure Wadsworth could hear it, and willing him to play along. "But they have quite a signal interest in discovering who sent you over here on a wild goose chase. For that is exactly what this is."

The sergeant's eyes got even smaller with suspicion. "You saying Tam Jenkins isn't here?"

"You have my assurance he is not."

"How about instead of your assurances, you give me a place where I can find him?"

"Tam Jenkins is lying in an ice house across the river, awaiting the results of a coroner's inquiry. As anyone in Braddock's Landing could have told you if you bothered to inquire. Her Majesty's interest is in who sent you over here to waste your time instead."

The sergeant set himself to thinking. It was not a pretty sight. "You saying Tam Jenkins is dead?"

"So did the coroner. There seems to be little question about the issue. On the other hand, there seems to be a substantial question as to who has an interest in the New York City Detectives Bureau chasing after a dead man."

The sergeant's eyes narrowed. "Maybe the person who killed him?"

"The coroner's verdict was against a person or persons unknown," Ransome said with a shrug. "I admit to Her Majesty's Government having a certain interest in keeping it that way."

"That so?" the sergeant said, reaching for his billy club.

It was a brutal weapon, made to hurt a man before it killed him. "What is arguably more germane to your interests is the fact that the Vanderbilts seem to have far more incentive to keep things quiet than Her Majesty's Government does," Ransome went on with a calm he didn't feel. "At least one can only assume that is why they sent you haring off here. Whatever the truth about Tam Jenkins's death, it is clear they are desperate to keep it from falling to the hands of Tammany Hall, or else they never would have showed their hand this clearly."

"What do you know about Tammany Hall? Or the Vanderbilts?"

"That it is always wisest to back the winning horse. However, in this case, it seems uncertain which horse that might be."

Metaphor—even a sporting one—seemed beyond this man's capacity. But at least his grip relaxed on the billy club. "You still haven't explained why Her Majesty the Queen is interested in some escaped convict."

Ransome smiled easily. "Because, of course, Tam Jenkins was far more than that."

The sergeant's eyes narrowed in sudden comprehension. "A spy?"

"We prefer the term operative," Ransome said. "And yes. He was one of the best. Until he decided it might be more profitable to strike out for himself."

That was clearly something the sergeant could understand. "Got ahold of some information he shouldn't have?" he asked with a cunning smile.

"Came to New York to sell it to the highest bidder," Ransome agreed.

"Any idea what this information might be?"

"Officially, all I know is that it could cause a diplomatic incident, which Her Majesty's government would very much prefer to avoid." Ransome lowered his voice confidentially. "Unofficially, it's been said that the Vanderbilts' concern with stern morality among the masses might not be exactly congruent with their private practices, if you know what I mean."

Even with the long words, the sergeant knew exactly what he meant. Just as Ransome knew the sergeant would swallow such a choice piece of bait as readily as he would swallow a pint of beer.

But the sergeant hadn't gotten where he was by being a creature of impulse and intuition. He tested the trap warily one last time. "Still oughta look around to make sure you're not lying to us."

"By all means. No need to take my word on it. Assure yourself there are no skeletons lurking in these cottage cupboards," Ransome said, stepping back as expansively as a butler throwing open a receiving room door. "But I would urge you to consider the possibility that far more important skeletons lurk in far more elaborate wardrobes across the river, and that right now the enemies of Tammany Hall are very busy seeking to afford them a decent burial while you waste your time here."

The sergeant took another look at the clearly silent village, then came to a sudden decision. "Let's go. Someone's tipped them the wink. There's no one here." He turned to favor Ransome with a glare. "If that's not Tam Jenkins in the ice house we'll be back. And you'll be sorry."

"By all means," Ransome said. He made a point of escorting them back to the wagon, seeing them off with a polite bow that honestly was probably going a shade too far. For the fact of the matter was, he did not feel himself exhale until several minutes after the sound of their horses hooves had died safely away, and he turned back to the office, where Wadsworth and the quarryman had emerged onto the porch, their faces slack with an expression that could only be described as gratifyingly dumbfounded.

Chapter 26

For once in her life, Libba was enjoying, rather than enduring, the monthly meeting of the Braddock's Ridge Ladies' Aid Society. It was the unexpected culmination of a series of unexpected events, which began that morning when Mama's request for an urgent private interview with Cousin Cornelia on a pressing personal matter was returned with the words "Not at home" scrawled across the envelope. Ordinarily, Mama would have been mortified. This morning, she had favored the returned missive with an unexpectedly malicious smile and had announced an entire day's worth of engagements—each of which contrived to cause them to bump into Cousin Cornelia. The Ladies' Aid Society was the third such foray.

The first time, Mrs. Braddock had swept out of the dry goods store as soon as they had entered. Mama had shrugged and purchased the several choice bolts of cloth Mrs. Braddock had been contemplating. Next, Mrs. Braddock had departed from the busy hotel lobby with such unseemly haste that she forgot her reticule, and Mama had sent one of the urchins lounging on the porch hallooing down the street after her to return "her dear cousin's property." But now, Mrs. Braddock stood cornered in the entrance to the Parish Hall of the Reformed church with no way to evade Mama's victorious advance other than pushing herself bodily past the aghast minister's wife.

"I would confess I would have had this conversation more privately," Mama said, not bothering to lower her voice, "but alas your butler informed us you were not at home this morning. And so, although I regret the unseemly appearance of a chase, I'm afraid I must press the issue of Sir Roderick Naughton and how exactly you are connected to him. For I very much fear my daughter's happiness might depend on your answer."

Mrs. Braddock drew herself up into a pillar of withering scorn. "I have no idea what you might be talking about."

"Why, the supposed father of the imposter you introduced to Braddock's Landing as Lord Hardcastle. I seem to recall that you performed a similar service for Sir Roderick Naughton many years ago. And since both of those introductions seemed to have considerable unfortunate consequences for my family, I fear I must insist on knowing how you made the acquaintance of Viscount Naughton in the first place, indelicate as the answer might prove." Mama asked. "Did you make his acquaintance in Tavistock? Or perhaps somewhere more . . . northerly?"

But before Libba—or anyone else—could ask what Mama might mean by that, boots rang up the steps to the parish hall, and, after a flurry of angry activity and furious remonstrance, a very apologetic sexton ushered in a lad that Libba recognized from the village stables.

"'Tis an urgent message from the quarry. I come all the way across the river with it!" the boy cried. "They said it was too important to be committed to paper. Made me memorize it instead. Repeat it over and over until I was letter perfect. Been told I have to deliver it direct to Mrs. Wadsworth and no one else."

A warning frown creased Mama's brow. "Were you perhaps instructed to deliver this message in private?" she asked the boy.

"Oh, no, Ma'am," he said. "No, he said nothing about privacy. All he said was that I was to tell you Byrnes's boys know where to find the pistol. Said Mr. Wadsworth needed to hide it right away. Before Byrne's boys get here."

Gasps and chatter erupted among the assembled ladies, but the lad scarcely seemed to notice. "That's exactly what he told me I had to remember to say to Mrs. Wadsworth," he said with an emphatic nod. "He said Byrnes's boys knew where to find the pistol and to tell Mr. Wadsworth to hide it before they got here."

Chapter 27

The boy Ransome had chosen from the stables was as letter-perfect as any actress he had known. But instead of disappearing down an alley after delivering his urgent warning, as instructed, the lad insouciantly strolled over to the trap where Ransome and Wadsworth were waiting.

"Is there some kind of problem?" Ransome asked him.

"Begging your Lordship's pardon, but here in America 'tis customary to tip a messenger," the boy replied. "Of course, manners may be different in England."

Ransome's incredulity at the boy's brazenness dissolved into a grin, and he felt in his pocket for a coin to add to the ones with which the boy had already been amply rewarded.

"Likely looking lad," he murmured to Wadsworth as the boy tossed him a cheeky wink and strode off whistling. "My advice would be to hire him quick before he finds a place at the other side of the negotiating table."

Wadsworth studied Ransome with the same wary disbelief as he had ever since he had finally found his voice back at the quarry. "I'm surprised you have not already pressed him into Her Majesty's service as you did the unsuspecting Tam Jenkins."

"My methods may be a touch unorthodox, but I think you can agree that it is in all our best interests to see Tam Jenkins consigned to the graveyard as quickly and quietly as possible."

There was a moment's pause, before an odd grin creased Wadsworth's face. "Might prefer it if you found another way to phrase it," he pointed out. His expression sobered. "Still, I don't mind saying, 'tis a deep game you play. I hope you're sure of yourself."

"Trust me, I'm always sure of myself," Ransome said.

Alas, while that had always been the simple truth in the past, it took only one glimpse of the exasperation on Libba's face as she emerged from the parish hall amid what seemed to be a stampede of ladies armed with needles and scissors to make Ransome realize that was no longer the case. And was likely to never be when it came to Miss Libba Wadsworth.

"I hope," he ventured, "that I might be allowed to make my explanations this evening."

"Come now, you're losing your touch," she sighed. "I would have thought plagiarism beneath you. Was not that trick invented by Sherlock Holmes? Or more precisely Arthur Conan Doyle?"

To his chagrin, Ransome felt his jaw drop as he groped for an answer—only to be cut off by Wadsworth scolding his daughter with tired humor, "Enough, miss! You speak of matters you know nothing about. And if you propose to offend Lord Hardcastle by refusing to at least listen to his explanations, I will explain things to you myself."

"Welcome as I would find the opportunity to bring this matter to light," Ransome intervened hastily, with an anxious glance down toward the landing where Byrnes's men had just arrived amid a flurry of shouts and whistles, "may I suggest that these explanations would be best saved for another time?"

After a moment's consideration, Wadsworth nodded. "Until tonight," he said, leaving Ransome to slide into the graveyard to await his prey.

He was painfully aware that he was about to take steps to shield a double murderer. And while a lifetime's career as a spy in Her Majesty's service had scarcely left Ransome with an overdeveloped sense of justice, he was nonetheless forced to admit that the thought didn't sit well with him, even if he could see no other way to end this whole mess. On the other hand, had the victims not been blackmailers and thieves, it would have sat far worse. For, if Ransome was being honest, their deaths made a tricky situation considerably less so. And so in fairness, he supposed he owed the murderer a debt of gratitude—enough, at least to offer to save his neck.

Taken all together, it promised to be as good an ending as any to what he hoped would be his last mission in service of the Crown.

Then he saw the flash of an all-too-familiar skirt hurrying across the church's tiny garden toward the entrance to the church's undercroft—where, he was morally certain, it was inevitable that the church's registry was stored.

Chapter 28

Determination drove Libba across the grass at a singularly unladylike pace. But Mrs. Philipse Braddock's stride as she took advantage of the commotion to quietly slide around to the back of the parish hall had been equally unladylike. In fact, it could only be said that she had fled with the furtive fear of a moonlit heroine in an illustration from a sensation novel.

It made no sense. Mrs. Philipse Braddock a murderess? Libba could scarcely bring herself to believe such a thing of even Miss Ripley. As for Cousin Cornelia, surely, if she had wanted someone dead, she would have simply hired an assassin, then refused to pay him, pleading his work was too shoddy.

By the time Libba could extract herself from the melee that had spilled out into the street in order to follow her cousin, Mrs. Philipse Braddock had vanished. For a moment, Libba simply stood there, telling herself she had imagined the whole thing. Then she saw the door to the church's undercroft swinging open. And while any level-headed girl might have been sensible enough to recollect that nothing good had ever come of one of Mrs. Radcliffe's heroines venturing down a set of stone stairs into the awaiting gloom, Libba did just that.

When her eyes grew accustomed to the half-light, she did not surprise Mrs. Braddock crouched guiltily over a moldering skull, nor did she find the bleached bones of an immured nun. Instead she saw the bundles of clothing that the Ladies Aid Society had already mended, neatly folded on the shelf nearest the door. But there, on top of the sturdy pinafores and patched shirts, she saw a pile of heavy woolen fabric that she recognized immediately, even though she had never seen it before. She touched it with shaking fingers. There was no question in her mind that she had discovered the Renegade's cloak—or at least the cloak with which the murderer had sought to disguise himself as the Renegade. But what was it doing here? Who had placed it here, and to what purpose?

She drew a deep breath to steady her nerves—only to be startled into a missish shriek by feet ringing down the steps.

"Mr. Ransome," she gasped, whirling to face him.

"In the flesh," he agreed. His eyes narrowed as he noticed her obvious discomfiture. "Is something wrong?"

"And why should you surmise that?"

"Because you are as interestingly pale as one of Miss Ripley's heroines and trembling as if a desperado were holding a jeweled dagger to your throat," he said. "Surely, by now you must be aware that if you have found something to trouble you, you may entrust me with the secret."

As he spoke, he reached for the stack of clothes. Without thinking, she reached out to stop it, and their hands brushed.

"I beg your pardon." Face flaming, she snatched her hand away. "Or do you deliberately propose to scandalize the Ladies' Aid Society?"

For a moment, he looked like he intended to do nothing else. And then he raised an eyebrow. "Enjoyable as I would find that possibility, I'm afraid my motive is far more prosaic."

"And that is?"

"The lad's rather dramatic announcement is likely to lead to some unpleasantness that I would very much prefer to spare you."

"What kind of unpleasantness?"

"Detectives are about to arrive from New York City."

"Pinkertons?"

"Worse," he said. He reached for the pile of clothing again. "Which means, although I am loath to press you on this rather than more . . . intimate matters, I'm afraid I am compelled to ask what you discovered."

Intimate matters? Had it only been days since such things were the greatest crisis she faced? Suddenly, it all seemed too much, and she simply gave in and showed him the cloak. "Perhaps you will have a better idea what to do with this than I do," she admitted. "I confess, I can make no sense of the situation. If this really were the murderer's disguise, what would he gain by hiding it here?"

"If you cannot see the answer to that question for yourself, I fear you are not as well acquainted with your American detective stories as your English ones," he said with a grin. "Can it be you have never read the tales of Mr. Edgar Allan Poe?"

She shook her head. "Only a piteous ballad entitled 'Annabel Lee.' Mama did not find the rest of his work quite proper."

"Perhaps because he died drunk in a gutter on Election Day," Ransome conceded. "Habits of intemperance and all that. Still, when he was lucid he wrote the most entertaining tales of ratiocination. In the one called 'The Purloined Letter,' he gives an incontrovertible demonstration that the best place to hide something is in plain sight."

His face grew serious. "This trick itself is harmless enough, but I would have you take my word that the Detective's Bureau is not. Which is why I would have you leave immediately. I have pressed your father to escort you and your mother back to Braddock House."

"Papa agreed to such a thing?!"

Ransome raised an eyebrow. "If I have managed to convince him of the logic of my position, surely you might be disposed to cooperate as well?" His face grew grave. "Please, Miss Wadsworth. Go home with your father and leave this matter to me."

Instead, Libba reached for the cloak. "But we should at least see if the pistol is here as well."

If you don't mind, we do not have *time* . . ." Ransome's eyes widened in alarm as she found the pistol immediately. "Have a care! It well may not have been discharged."

"Well, of course it has. It was used to kill Tam Jenkins. Why would the murderer take it otherwise?"

"To sow confusion. Muddy the waters, as bottom feeders will. But please, Miss Wadsworth, time is running short."

She barely heard his protestations. She was too busy staring at the yellowed sheets of paper that had fallen out of the cloak along with the pistol.

"*More* letters," she sighed, as she stooped to retrieve them. "Honestly, is there never to be an end to such a thing? You'd think the world had nothing better to do with its time than pen one another indiscreet missives."

But Ransome was too quick for her, and she only had time to make out one line before he had scooped up the letters and pocketed them, saying, "Please, Miss Wadsworth. I can assure you this is none of your concern."

None of her concern? She blinked against the memory of the block capitals, stark against the cheap paper, unable, at first, to make sense of them. A TITLE IS NO DEFENSE AGAINST BIGAMY . . .

"How can you say that?" she stammered, when their meaning at last became clear. "This must be the secret with which Tam Jenkins sought to blackmail his way to my hand."

"It would seem," Ransome allowed.

But . . . what sort of secret was this meant to be? Bigamy? She was not so sheltered as not to understand the meaning of the word. But Papa? Mama? Even as she dismissed the idea as impossible, she recalled the way merely the word "elopement" reduced them to silence. Had that fabled disastrous elopement not been foiled after all?

Libba shook her head in answer to her own unvoiced question. "It makes no sense. This note mentions a title, and Papa is no nobleman."

"If you don't mind, we do not have *time*—" Ransome's mouth snapped shut, and abruptly, he changed tack. "Surely a woman of your obvious perspicacity has noticed that I am, in fact, possessed of a title. So if you do not suspect your father, I suppose I must ask for formality's sake, would you accuse me?"

"Must you make a joke of everything?" she sighed.

"'Tis no joke whatsoever," he said. "For if you eliminate

the convenient tramp, the odious Miss Ripley, and a member of your household from the list of murder suspects, what poor options remain beyond a nobleman who is being blackmailed over a past seduction that stood to ruin his marriage prospects now. And who comes closer to fitting that description than me? So I must ask you directly, Miss Wadsworth, do you think me capable of such behavior?"

Clearly, it was not a question he expected her to answer, and yet she heard herself sigh again. "Which part?"

Ransome's eyes widened. "I beg your pardon?"

"'Tis a simple enough question," she told him. "Which behavior would you have me deem you capable of? A bigamous marriage to an heiress? No—if only because such complications could only jeopardize your openly mercenary approach to marriage. Beyond that, I apologize that I can only speculate, but from what I've gleaned from your conversation, if there's no question of marriage involved, you seem to prefer the more practiced embraces of the houri to any innocent country lass."

He choked out a strangled syllable, before recovering himself. "And there your speculation fails you, Miss Wadsworth, I can assure you. If you doubt my word, I would be delighted to provide you with a demonstration."

He reached for her hand again, but she snatched it away before he could distract her. "But would you lie to me?" she went on. "Are there parts of your life that you wish not to share with me? And would you deceive me to hide them? Not out of any real desire to protect them any more than to protect me, but rather out of a sheer, perverse love of lying? That you would never settle for the unvarnished truth, when a so much more satisfying one can be spun out of the whole cloth? Well, then, yes, Mr. Ransome, not only do I believe you capable of such a behavior, I believe you rather delight in it."

There was a moment's stunned silence. And then Ransome grinned. "Well, now, that's about as fair an answer as I could expect," he allowed. "Or deserve. Now would you please be so good as to leave and save me courting any further scandal by throwing you over my shoulder and hauling you out of here bodily?"

Chapter 29

Ransome had to confess himself gobsmacked. Gobsmacked enough to take one last, fatal glance at the yellowed letter from Sir Roderick Naughton that reminded the newly-wed Mrs. Philipse Braddock of their previous *intimate* friendship, and begging the favor of being sponsored for the New York Season and being introduced to some *suitable* young heiresses—especially her cousin Miss Lydia Braddock, about whose beauty he had already heard so much. As for the special marriage license signed by both Sir Roderick Naughton and Miss Cornelia Livingstone, well, Ransome had to admit himself blindsided every bit as badly as when Macaulay himself had called him to the command tent to suggest that Her Majesty might be better served by an orchid-hunter gone native in Sikkim and the Tibetan frontier than another captain with no appetite or aptitude for Army life. Or the moment the cable had reached him, requiring his immediate return to London to receive some familial news that might be to his advantage.

Unfortunately, he was so stunned that he did not re-cognize the implication of the muffled shriek that abruptly ended Libba's retreating footsteps until Gaddis loomed at the entrance to the undercroft, an extremely lethal-looking pistol held at her chin.

And for the first time in his life, Ransome knew what panic felt like. "You do not want to do this," he said.

"What I want is for you to hand me those papers."

"And then what? You'll shoot me and leave me here with the evidence that I was the murderer?"

"Exactly," Gaddis said. "The only question left to you is whether I kill the lady in a tragic murder/suicide, or leave her here to defend herself against charges that she shot you in self-defense when you tried to ravish her."

Ransome drew a deep breath. "You do understand it will never work?" he asked with a steadiness he did not feel. "Byrnes's boys have already landed, and it's only a matter of time before they arrive here. Even if you have a private railway car at the ready, I am certain you will not be quick enough to prevent them searching you. Just as I am equally certain that we both agree that it would be a disaster if these papers fell into Inspector Byrnes's hands—for both the Vanderbilts and the Crown. As I have already explained to Inspector Byrnes's men, Her Majesty's Government is most anxious to prevent a scandal."

Gaddis snorted. "Oh, please, Lord Hardcastle. Your scandal happened twenty years ago. I may not understand what you're playing at here, but I do know the body in the ice house is decades too young to be who you claim he is. Your Tam Jenkins is a fairy tale, but the man lying dead in the ice house is quite real. And as far as I can see, of all the people in this room, you have the best motive to kill him."

"I pray you, do not insult either of our intelligences. We both know who killed Ta . . . our imposter," Ransome conceded the minor point with a shrug. "I assume you removed these papers from his body after you shot him? And now you plan to use them as leverage if Mrs. Philipse Braddock ever gets wind of your financial misdeeds? How much have you stolen from her?"

"It would seem equally likely that you killed him because he was about to reveal you as a spy for the crown."

"I prefer the term 'confidential agent.'" Ransome favored him with a bland smile. "But why are we wasting time quibbling over a dead man's fate? I do not seek justice for the man any more than you do. I can personally attest to the fact that he squandered twice as many second chances as most men are given in a lifetime. So while I will admit to a certain lingering resentment about your clumsy attempt to coerce my cooperation, our shared interest in this matter compels me to offer it to you freely instead."

It was a reasonable offer. Dammit, it was generous offer. Better by far than this man deserved. Bloody hell, he was offering the man the chance to walk away from murder scot-free. "For the love of God, man, why can you not see that you have no other choice? Byrnes' boys are on their way. Is any of this honestly worth hanging for?"

The question—reasonable though it might have been—was never destined to be answered. Instead, a flurry of motion erupted from the depths of the undercroft and snatched up the Renegade's pistol in a swirl of skirts from where it lay atop the folded cloak. The gesture was so theatrical that Ransome could only see it as a fitting capstone to this farce. Indeed, Mrs. Philipse Braddock made a surprisingly excellent madwoman—all glittering eyes and muttered imprecations. If this turned out badly, he was certain Miss Ripley would have ample material to memorialize her in a poem.

One glance at the gun pressed at Libba's throat was enough to make Ransome recall every last one of his mother's pained remonstrances about his unfortunate taste for *levity*. "You grow exercised and for no good reason, Mrs. Braddock," he said. "Our motives may differ, but our interests are the same. Her Majesty has no more interest in this matter seeing the light of day than you do."

"Shoot him!" Gaddis cried. "Shoot him as a spy and a bounder! Shoot him if you do not want the story of this particular Braddock Bride hawked by newsies on every corner of New York City."

"You!" She whirled, training the pistol on Gaddis with trembling hands that to Ransome's professional eyes were far more dangerous than a sniper's deadly aim, then spun back on Ransome uncertainly.

But before she could decide which of them she truly wanted to kill, the world erupted in a dull roar of smoke and sound as the Renegade's Pistol seemed to explode of its own accord.

Chapter 30

Libba felt only vaguely the sudden release of Gaddis' choking grip before Ransome forced him to the ground and relieved him of his revolver in a manoeuver that hinted at yet another aspect of his life that she suspected he would prefer remain concealed. Leveling the gun at Gaddis, her intended scrambled to his feet and turned to Libba, his face dark with concern.

"I trust you are uninjured?"

She nodded numbly. The only thing injured was her pride, and that wound was substantial. In fact, she was well and certain that the tale of the Renegade finally rising to fire a pistol ball to defend the honor of a Braddock Bride would supplant all other versions of the legend.

Mercifully, Ransome evinced no inclination to dwell on such a scandal, and instead turned his attention to Cousin Cornelia, whose coiffure was as much an ashy, smoky ruin as her sleeves. "And you, madame?"

She offered no reply beyond icy silence—as a true lady would. And if Ransome grinned at her response, he managed to bite it back as he gestured with the pistol toward the entrance to the undercroft. "No matter. Time enough to sort that out later. But in the meantime, may I suggest this would all feel somewhat less theatrical, if we were all to step back outside? At the very least I might suggest we attempt to spare the ladies what scandal we can."

"You? A spy? Seeking to avoid scandal?" Mrs. Braddock asked with withering scorn. "And to think I received you as a *gentleman*."

"Well, technically you received a blackmailing imposter as a gentleman," Ransome pointed out.

"A man who sought to impose himself on the first families of New York. God in heaven, does the girl have any idea what she has done?" Cousin Cornelia turned on Libba venomously. "You, you stupid girl. Do you have any idea of the enormity of what you have stumbled into? That man is a spy. An operative for Her Majesty's government. Your father is ruined, and it is all your doing!"

"As I am rapidly growing weary of repeating, I *was* a spy," Ransome sighed. "And at the risk of committing a fatal indiscretion, I must insist that Her Majesty sent me to retrieve a few indiscreet letters as a personal favor to her connections among America's First Families, but I seem to have unearthed a veritable post office of scandal."

Any reply Mrs. Braddock might have made was cut off by the sound of shouts, whistles, heavy wheels and pounding footsteps that began to emerge from the edge of the churchyard.

"Byrnes's boys," Gaddis hissed.

"Most likely," Ransome concurred.

And at that, Cousin Cornelia decided to faint.

Taking Libba's arm, Ransome pressed her toward the fallen figure, and said quietly, "I would beg you trust my instincts in this matter, and focus your complete attention on attending to Mrs. Braddock. I would have you not speak to these men."

At least, Libba thought philosophically, he had been gracious enough not to use words like "learned your lesson," which, in her considered opinion might have been all too a propos. So she knelt and did exactly what he proposed.

"Seize him!" Gaddis cried, pointing at Ransome, as the wagon hove into view. "This man is armed and dangerous!"

They were-hard looking men, harder by far than the Pinkerton, as much a mob as a police force. But Ransome approached them as casually as if he were greeting them at a soiree.

"Quite on the contrary," he said, offering both guns to the sergeant. "These weapons are valuable evidence, which in the spirit of the full cooperation between the Detectives Bureau and Her Majesty's government in this investigation, I am privileged to present to you now. Here is the missing dueling pistol, which you will discover has just now been fired—under somewhat singular circumstances that Mr. Gaddis might be more able to explain than I can."

"Lies! This man is nothing but a spy and a troublemaker," Gaddis snapped.

"Stipulated," Ransome said. "But irrelevant. What, however, would be extremely relevant—at least in my humble opinion—would be whether the bullets the coroner retrieved from the bodies of the putative Lord Hardcastle and our unfortunate local postmaster match this other weapon."

"And if they did, what would that prove? Self-defense. Any judge in New York will agree; I know them all! Mark my words; you do not want to do this. My friends will have me out of jail in a day!" Gaddis's angry tirade was cut off abruptly, as, at a nod from the sergeant, two of the burliest detectives seized him.

"Well now, we'll see about that." The sergeant smiled, revealing stained teeth, as he turned back to Ransome. "Thank you, your lordship. Pleasure doing business with the Crown, I must say."

"Our pleasure entirely. However, I am afraid I must introduce a decidedly unpleasant complication at this moment. For I must request that you seek no more answers about Tam Jenkins beyond ascertaining that this is indeed the murder weapon." Ransome paused, shooting the struggling Gaddis a disgusted look. "And while I am well aware that may entail sparing this man his just punishment, the business of Tam Jenkins is not England's finest hour, and I must crave your indulgence in allowing us to put this matter quietly to rest in a way that avoids any embarrassment to the Crown."

The sergeant's eyes hardened. "You want us to let a murderer go free?"

"Not just a murderer. A murderer and a blackmailer, seeking to sell the secrets of several highly placed ladies to the highest bidder." Ransome raised an eyebrow. "And I feel impelled to point out that, in that latter capacity, he might well be of much more service to your Bureau alive than dead."

"I will never—" Gaddis snarled.

"That is why I am offering you the murder weapon as, for want of a better term, collateral," Ransome went on, as if Gaddis had never spoken. "There's something about the threat of hanging that tends to ensure a man's cooperation."

The sergeant grinned. Gaddis snarled. And Cousin

Cornelia's eyes fluttered open and focused on Ransome. "You," she hissed, "are no gentleman."

"No," he agreed cheerfully. "I'm a peer of the realm. Entirely different thing altogether."

Turning back to the sergeant, Ransome handed him the hastily gathered papers. "Pray forgive the lady. She is overwrought. She apparently feels there is some scandal in her past Mr. Gaddis and his associates might hold over her." Ransome cast Mrs. Braddock a frankly malicious smile before he added confidingly, "Of course, Her Majesty is not concerned about any scandal that does not pertain to the unfortunate history of Her operative. Yet, while courtesy demands that one did one's best not to be *prurient*, one couldn't help noticing a rather salacious exchange of letters between a lady of one of New York's first families and an apparently quite strapping groom. Or maybe the strapping groom in question was of another kind altogether. As I said, none of my affair, and I read no further when I had ascertained that it did not pertain to my immediate remand. I mention it only because I am confident that you will do the gentlemanly thing and burn those letters before they find themselves hawked by every newsie on every street corner. I have been given to understand that the tabloids in your fair city can be less than scrupulous."

The sergeant's smile widened as he glanced at Mrs. Braddock so insinuatingly that Libba could almost feel sorry for her. "You got my word," he said with heavy-handed irony. "The Detective's Bureau pride themselves on always doing the gentlemanly thing."

Any further debate was cut off by the sound of footsteps racing across the lawn. Ransome's gaze sharpened in alarm—arguably at the prospect of facing Wadsworth's wrath—as Mrs. Braddock prudently seized the opportunity to faint again.

"Given your natural devotion to good manners," Ransome said to the sergeant with a casualness he clearly did not feel, "might I also suggest that you continue your discussion with your prisoner elsewhere, so as not to further distress the lady?"

The sergeant's grin widened. "I'd be happy to call on her at her own home. If you could just give me the particulars as to when she might be receiving?"

Ransome obligingly pulled out a memorandum book and furnished the sergeant with an address—although Libba was hard-pressed to imagine whose address it really was. But what did it matter, for the other detectives were already bundling Gaddis into the police wagon, ignoring his angrily shouted protests about his friends. Their flurry of activity swelled, then dissolved into Papa trying to look stern-faced as he did his best to support Mama, who seemed to understand that the only possible ladylike thing to do was collapse alongside Mrs. Braddock, but was having far too much fun to consider any such notion.

Following them—or perhaps following her unerring nose for scandal—was Miss Ripley. Ransome's smile grew even more malicious when he saw her, and he hurried to the churchyard gates, calling to stop the departing police wagon, "Sergeant, a moment if you will. For I fear I would be remiss in not presenting to you the Sappho of Braddock's Landing, despite the urgency of your other commitments. Truth be told, her poetry flies a bit above my head. I'm a simple man such as I suspect yourself to be. But I must needs inform you that you that she has been one of Her Majesty's most important operatives. Of course, she's been forced to disguise herself beneath the unbecoming mask of a disappointed old gossip-monger. But I can assure you her intelligence is superlative. A regular Irene Adler, the service branches always say."

It was a flagrant fabrication, even for Will Ransome, and Libba had to bite back a snort of unbecoming laughter as Miss Ripley's complexion waxed puce from its customary sallow. "Lies," she protested. "All lies."

"Oh, no point in unbecoming modesty. You've been the ruin of many the man that threatened the Crown." The mischief in Ransome's face grew perhaps more than a little unbecoming as he warmed to his theme, "It was her early upbringing in the Orient, you know? Child of missionaries, and yet she learned the secrets of the houris—"

"Houris, Mr. Ransome," Mama choked. "I am uncertain that I am acquainted with the word."

"Of course, you would not be. And under other circumstances, I would never sully a gently bred woman's ears."

But the sergeant had already hopped down from the wagon and was hurrying toward Miss Ripley, his smile suddenly unctuous. "Well, in the spirit of cooperation between our two great nations, I can only thank you for your honesty in making such an asset known to us—as well as offering our grateful assurances that we will make the best use of such an asset as we can. So if the lady would be so good as to just provide the particulars of when she might be receiving, we'll be on our way and trouble Braddock's Landing no more."

Chapter 31

Libba stood on the edge of Cora's Leap, cocooned in merciful silence. The echoes of the chaos at the church had finally subsided beneath the sound of the waves lapping at the shore of the river beneath. Gaddis's hissed threats were as substantial as the clouds reflected in the river. The afternoon breeze had wafted away the memory of Cousin Cornelia pushing away Mama's *sels volatiles* with the same contempt that she had received questionable introductions her entire life. Miss Ripley's spluttered protestations that her parents were missionaries and the strictest of Methodists were as faint as the cries of the gulls.

"So what are we supposed to witness?" an all-too-familiar voice broke the silence. "The released lovers ascending, locked in an eternal embrace, as in that Wagner fellow's opera?"

"Please no more of your ludicrous stories." Libba turned away from the cliff. "I think you and I both know we were dealing with nothing more than a happy accident from a gun that had gone too long uncleaned."

An odd look crossed Ransome's face. "If you mean to

suggest that it is ludicrous to believe in the existence of such heroes as the Renegade, I can assure you they do, in fact, exist—even if I will never prove one of their number. And I am saddened, truly saddened, to think that I was the man to so shake your belief. Indeed, it is a sin for which I should never forgive myself."

She sighed. "Spare me the rhetoric of that stupid legend."

"I did seek to spare you that and much else."

"Including the fact that you are a spy on top of everything else?"

He crossed his arms across his chest and studied her. "As for the latter question, it's really a matter of the past tense. When speaking of my present situation . . . well, shall we say determined to retire into respectability, but forced into action by circumstances? And, further, looking forward with pleasure to being completely reformed. Love of a good woman and all that?"

There might have been the faintest of hopeful questions underlying those last words, but she steeled herself to ignore it. "Please," she snapped, "would you at least pay lip service to respecting my intelligence?"

His eyes narrowed dangerously. "Why, Miss Wadsworth, I am all for lip service. That is, if you do not find me too forward."

He reached for her, then stopped himself with a muffled curse, and ran his hands through his unruly hair instead. "Dammit, I never thought I'd see the day I'd regret being forced to resort to words. But pray be reasonable. Do you think I would have made such a hash of things if spying were my only motive? For I did not lie when I said I was rather a good spy. In fact, I should have said I was one of the best. And if you have thought involving the Detectives Bureau and making public incriminating letters are the stuff of expert spycraft, think again. Do you think I could have ruined things like a rank amateur if I weren't mad for you? Completely, *disastrously* in love?"

"So, now I am a disaster. How refreshingly honest."

"Yes, a disaster. Professionally speaking, there is no other word. It is just as well the cursed earldom put an end to my spying days. You're a vulnerability a spy cannot afford." He snorted in disgust. "Frankly I never could stomach tales like that of your cursed Renegade. Never could understand how a man could be fool enough to lose all sense of rational judgment over a woman. One true love, indeed. Always thought a sensible man could see that there were a dozen more where the first one came from." He raised an eyebrow at her shocked expression. "There. That's me. The plain, unvarnished truth of what I am. Not exactly a girl's dream, is it?"

He cut off her stammered protest with an angry wave of his hand. "It matters not. Because it seems I've been taught a lesson worthy of the Sappho of Braddock Ridge herself. Now I believe I even understand why a man would be willing to die for a woman. Because I understand exactly how it feels to know I would die if I cannot have you."

They were words she could never have imagined Will Ransome speaking except in jest, but try as she might, she could not hear even the faintest trace of irony beneath them. "So do you deny you were sent to Braddock's Landing to retrieve Tam Jenkins' letters?"

He met her eyes. "I deny it completely," he said steadily. "The tale of our operative turned rogue and blackmailer was nothing more than a convenient fabrication."

"Convenient to whom? What purpose could it possibly serve beyond a sheer perverse love of lying?"

He drew a deep breath. "Dammit, I know you mistrust my easy way with words—and with good cause. But I beg you to trust me when I tell you that it is in all our interests that the case is allowed to remain closed."

"But *why*? What were those papers?"

Her heart sank as he shook his head. "Another man's secret," he said firmly. "Not mine. And perhaps one day he will choose to explain it to you. But I cannot."

"How can he do that if he is dead?"

"Enough! I have told you the truth, and I tell you that is all I can say!" His face twisted, half in humor, half in exasperation. "By all that's holy, you would make a fine addition to Her Majesty's Service, if only for sheer persistence. And perhaps one day you may find yourself recruited. But for now, I would talk of no other men, but this man. Me. Will Ransome, the suitor. Not Tam Jenkins. Nor Lord Hardcastle, earl or spy. Not as admirable as many men, and perhaps not worthy at all. But a man who would do anything to have you. Beg, borrow, steal, cheat. Work my fingers to the bone. Wear a bloody ermine robe if it came to that."

Her treacherous heart leaped with mingled humor and affection as she pictured him trapped, catlike, in an earl's regalia instead of the starched collar with which he seemed to wage an ongoing war. Deliberately, she pushed the picture away. "And lie?" she asked.

"Never," he said. "Oh, I concede I might lie for you, but I would never lie to you."

"And how can I believe that? For is not a taste for embellishment your very life's blood?" She cut off his snorted protest with a wave of her hand. "So how am I to believe that I am the exception? How can I believe, Mr. Ransome, that you would never settle for the unvarnished truth of a wife, when a so much more satisfying one can be spun out of the whole cloth?"

There was a moment's stunned silence. And then Ransome grinned, and she realized her resistance was about to crumble. Just as she realized she really didn't mind all that much—if only he'd stop talking and put that glib tongue to much better use.

"I believe we have already discussed that issue before— over the unhappy set of pastels you were so bent on tormenting. But this time, I can only beg you hear me and believe me," he said softly—so insinuatingly to allow no other answer. "Why would I flatter, lie, or even embellish, when there could be no lie more satisfying than the unvarnished truth of you?"

This time, when he took her in his arms, he brooked no resistance, his mouth crushing down over hers, as he triumphantly claimed what Libba was forced to concede had been his all along.

Chapter 32

If it had been up to him, Ransome would have simply continued to pursue matters in the Folly until the time came to sweep Libba into his arms and carry her up to their marriage bed. Unfortunately one last task remained before he could be certain that Tam Jenkins was well and truly buried.

He found his prospective father-in-law smoking his pipe on one of the cliffs overlooking the Hudson, lost in thought.

"If I might have a word," Ransome said, lowering himself to sit beside Wasdworth. "I am happy to inform you that your daughter has been kind enough to accept my offer of matrimony, despite my, shall we say, chequered past."

Wadsworth nodded, his gaze never wavering from the river beneath. "I'll see to the settlements immediately."

"Eager as I am to seal the happy arrangement, I no longer think there is any cause to rush." Ransome waved a hand back toward the house. "Women will have their weddings, after all. I am sure the female dependents would never forgive me if I denied them their chance to argue over the arrangements."

"Petticoat invasion of Braddock's Landing, eh?"

"Regular army of them," Ransome agreed, then added quietly, "So many that I'm certain no one would notice a few additional ones from the Jenkins side of the family tree."

Wadsworth's head snapped around, and he started to spit a furious denial. Then, abruptly, he shrugged his defeat. "Stupid damned moment of sentimental weakness. I just wanted to see them once more. Came damned close to ruining everything."

"Happily, I think I can safely say circumstances have changed."

Wadsworth's face set. "There'd be those who'd say circumstances never change. That try as you might, you can never put the past behind you."

Reaching into his coat, Ransome pulled out the remains of the bank draft, as well as Naughton's correspondence with Mrs. Philipse Braddock. "And there would be those who'd say burning these would be a very fine start indeed."

For a moment, Wadsworth just stared at the papers in the same silence he had been contemplating the river. Then he sighed. "I assume you require some kind of explanation?"

"Not at all. I'm fairly certain I have extrapolated the basics of the situation."

"I'm sure you have." Wadsworth smiled despite himself, as he took the papers, but he sobered immediately. "Wretched business altogether."

"Could happen to any man," Ransome said. "I must admit to a few misapprehensions about the criminality of my activities in the past, as well as more than one hasty exit from a prison cell."

"All the time looking over one's shoulder." Wadsworth

pocketed the papers mechanically. "Wondering when the truth might threaten to surface once more."

Ransome studied him for a moment, then settled companionably next to his father-in-law.

"So did you come to New York City for revenge?" he asked.

"I'd have had a right," Wadsworth snorted. "My freshest horses, my fastest sloop. All put in service of Cornelius Livingstone so he could rescue his empty-headed daughter. 'Twas not my fault if the girl was already wed by the time we caught up with them. There is no one who could have done it faster—I give you the word of a man who outran Her Majesty's tax collectors for a decade."

Ransome nodded. "And Livingstone used that as an excuse to renege on your bargain?"

"There was never a bargain. Oh, I admit, he offered me plenty of money, but I never would have risked it, had not that scoundrel Naughton already attempted the same thing with my sister." Wadsworth's face flattened. "But the bastard always meant to betray me. And I still canna forgive myself for not seeing that. Naughton, he simply paid off, but smugglers counted for less. Or maybe he knew that I would have thrown his money in his face. Whatever his reasons, he betrayed me to the authorities and had me hauled off to the hulks in order to eliminate the only other witness to his daughter's disgrace."

"Fair enough cause for revenge from my point of view," Ransome said. "I've seen men gutted with a fish hook for less."

"A bit messy for my tastes, if you don't mind." Wadsworth's gaze grew distant. "Truth be told, I'm not sure any more what I intended when I escaped beyond refusing to endure the years I was to serve at Her Majesty's pleasure. If I'd killed Livingstone, I'd swing for it, and if I revealed Cornelia Livingstone Braddock was bigamously wed, I'd have been sent straight back to the hulks for my trouble. Neither option truly appealed. But the only other option would have been blackmail. And no matter how hungry, how tired, how angry, I might have been, I would never have sunk that low. 'Tis a filthy trick."

"Defenestration's always another possibility," Ransome said meditatively. "Then again, perhaps we can be satisfied by simply imagining the fate of a blackmailing swine in the hands of the Detectives Bureau."

But Wadsworth hardly seemed to be listening. "As I said, I don't know what I intended. What I do know is that fate gave me a chance to best Cornelius Livingstone in a business dealing, and although it was a small enough victory—a dispute over the price of a load of stone while I was nothing but John Braddock's quarry manager, I knew I had found a much better way to revenge myself." He came back to himself with a snort. "All of it, water under the bridge. Or so it should be. Cornelius Livingstone is long since dead, and what happens to his daughter is none of my concern."

"You have far better people to concern yourself with," Ransome agreed.

With a sigh, Wadsworth went back to looking at the water. "She'll have to be told the truth, of course."

"Libba? If I may be permitted the familiarity of referring to my intended as such?" Ransome raised an eyebrow. "And what truth do you feel has been withheld from her? That I have exaggerated the facts of the notorious Tam Jenkins case to my own advantage, rather than in service to the

Crown? She has already taxed me with the fault and chosen to forgive me. As your daughter is so often reminding me, you did not breed a fool, Mr. Wadsworth."

"I'll say not." Wadsworth fell silent, then the ghost of a smile appeared on his lips. "Service to the Crown, eh? Still can't say I really like that. Frankly found it easier to trust you when you were just an honest blackguard. Smugglers' honor and all that."

"Perhaps it would help to think of me a dishonest blackguard instead?" Ransome offered. "Which is why you can rest assured I'll not be the one who tells her. For my own humble exploits could only pale in comparison. And since I have just managed to turn Libba's head from the paragons of the circulating library for long enough to notice me, I have no idea what my chances would be if a new hero suddenly arose in her life."

"More like a footpad from the penny dreadfuls," Wadsworth snorted. He shook his head. "Too much imagination. That's always been the girl's problem. She'll lead you a merry chase; mark my words."

"And it is a pursuit I eagerly anticipate," Ransome assured him. He drew a deep breath, suddenly as intent on studying the river as Wadsworth. "But at the risk of intruding my opinions where they are unwelcome, I feel impelled to point out, your wife is no fool, either."

Wadsworth turned on him. "Come now, we're both blunt men. Why are you suddenly dancing around your words as if you were in a drawing room? If you have something to say to me, come out and say it."

Ransome inclined his head. "Whether you tell your daughter can only be your decision—although I must honestly suggest that she would rather enjoy the romance of the tale, if perhaps overmuch. But may I be so bold as to suggest that your wife, sir, needs to hear the truth. She is still tormented by the thought that she is somehow at fault in the matter."

"The only fault was that coward's approaching her instead of me," Wadsworth snapped. "I didna kill the man, as you well know, but I could have. How dare he expose my wife to such a sordid mess?"

"I think your wife is less delicate than you give her credit for. But nonetheless, the point is, she has been exposed, and she deserves to understand the rest of the story." Suddenly eager to find his way back to the Folly, Ransome scrambled back to his feet, pausing only to add, "And if you were a wagering man, I would lay you solid odds that when she hears the truth of the story, she will be as taken with it as if she was to personally witness your Renegade and his lady returned to each other's arms at last."

Chapter 33

It was not Lucius Wadsworth who squared his shoulders before he tapped on the door of his wife's bedroom. It was a wary escaped convict, torn between revenge and fear, still struggling to remember his name was now Luke Watkins. And the fear that had chilled him as he lay manacled in a ship's hold was nothing compared to the fear he felt when he saw his wife unpinning her hair at her dressing table.

"I dinna ken whether a gentleman hides behind a lady's skirts," he began and stopped in dismay as his carefully mastered elocution abandoned him even more ruthlessly than his courage threatened to do. He drew a deep breath and forced himself to go on. "But a man does not. I'll nae have you believing you brought scandal and murder into Braddock House, when the fault was mine and mine alone."

"You speak of the unfortunate matter of those letters." She turned from the mirror, the stray curl she twisted the only sign of her distress. "I owe you my gratitude for redeeming my jewels so unselfishly and discreetly. 'Tis better than I deserve. I'm afraid I'm a terribly foolish woman."

"You're never foolish, even though you play at it. Poor woman's head indeed—you were as quick on the Portland cement as any man. Just my good fortune you decided you're more interested in moving in the first circles than running a quarry, or I'd be of no use to you at all."

She twisted the curl with more force. "Although I find I have quite lost my taste for moving in the first circles, you have my assurance I will not seek to take over the running of the quarry instead. I am certain I can find something more constructive with which to occupy myself. Good works, perhaps. I understand it's a customary form of penance."

Damn the woman. Damn the turn this conversation already seemed to be taking. And damn him for a coward who was already groping for an excuse to flee the room leaving needed words unspoken.

"Best not to trouble ourselves overmuch with blame," he said. "Particularly when it comes to those letters. You have my word that they have nothing to do with the current situation. They have lain undisturbed in my strong box ever since I intercepted them twenty years ago."

Her grip on the curl loosened. "Intercepted, Mr. Wadsworth?"

"I apologize for that, but it was the only way. I couldna let you run off with him. He would have been the ruin of you. Would have abandoned you just as soon as he discovered he couldn't get his hands on your money."

He winced as he saw the shock on her face. Once more, he'd been too blunt. Well, if twenty years trying hadn't taught her she couldn't make a silk purse out of this particular sow's ear, there was nothing he could do. And bluntness was what the occasion called for. Best get this out as quickly as possible, like ripping a bandage from a crusted wound.

"I couldna explain the details of the situation to you then, so I just took the letters and hid them away. But I would like to venture an explanation now."

She barely seemed to hear him. "You are saying you hid those letters away in your strong box at the time when I wrote them?"

"And there they have lain undisturbed for the past twenty years. I give you my word."

"Undisturbed and unopened, and for that I must thank you." She frowned. "But may I ask why you kept them if you never had any intention of reading them?"

He raised an eyebrow. "I held them against the possibility we would ever have this unhappy conversation. For how else could you be entirely certain that that I never opened those letters, nor never sought to?"

The silence that followed frightened him more than anything in his life. And then she bowed her head and said, "I would like to think there would never have been any doubt in my mind with or without such proof."

"Wellna, there's no point in testing waters you dinna need to. Forgive my frankness, Mrs. Wadsworth," he added hastily as he saw the flush stain her cheek. "But I would have matters clear between us for once and for all."

She stiffened, then wordlessly offered him a chair, but he refused. Damned thing looked like it would collapse beneath him. In any case, he preferred to keep the option of a quick exit after he said what he had to say.

"Whatever letters you may or may not have written in the past, they were not the letters with which the postmaster sought to threaten you," he told her, as evenly as he could. "Nor were they the secret that the man who pretended to be Lord Hardcastle threatened to expose in exchange for our daughter's hand. It was my secrets those blackguards tried to hold over our family."

"Pray stop, Mr. Wadsworth," she gasped, springing to her feet. "If that was well and truly why you killed them, you need not answer for that to me. I would have pulled the trigger myself given the chance."

And dammit if he did not believe her. It was all he could do to fight down a smile. "I didna kill them," he said. "Gaddis did me that favor. But I canna say I mind seeing them dead."

She frowned as she sank back onto her chair. "Then if you did not kill them, what dread secret would you confess to me?"

He turned away from her, uncertain where to begin. Damnation, he was losing his nerve again. Trying to talk around what was simply unspeakable. A hell he still hadn't forgotten after all these years.

"The arrival of the imposter allowed the postmaster to realize the significance of some bank drafts I had regularly sent to . . . a lady in England."

She met his eyes levelly. "A female dependent, I can only assume?"

"My sister."

"You have a sister I have been unaware of, Mr. Wadsworth?"

"And a mother. Circumstances . . . have prevented me introducing you . . ." He flushed. "I've been sending them money all these years."

"As would any dutiful son. What shame could there be in that?"

And at last he was faced with a moment that he had spent a lifetime seeking to avoid. "The shame lay in the name on the bank drafts. Jenkins. My sister's name is Essie Jenkins. Of the Cornwall Jenkinses," he added with a twisted smile.

She eyed him sharply. "From that am I to infer that you are somehow connected to Mr. Ransome's spy?"

"Yes. And no." He drew a deep breath. "The body in the ice house is not that of Tam Jenkins. I am—was—Tam Jenkins. I was sentenced to fifteen years hard labor in Her Majesty's hulks in Bermuda." He choked at the memory, the unfairness, then swallowed hard, and forced himself to spit out. "I would have been dead within two. And so I escaped. That is the matter that both the postmaster and the man who now lies dead in the ice house would have held over my head. Not any past indiscretions on your part."

He did not know how he expected her to react. Tears, anger, accusations, recriminations, he was prepared for anything—except, it seemed, the question she asked.

"Escaped? How?"

He was too stunned to do anything but tell her the truth. "There were pirates. They were known to offer freedom in exchange for . . . certain skills. Skills I happened to possess."

"You were a pirate, Mr. Wadsworth?"

"Dinna last long. I was not cut out for it," he assured her. "I leapt off the ship at the first sign of land, and swam straight to America. Took the pirates by surprise. Most men in our line of work never learn to swim, figuring 'tis better to drown than die at the hands of the hangman. I was never quite that philosophical."

She nodded bemusedly. "So if I am to believe that you are that Tam Jenkins of the Cornwall Jenkinses, am I also to infer that when you refer to your line of work, you mean smuggling?"

And dammit if she did not sound interested. "At one point in my life, I was a smuggler, Mrs. Wadsworth. And rather a good one I might say."

"I believe Mrs. Humphries might have regaled us with a tale or two. Something about brandy in a police wagon," she concurred.

"It was port. And I wouldna have settled for less than the Royal Mail to see it safe to London," he snorted. "Leave it to a vicarage tabby to get it wrong."

She took a deep breath, then met his eyes again. "Mrs. Humphries also suggested that you were at last brought low by rescuing a woman from a Wicked Viscount."

"I never would have been caught if it hadn't been for that bastard—Apologies, Mrs. Wadsworth," he corrected himself. "That ne'er-do-well Sir Roderick Naughton."

"The man who would have dishonored me, had you not intervened."

It was a statement, not a question—as if she saw the wretched truth of those events so many years ago. And suddenly the words seemed to come more easily.

"I knew him in Cornwall. Before the hulks and pirates and all. Had quite the reputation even then. Famous for his love of that old English concept, *droit du seigneur.*" He smiled at her surprise at his perfect pronunciation. "I learned passable French on the docks, but everyone who lived on Naughton's lands came to learn those three words, including my sister."

"I must say I am sorry that we had no chance to make your family's acquaintance while we were in England. It is an oversight I would rectify immediately." She spoke as casually as if she were contemplating drawing up a guest list for tea.

"It seems Ransome has already taken steps in that direction—he even plans to spirit them to the wedding."

"Our future son-in-law continues to prove himself a remarkable man." She fell silent for a moment, then continued to quiz him. "And so when Sir Roderick Naughton appeared in New York, you thought to warn me of your sister's experience, despite the danger to yourself?"

"Not just my sister. God alone knows, no one cared about her suffering. But when it came to him eloping with Cornelia Livingstone, the American heiress—"

"Cousin Cornelia really did elope?" The smile that lit her face was enchanting.

"Not just eloped, but was bigamously wed. That is what Sir Roderick sought to hold over her head to force her to introduce him into New York society. And I can only guess that his son stumbled on the same secret and sought to put it to similar use."

The enchanting smile grew more than a little malicious. "But what scandal! Are you quite certain, Mr. Wadsworth?"

"Naughton would have stopped at nothing to carry off such a fat prize—begging your pardon, Mrs. Wadsworth, I refer only, of course, to the size of her dowry. And so I offered her father my fastest horses and my swiftest sailors in the name of justice. Alas, when we arrived, it was too late. Naughton had already wed her." His voice tightened. "But instead of thanking me, her father betrayed me to the law—as he had intended all along. I was the only witness after all."

The smile vanished. "And you could bring yourself to set foot in her ballroom?" she hissed.

He raised a shoulder. "Not up to me to judge the manners of the first circles."

"Who would have better right?" she asked. Not waiting for an answer, she went on. "Is that why you came to New York when you escaped? In order to avenge yourself against the family that had wronged you so cruelly?"

"Revenge? Maybe." He shifted uncomfortably. "At this point I couldn't say what drove me here—any more than I could truly say what I hoped to accomplish when I threatened to expose Naughton. For if I, um, admired you from the first day I met you, I swear I never aspired to be . . . to be as fortunate as I now find myself."

"But if you had been forced to make good on your threat—"

"I would have been dragged in chains back to Bermuda," he said. "Hanged, perhaps. But I risked that willingly."

"As willingly as the Renegade."

He searched her voice for a trace of irony, and flushed when he couldn't find one. "Well, now, it wouldna come to that. I am—was—a slippery enough creature in a pinch." He shook his head. "I planned to flee to the West. It's hidden many a worse soul. I . . . certainly never presumed to intend the rest. But then your father collapsed, and the quarry needed running."

He longed for her to say something. Anything. Shriek. Wail. Throw her hairbrush at him. Banish him from her presence forever. But she simply stared at him with those wide blue eyes, as if she had never seen her husband before.

"Do you still smuggle?" she asked.

And once more he found himself at a loss for words. "Nay," he finally managed to say. "'Tis a young man's game."

"I should hope so." Her voice grew severe. "It wouldn't

do, Mr. Wadsworth, to have you pulled up dripping at the ferry landing in order to be hanged. I shan't stand for them hanging you, do you hear me?"

He stiffened. "Have no fears on that account. If matters ever come to such a pass, I'll make an honorable end of things before I let such a sordid tale redound on you."

Her eyes flashed. "I beg your pardon, Mr. Wadsworth, but you insult me with your misunderstanding. As if I could ever be ashamed of a man willing to go to the scaffold for a woman's honor, even when unjustly accused of being a criminal."

They were the words he had longed to hear his entire life without any true hope of hearing them spoken. But now that he had, he couldn't help but think he must have dreamed them. "Well there'd be those on her Majesty's revenue service who would might see fit to disagree with that last part," he admitted. "But I thank you for that, Mrs. Wadsworth. From the bottom of my heart. And now perhaps 'tis time that I trouble ye no more."

He turned to go. But as he reached for the handle of the door, her voice trailed after him.

"Mr. Wadsworth?"

He turned. "Yes, Mrs. Wadsworth?"

"Would you care to accompany me on a stroll around the rose beds?" she asked, repinning her hair more deftly than any ladies' maid ever could. "For I would far prefer to hear of the adventures of Tam Jenkins from a more reliable source than a vicarage tabby. And I believe the thorns would provide ample protection against any postmasters or imposters with an impulse to eavesdrop."

He snorted with unwilling humor even as his heart leapt. "I'm not sure most of my tales are fit for a lady's ears.

Especially the one that involved a certain highly placed government minister forced to escape a lady's bedroom via the same Royal Mail delivery as the port—and how he explained the stains to his valet."

Her sudden silence made him look up.

"Mr. Wadsworth," she said, a touch severely, "I trust you are not developing your son-in-law's propensity for tall tales?"

"Oh, I'll never equal that young man's tongue."

"One wonders, Mr. Wadsworth. One is seriously given to wonder." But her eyes were warm with humor as she reached for her wrap. She stood gracefully, only to frown as she saw that he still hesitated. "But, fie, Mr. Wadsworth. In all these years of marriage, have I still not managed to teach you that it is the height of incivility to refuse a lady her foolish whims? Would you persist in denying me hearing the truth of Tam Jenkins from his own lips?"

He moved to take her arm with the same numb disbelief that he had experienced when he realized he had been betrayed all those years ago. But the emotion that colored his voice this time was very different indeed. "I give you my word that all you'll ever hear from me is the truth about Tam Jenkins—even if it involves confessing the awkward scene that ensued when Miss Livingstone's King Charles spaniel betrayed her by depositing on the rug the missive he had accidentally swallowed earlier. If I recall correctly, I believe the incident occurred while Mrs. Livingstone was in the midst of entertaining her afternoon callers."

And if he bit back a hint of a smile at the last, he was wise enough not to allow his wife to see it as they strolled out into the night air and down toward the privacy of the rosebeds.

It could have been nothing but a trick of the moonlight, a play of light and shadow against the panes of the terrace doors that caught Libba's eye as she lounged in Ransome's arms. Surely, the reflection she glimpsed could be nothing but a reflection of her contentment with the prospect of yet another foray into the increasingly fascinating realm of scientific experimentation. Yet, as a cloud passed across the moon, she could only believe that the ghostly figures of the Renegade and Lady Cora arose in the depths of the glass, reunited at long last in a rapturous embrace.

Then the cloud shifted, and the mists of legend dissolved beneath the cool, clear light of a full moon. And Libba sprang to her feet.

"Papa?" she gasped. "Mama! *Really?*"

Acknowledgments

Once again, I'd like thank my newfound family at Amphorae Publishing Group: Donna Essner, Kristina Blank Makansi, and Lisa Miller. I'd also like to thank the indefatigable Carolina VonKampen for charting an effortless course through the muddy waters of social media.

The Suckley family of Wilderstein in Rhinebeck, NY are not likely to recognize themselves in my fictional Wadsworths. However, they may well recognize the house's spectacular view of the Hudson, which inspired Cora's Leap. In any case, I offer my profound thanks to the tireless volunteers who have restored and continue to maintain this wonderful historic home (as well as putting on the glorious annual garden party where I first wandered to the cliff's edge, thinking "Surely, this needs to be haunted by someone").

And, as always, I would like to thank George Baird, who really does help with the research.

About the Author

Erica Obey graduated from Yale University, and her interest in folklore and story led her to an MA in Creative Writing from City College of New York and a PhD in Comparative Literature. She began publishing articles and then wrote a book about female folklorists of the nineteenth century before she decided she'd rather be writing the stories herself. There are three places you can find Erica when she's not writing: on a hiking trail, in her garden, or at the back of the pack in her local road race. Her favorite kind of vacation is backpacking across Dartmoor or among the hills of Wales in order to find new and exciting legends to inspire her own writing. *The Curse of the Braddock Brides* is her third novel and the first in a series of historical suspense romances inspired by the stately homes of the Hudson Valley.